THROUGH THE EYES OF DESPERATION

THE RED VERSION

ARON BEAUREGARD

BAD DREAM BOOKS

ISBN: 978-1-961758-98-8

Cover & Interior Art by Anton Rosovsky

Cover wrap design by C.V. Hunt

Edited by Jason Parent

Printed in the USA

WARNING:
This book contains scenes and subject matter that are disgusting & disturbing; easily offended people are not the intended audience.

For the iLLest ones,
Day Day & J.P.

FOR SIGNED BOOKS, MERCH,
AND EXCLUSIVE ITEMS VISIT:

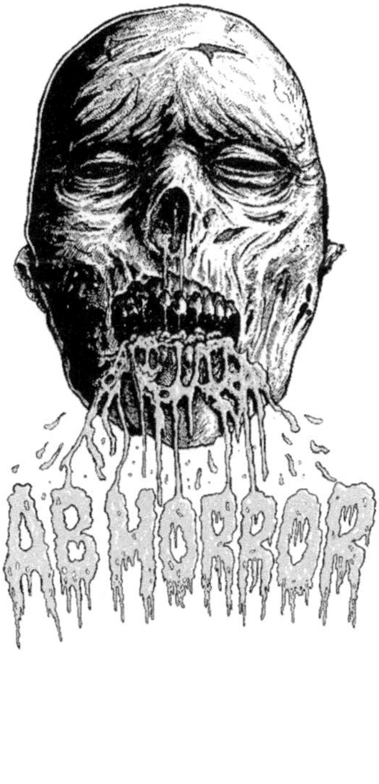

"Back home, they would've put me in jail for what I'm doing.
But out here, they're giving me awards."

- Ace Rothstein

MORNING GLOOM

Something about this time felt different.

As Patrick Blanchfield drove through pouring rain, an uneasy feeling poked around in his guts. He pulled up to the street curb, sending a mini tsunami of water onto the sidewalk as he parked. He turned off the engine, and his gaze drifted to the glove box.

A man could only press his luck so many times before he pressed it too hard. He wasn't the luckiest fella to begin with. Anyone who looked at his face knew that much.

His eyes pivoted to the rearview mirror. As his reflection projected back, it was easy to see why he'd been nicknamed Red. If his short, fiery ginger locks weren't enough to warrant it, the port wine stain clinched the pseudonym. The birthmark started at his collar and stretched over his chin and part of his cheek. The unnatural pigmentation was red as rare meat in his youth, but by the time it transitioned to its purplish present shade, his nickname had already been solidified.

The odd splotch made Red's throat look like it'd been freshly slit. Given Red's line of work, an unhappy accident of the kind didn't always seem so far-fetched. Sometimes, the birthmark felt downright prophetic.

Eat
Diner
Diner

Yet there he sat, still breathing, and continuing on his uncertain path.

Red couldn't tell if he was feeling intuition or just indecision. He opened the glove box, where a wrinkled, white envelope sat atop various automotive paperwork. Biting his lip, he again wondered if he should go through with it.

Squinting, Red tried to see through the monsoon into the diner window. Aside from the staff there weren't too many people inside the joint. There was a chatty elderly couple occupying a table in the corner, an exhausted night-shift construction worker on a stool near the grill, and at a table by himself sat his guy, Jack Tunney.

Red took a deep breath. He did his best to keep calm while he reassured himself he was making a sound decision—in his mind, it was the only decision. Even so, he wondered if he was overplaying his hand. Most any choice he'd ever made was shit, a long track record proved that much. He forced himself to ignore the edgy feeling nipping at him that he couldn't seem to shake.

"Fuck it," Red said, grabbing the envelope. He slid the paper inside his front pocket, zipped up his jacket, and headed toward the diner.

A few bells jingled when Red opened the door. Jack Tunney sat by himself, looking down at the runny egg on his plate. It was less runny and closer to raw. He used his fork to push some of the gelatinous jumble into the burned strings of hash browns.

After a moment, Jack's eyes found Red's. The aftereffects of the torrential downpour lingered, the dampness soaking Jack's water-saturated trench coat hanging around the top of his chair.

Shaking the raindrops off his jacket, Red approached the table. He took the seat across from the yolk-stained plate in front of Jack.

Jack grumbled. "You sure do like makin' me wait."

"Let's just say it's been a shit day," Red said.

"Yeah, well, way to share the wealth."

Red had a feeling inside like his dog just died. His bloodshot pupils, disheveled hair, and general demeanor should've been a hint for Jack. He hadn't been getting much rest. The furthest thing from Red's mind was holding a pity party for him because he was a few minutes late.

"Cry me a river," Red said.

Jack shook his head. "You're all sunshine on a rainy day. What's your deal?"

"Did you come here to do business or play therapist? I really ain't in the mood."

"Relax, kid. Maybe I'll do something to improve your day more than you expected."

A brief twinkle of hope rumbled inside Red. He straightened his shoulders.

"You found her?" He couldn't remember the last time his tone had such pep.

"No, but I got a tip. Actually, not *just* a tip. I'd call it a promising lead."

"From who?" Red fidgeted in his chair. He couldn't contain himself.

"Some junkie downtown."

Red rolled his eyes.

"Ease up," Jack said. "While the source might not be reputable, he had some details that no urge for a fix could enlighten him with."

"What kind of details exactly?"

"I didn't even feed him a name, just asked him if he'd fucked anyone with tattoos. I didn't even tell him what kind of tattoo I was looking for, but when he told me about a whore he'd seen with a little scorpion inked above her twat, suddenly, the ten bucks was worth it."

Red felt a curl of disgust pucker his lips and his eyes light ablaze with anger. "She's hookin' again—probably never stopped. That's just like her. Same ol' Britt. She'll never fuckin' learn." An exhale of disappointment left his lungs as he felt the blush of rage painted over the unstained areas of his face. Red clenched his fist as he bit down on his bottom lip and shook his head.

"Afraid so, but hey, at least I have a trace of somethin' to follow now," Jack replied, reaching for his coffee.

"Did he say anything about Des—"

"Speaking of which," Jack said cutting him off, "that reminds me. If you want me to follow up on this, you've still gotta make things right. I'm gonna need the standard payment—in advance—plus a little something extra for travel."

Red's brow furrowed—it seemed like every time they met there was a price hike. "How much more?"

"Oh, I don't know, another grand should do the trick. In addition to the standard pay—"

"I heard you the first time."

The situation was beyond expensive now, but paying the man was the only thing that brought promise to Red's sad life. A lump rose in his throat. The news was difficult to swallow, but he did so anyhow.

"She couldn't have gotten far," Jack continued. "That fiend said he fucked her just a couple days ago. I'm aiming to move on this tomorrow, *if* you got the cash that is."

Red reached into his jacket and fished out the envelope. He put it down on the table and pushed it toward Jack.

"That's enough for the normal payment, but if you—"

"I told you, I need it all upfront—"

Red slammed his fist down on the table. He couldn't hold his fury inside any longer. The dishes and glass clanged. The few stragglers in the diner and even the guy working the grill looked toward the commotion.

"Let me fuckin' talk!" Red barked.

Eyes widening with surprise, Jack looked around at the rest of the patrons and the cook, then back to Red. "Okay, okay, just relax. Keep your goddamn voice down."

Red didn't answer his request. While he did drop his volume some, his intensity remained. "Like I was saying, this is your normal payment, but if you give me a few days, I'll have the rest. I'm good for it."

Jack couldn't help but smile.

"I'd be lying if I said this was the first time I heard that one." Jack retrieved a cigarette from the coat hanging on the back of his chair. "But…" He lit the smoke and inhaled. "But I like you, Red."

Red froze, holding back his anger and anxiety. The constant stress was pushing him closer to the edge.

"Yeah," Red said, "but you don't like me because I tell good jokes, or because I'm the kinda fella you'd like to see your daughter beside. You like me because I've been paying you thousands of dollars for the last several months without fail. So don't sit here and act like you're doing me a fuckin' favor. Just finish the goddamn job that I paid you to do."

The smoky grin remained steady on Jack's face.

"Hey, you can't smoke in here," the cook said.

Jack slipped the envelope into the pocket of his trench coat and took another deep drag of his smoke. He narrowed his eyes at Red as he replied to the cook. "No problem. It looks like I've got somewhere to be now anyhow."

A GAME OF INCHES

Rosie's was bustling. When Red crossed the threshold of the bar, he took in the scumbag atmosphere. The clatter of pool balls and funky aromas of smoke and body odor were both nauseating and familiar. Dozens of gritty characters shifted about the dimly lit dump.

Grumbling could be heard in every corner of the joint. Arguments between the seedy bar's hedonistic patrons continued to blossom, intermingling with the velvety voices of the sportscasters on the televisions.

Red found himself distracted, still thinking about the news Jack had given him earlier that morning. He approached a seat at the far end of the bar. He always gravitated to the corner because it was tight and usually never overly occupied.

Looking down at the hands of his watch, Red's eyebrow twitched.

Shit, it's probably finishing up right now, Red thought.

He plopped down on the stool and looked up at one of the several TVs mounted behind the bar. As he recalled his reason for being there, his heart started to thud. He reached his sweaty palms inside his jacket and retrieved an index card that was folded once over.

"The usual?" a gritty voice asked.

Before he could unfold the paper, Red's gaze drifted up to the bartender. Rosie was a big fella. His long, braided hair, chipped front tooth, and the Samoan tribal tattoos that covered his upper body offered an intimidating glimpse at his persona.

"Hey, Rosie. Yeah, Miller works," Red replied.

"Bottle, right?" Rosie asked.

"Yeah."

"You alright, man? You look a little shook."

"Ask me in about five minutes."

Red forced a grin, but inside he was scared shitless.

"Whatever you say." Rosie set a slightly chilled, brown bottle in front of Red.

"Hey, can you put the Giants game on?" Red asked.

Rosie reached for the control. "Gimmie a sec."

Red kept his eyes on the bartender as the big man clicked the remote in the direction of the TV. He never liked to watch the actual games; they were like torture. Each positive play the opposing team made was like a dagger in his heart. He avoided the emotional aspects and just watched the endings. As the channel shifted, Red unfolded the index card. The black ink contained several lines of scribble: *Three-game parlay, OAK over ARZ by 5, NE over SF by 1 ½, PHI over NYG by 2.*

Oakland, New England, and New York were already circled on the card and a checkmark sat beside the first couple of listings.

Two of the three bets had already landed, which was two more than was typical. With all of the one o'clock games already completed, the results kept the pool of dread bubbling in Red's stomach. He'd spent the entire afternoon with a gnawing anxiety biting at his entrails.

Shuffling in his seat, Red looked up at the screen. He hadn't been able to sit still for hours. If the third bet somehow landed, the outcome of the contest would undoubtedly change his life forever.

"Fuck, fuck, fuck," Red whispered.

The game clock showed only 3 seconds remaining and the score was knotted at, 20-20. The Giants' kicker lined up at the 45-yard line in the center of the field. The rain soaked his uniform and the turf. As he attempted a practice kick, his plant foot slipped and he landed on his ass. In the mucky, natural grass, the kick was anything but a sure thing.

They never fucking win, Red thought, trying to comfort himself. *It's a 55-yarder in the goddamn rain on a natural field. He'll miss, and the birds'll pull it out in overtime.*

Red lifted the bottle as the players got into position. He guzzled nearly half his beer, desperately waiting for the ball to be hiked.

The snap was good.

The hold was good.

The kick was clean.

As the pigskin spun end over end, cutting through the pouring rain, time seemed to freeze. As the bottle dropped from Red's lips, he leaned into the bar. His eyes remained glued to the screen as the football's trajectory started to hook.

When the ball reached the goalpost, it smashed inside the left crossbeam.

Doink!

The noise resounded in Red's head.

"No," he whispered.

Despite connecting with the inside of the post, the ball was still moving forward with enough power to slip inside after the deflection.

The kick was good.

"Nooooooo!" Red screamed, raising his Miller into the air and smashing it down on the bar.

The bottle broke, glass erupted, and a big hunk cut deep into his hand. Beer puddled all over the countertop, with highlights of his blood.

"No!" Red yelled again. "This—this can't be happening! They never win!"

Several barflies took notice of his outburst, but Rosie was the only true concern.

The big Samoan's eyes popped. "What the fuck are you doing?!" Rosie screamed.

Red was too lost in his fears to answer. As blood oozed out of his hand, he remained staring in disbelief at the TV.

Rosie couldn't have known what his problem was and didn't seem to care. He quickly maneuvered around the bar to address the outburst. Gritting his teeth, the bartender cocked back his hammy fist and slammed it into the side of Red's face.

Red dropped to the floor—his lights flashed off before coming back on. He turned on his side holding his bloody hand over his ear.

"You wanna fuckin' break shit around here?!" Rosie yelled, grabbing him by the back of his shirt and pants.

He dragged Red to the exit and spun him face-first into the steel bar fixed to the door, opening it with his head. The metal connected with his right eye, instantly swelling it.

When Red landed in a puddle on the concrete, his mind was muddled. While the fresh beating left him a bit disoriented, it didn't erase the bad news that continued to dominate his thoughts. As he lay on his back, staring up at the gray clouds, all Red could think was, *I gotta get the fuck out of town.*

THE HAND THAT FEEDS YOU

The road in front of Red was distorted. It wasn't solely because of the downpour falling on his windshield, but also due to the puffy flesh that surrounded his right eye.

As he pulled up to the dilapidated apartment building, Red's face ached. He groaned while using his good eye to scan the area for a parking space. Somehow, there were several just ahead—a rarity in the congested slice of the city where Red resided.

Well, I'll be damned, Red thought. *Something's finally gone right for once.*

He would've much rather had the games go his way, but at the very least, he hoped it was a starting point for his luck to pivot.

Red used his good hand to guide the car up to the parking meter while clasping a blood-drenched napkin in the other. *I'll be in and out.* The cut on his hand was deep and probably could've used a stitch or two, but he didn't have time for all that. In the back of his mind, he feared that he was probably already running late.

Red popped out of the car and pushed his way through the building's front doors. He staggered up several flights of steps before making his way into his apartment.

Right when he entered the kitchen, he went for the freezer handle. Buried in the back, behind countless TV dinners, sat a box of three cheese ravioli that looked like it had been in there well past the expiration date. He pushed through the frayed corners of the packaging and stuck his fingers inside.

"Patrick? Is that you?" a shaky female voice asked from a room over.

"I need the cheese," Red mumbled to himself, pulling a wad of stiffened twenties from the container.

"Patrick?" the voice persisted.

"Yeah, Ma!" Red yelled out, upping his cadence. "We—we're gonna go on a little trip today, okay? Like a last-minute vacation."

"What?! Really?!" she squawked.

He dropped the empty box of ravioli on the floor and closed the freezer. Red quickly shuffled around the fridge to the living room entrance.

"Yeah, why not? I got a few nights at a nice little…"

Red stopped dead in his tracks.

"I told you, my Patrick is the sweetest boy," Mrs. Blanchfield said.

She was staring up at a large man in a soaked trench coat beside her. His bulbous nose was peppered with blackheads, and a sickening patch of dry, chafing skin sat between his bushy eyebrows, above his five-o'clock-shadow. Wet, disheveled hair crept out the sides of his brown hat. A fly circled his body, seemingly attracted to his odorous musk.

"B—Buggs," Red mumbled.

"Hey, Red!" Buggs grinned. "How 'bout that? Just the guy we was lookin' ta see!"

Buggs' raspy tone was friendly enough, but Red knew it was all show. His memories of the man were forever burned in his head. He knew about Buggs—everyone did. They called him Buggs on the count of the insects that seemed to cling to him like stink on shit. Rain, sleet, or snow, there was always a fly or two doing the rounds on him.

But the second reason was far scarier than his poor hygiene. The unlucky people who had to face Buggs under sudden circumstances were always the ones at the end of their rope. The people who owed big. The people whose only way of squaring up was cashing out completely.

The streets called him Buggs because that's what the people who encountered him ended up covered in. He was a walking omen, one that foreshadowed bodies getting stuffed in the dirt as he delivered their decaying husks as a meal for the insects. Red had survived his first unexpected encounter with the man, so it was only natural that a paralyzing fear wormed through his stomach.

"We was just in the neighborhood," Buggs continued, "and figured we hadn't seen you in a while, why not pop in? Oh, and, Mad Dog sends his best."

"His *best*," Dane echoed.

Red was so panicked by the presence of Buggs in his living room he hadn't even seen the bony, sunk-in face of Dane Fuller lurking nefariously in the background.

Dane's frame might've been scrawny, but what he gave up in girth he made up for in grit. A stone-faced killer's eyes glared under his fedora. He was the kind of cat that didn't scare, he just stuck his claws deep into whoever crossed him. Red had even heard a rumor floating around the streets that he'd offed his first cousin over a small financial quarrel.

His own fuckin' cousin, Red thought.

"Are you hurt, dear?" Mrs. Blanchfield asked. "What's wrong with your hand?"

Red quickly shoved the bloody napkin in his jacket and the handful of money into the opposite pocket. Despite his mother's failing sight, the blood was bright enough for her to pick up on.

"No, Ma. I just nicked my finger is all—"

"Actually, it's a good thing we're here," Buggs interjected, looking down at Mrs. Blanchfield. "With this big, ah, trip you got coming up, we better get your luggage packed. Ain't that right, Red?"

Red nodded his head.

Buggs looked back at Dane. "Why don't you take the lady into the bedroom and help her get her things together."

"Sounds like a plan," Dane said.

"What?" Mrs. Blanchfield asked.

Her confusion was only growing. For the first time she was starting to sense something was off with her son's attitude. She locked eyes with Red. "Is—is everything okay, sweetie?"

Dane stepped beside Red's mother and took her frail hand.

"These are my friends," Red replied. "It's okay, they're just here to help."

A smile found Mrs. Blanchfield's wrinkled face as Dane assisted her up from the recliner. Red's lies were enough to give her some comfort.

The fly swirling around Buggs finally docked on his hat. The big man watched Dane escort Mrs. Blanchfield out of the room and close the door behind them.

"She's just the nicest little old lady," Buggs said, cracking open his trench coat. He extracted a long, black baseball bat. "She talked about your father. If she only knew..."

The comment angered Red but his anxiety outweighed all other emotions.

Buggs brandished his yellow teeth. "Guess she's been single for a while now."

The discomfort in Red's intestines only intensified as he watched Buggs raise the bat in front of him and admire its width. The fear tightening his chest was only slightly diluted with rage. Red glanced at the watch on his wrist, trying to forget the dark secret that had been revealed to him months prior. A secret that had been eating at him every day. But the details weren't something that had any chance of comforting his mother and wouldn't change anything, so why reopen the wound? It was *his* burden to bear.

"She ever been with a spook before?" Buggs asked.

"W—what?" Red stammered.

"What? You got shit in your ears?"

"No."

"She ever fuck a black guy?"

Red hung his head, contemplating how to answer the incendiary question. "I don't know."

Buggs' eyes shifted back to the bat. "I guess it don't really matter. This thing's bigger than any prick I ever seen. You know what I'm sayin'?"

Red didn't want to imagine where he was going with the setup and just nodded.

"I mean, not that I'm going around lookin' at pricks or anything. She's just so fuckin' sweet though. It'll be a damn shame if I have to stick this fuckin' thing inside her. An old cunt like her might just up and croak. Might be too much for her."

"What the fuck is that all about?" Red asked.

"Your face don't match up to the words it's spittin' out. It don't look like the face of a fella in the dark. It looks like the face of a guilty cocksucker." Buggs squinted his eyes glaring at the egg on his cranium. "And that lump on your head makes me think you got more problems than just me and Dane. And while you may very well have more problems, let me assure you, them problems ain't bigger than *us.*"

"I don't know what you're talking about," Red said, continuing to play stupid.

Buggs grinned. "Okay, fine. I'll humor ya."

Red swallowed hard and as the sweat seeped out around the crown of his head, the blood from his hand started to soak through the front of his jacket.

Buggs tapped the bat against his leg. "After the first two games hit today, the boss had me call over to make sure Jasper had the money ready if the third bet hit. Funny thing though, Jasper says you never laid money down on no parlay. In fact, he said you ain't laid no money on *any* bet since he can remember. So, instead of wasting my time playing dumbfuck, why don't you tell me why all the bets we thought we placed for the last six months never hit his sheets."

Red became his nickname—he felt face rise to a boil. He felt like a cornered animal with no pack. A loner, but not by choice, by abandonment.

Buggs took a step closer to him, swinging the bat at his side. "You only had one fuckin' job, lay down the money. But instead, you stole it. I don't know what you did with it, but I hope it was worth it. I gotta give you credit though, it was a good little scam you had going. If the parlay hadn't hit, who knows how much money you would've pinched from us. But now, because of your greed and deception, people are gonna get hurt. There's no gettin' around it."

"Wait!" Red begged. "There's gotta be a way for me to get the money back!"

Buggs' sinister grin widened. "Oh, there is, but let's just say the odds ain't in your favor."

"All I need is a few weeks—maybe a month—"

"Mad Dog doesn't like to wait, and the truth of it is, you and I both know a two-bit piece of shit like you can't come up with that kinda scratch no matter how many cocks you suck. Furthermore, when you became the bet bitch, it was made crystal fuckin' clear that there was no fuckin' up. You knew what would happen if you tried us again, but you did it anyway. You didn't learn. You bet against us, and you lost. So that only leaves us with one option… Shadows."

Red got light-headed when Buggs spoke the words. His heart smashed inside his ribcage. He pretended that he didn't even hear him say it. "I'm telling you, if I just get a little time—"

"Listen, scumbag, you don't tell me shit! You understand me?" Buggs pointed the tip of the bat at his face. "You're going, and if you're not back at this apartment with every fuckin' penny of that money in exactly four days, then I'm gonna break each brittle bone in that sweet old lady's body. I'm gonna rip that dusty cunt open so wide her hole'll be big enough for her to give birth to you as you fuckin' stand. And I'll make sure she's alive, for every godforsaken minute of it."

Tears started to streak down Red's face.

"There's no crying in baseball," Buggs said with a phlegmy chuckle.

"Please, my ma doesn't have anything to do with this."

"She does now. Don't act like you don't remember. It wasn't that long ago that you helped us clean up. You saw how messy it gets. Mad Dog told you himself—if somethin' like this happened, then it wasn't just you that was gonna feel it. But don't you worry, me and Dane are gonna take real good care of her while you're out. For exactly *four* days that is. And if you ain't back here by then, just remember, what happens to her," Buggs pushed his finger into his chest, "is all on you."

"Can—can I at least say bye to her?" Red asked.

The ice-cold stare that Buggs projected toward Red was an answer in itself. But just in case, he was willing to clarify. "You can go get that money right *now* before I even up your fuckin' head. And I'd hurry, time's a-wastin'."

SPACE NUMBER SEVEN

The car ran idle as Red looked at the crumpled sheet of yellow paper in his bloody hand. It was a parting gift—the lone set of instructions Buggs had left him with. Red rolled down his window to get a better look at the structure. The chilly evening air nipped his face.

The address inked on the faded blue line matched the decrepit parking lot. For an abandoned garage crumbling on the outskirts of a tiny ghost town, it had a lot of cars, but for some reason, no people.

Red's eyes jumped back to the note on the paper: *park in space number seven and wait.*

As he pulled into the dark structure, Red quickly located the parking spot. Seconds after he pulled in beside a blue Cadillac, his rattling fingers killed the ignition and he exhaled deeply. There was a reason for his labored breathing. Red knew what he was in for, but at the same time, he didn't.

Were the stories he'd heard about the casino true? The rumors in the streets told of the ultimate winnings, but on the other side of the coin, losses that there were no bouncing back from. The recollection made him shudder. If all the chatter matched the reality, then there wasn't much hope for him or his mother.

As he sat in the car, knee bouncing, Red checked his mirrors often. He tried to clear his mind and stay alert, but the reason he'd gotten tied up in this whole mess wasn't something he could forget.

It went back to before he became a bookie or had his life-changing run-in with Mad Dog. Long before he'd ever smelled Buggs' rancid musk or laid eyes on Dane Fuller's maniac smirk. In fact, it didn't have anything to do with any man at all. Red didn't like thinking about the past, but when every day seemed worse than the last, he found himself doing it all the time.

A YEAR PRIOR

MACABRE MEMORIES: PART 1

In the darkness of the apartment, Red admired Brittany's hourglass outline. He watched as she leaned off the mattress and rustled through her purse with her back to him. The desire to be inside her still burned despite knowing that several men had already felt her warmth that day alone.

The heroin helped his mind stay blank and his heartache numb. They'd had some promise when they'd first met—neither of them had led charming lives, but at least they had each other. As Red's hand slid up her leg and felt on her ass, it became obvious they didn't even have that anymore.

"Get off me," Brittany scowled. "I had enough of that today already. I need a fix."

Red checked the face of his silver wristwatch and felt the frown contorting his lips. "Another? It's only been a few hours since we—"

"I don't give a shit about before! I'm talkin' about now."

As Red continued to look at the timepiece, a solemn feeling took hold of him. The keepsake was his only connection to his father. A man who he'd never known, but still a man his mother was terrified he'd become. By all accounts—the way his ma talked and the way the streets talked—his father had few redeemable qualities.

While his mother understood why he took a liking to the thing, she didn't like it. But besides a few old pictures, it was the only thing Red had. Since the silver watch had touched his father's flesh, in an abstract way it helped Red feel slightly connected to the man he'd never known. And if nothing else, Red looked at the watch as a reminder to stay straight. Otherwise, Red would end up the same: an unsolved case, a sad life cut short, riddled full of bullet holes, and turned to dust inside a furnace. Hopefully, one day he wouldn't need the motivation. But more recently, that was seeming less and less realistic.

I'm headed for the same… maybe worse, Red thought.

"I'm fuckin' tweakin' right now," Brittany said. "Feel like my heart's gonna explode. I gotta pick up."

Her fiendish gripes snapped Red out of his reverie. "But we're outta cash, even if we wanted to—"

"I'll go see the old man."

Red sat up. He could feel sickness and angst rising inside him. They'd been steadily upping their heroin doses, and as their tolerance heightened, the habit was becoming a bigger problem by the hour. They were both addicted to an expensive drug and without the financial support to keep the demon subdued.

"No, Francis is a fuckin' creep." Red shook his head. "I heard weird shit about him."

"Everyone's weird out here," Brittany said standing up and slipping on an outfit. "Whaddya think makes you so special?"

"I ain't sayin' I'm special but he gives me the creeps."

"He's harmless. Francis' a hell of a lot safer than most of the other guys I gotta get down with to keep this house in order. What's the matter, you suddenly wanna speak up because you're afraid of an old man?"

Red knew Brittany was right. Francis was a strange, older guy with an infatuation for local prostitutes, but nothing more. He looked out the foggy window into the dark alley. "No, I just…"

"Just what?"

"It ain't about Francis, it's about gettin' to him," Red explained. "It don't bother me so much when you're out during the day, but when it gets dark, all the crazies come out."

"I ain't scared," Brittany said.

"It ain't about being scared. It's about being safe."

"Then come with me."

Red bit his bottom lip. All the talk of more smack was getting into his head. He probably would've been fine if she could've kept quiet.

"What about Dessi?" he asked. "We can't just leave her alone this late at night."

"She could sleep through an avalanche." Brittany slid back down to the mattress and squeezed Red's cock through his boxers. "We'll be back in forty minutes. And maybe, after we get back, I'll be in a better mood."

Red tried to consider their daughter alone in the other room—would Dessi be all right by herself for a little while? The pressure of the guilt inflating Red's frame matched the pressure being applied to his dick. As his erection solidified, Red opened his mouth to argue, and Brittany slipped her tongue inside it.

MACABRE MEMORIES: PART 2

When they arrived on the doorstep, it didn't take long for Francis to answer. The look on the wrinkly man's face was not happiness. He seemed tired and filled with ire.

"Why the fuck are you here?" Francis asked, yanking at the crotch of his pajamas.

Brittany donned her best seductive smile—her teeth were covered in plaque buildup but straight. Despite her daunting drug issues, she was fortunate that all her beauty hadn't been stolen from her yet. "I just thought you might be interested in a late-night trade." She bit her chipped fingernail gently. "A little tight pussy for a little powder."

When she reached for the old man's cock, he slapped her hand away.

"Hey!" Brittany yelled. "The fuck's up your ass?"

Red grimaced. Seeing his girlfriend's rejection bothered and relieved him at the same time. He was stuck in a sick, unwinnable situation.

"Listen, I like you, Brittany," Francis said. "I like all the girls. I just wanted us to help each other."

"Me too, babe." Brittany changed up her cadence again. She was back to playing nice and willing to forgive. "So, just let me come inside and I'll make everything better."

"I can't. Please go."

When Francis tried to close the door, Brittany blocked it with her arm. "What—why?"

Francis' eyes flared like he'd been waiting to say it but trying to avoid it. "Because every fuckin' time I let you come inside, things go missing! It's one thing to be a whore, but it's another to be unfaithful and ungrateful!"

The words cut deep into Red's soul. He was doing his best to hit the streets and try and scrape together some money for their family. And in the evenings, he took care of their daughter while Brittany was out doing her thing. But that word: unfaithful. The old man was right.

Brittany would take off some nights and come back with no money. But Red could tell she'd gotten fucked. She'd had that certain look in her eye and scent on her body. Brittany's behavior had lingered since their toxic relationship started. Since before Dessi was even born. His daughter's innocent face flashed in his head. Francis' comments triggered the question in his mind for the thousandth time.

Is she even mine? he wondered.

Dessi didn't share his eye or hair color. Red didn't know a whole lot about genetics, but just from the sight test alone the girl looked nothing like him. He hated asking himself but that wasn't truly what he was ashamed of. The part that bothered him the most was that he cared. That if it was somehow proven he wasn't the girl's father, he might find relief in such a revelation. An excuse to cut ties with Brittany and start over. To not be the constant cuck that sits by idly while his girlfriend gets railed by every dirtbag in town.

The selfish side of him wanted to forget about Dessi and Brittany, like their entire lives as a family were some fabricated nightmare—a horror movie. Much of it had been. Sadly, Red wanted nothing more than to see their movie conclude.

"Bullshit," Brittany argued. "I didn't take anything from you."

"Britt, let's just get outta here," Red pleaded.

"Step back!" Francis yelled trying to get Brittany's arm out of the doorway.

"I ain't leavin' until I get what I came for!"

Francis pushed her backward, closed the door, and locked it.

Red alertly caught Brittany in his arms as she slipped off the steps.

"You junkies better get lost, or I'm calling the cops!" Francis threatened through the glass window before closing the curtain.

Brittany rushed back up to the glass and banged her palms against it. "Fuck you! You old, limp-dick bastard!"

"Britt, chill," Red said. "We've gotta get outta here before he calls the cops."

Brittany's face changed as an idea hit her. "Follow me," she whispered.

As Red trailed her around to the bushes that surrounded the house, she called him closer.

"We need to leave," Red said. "He's pissed."

"He ain't callin' the cops," Brittany said.

"What do you mean?"

"I mean he's got enough dope in there for an entire Mötley Crüe tour. He's an old fucker, but he fucks like a teenager—two, three times a day. He don't sell it or use it, just keeps a hefty amount on hand to pay the girls with."

"So, what?"

"So, he's bluffin'. Ain't no way he's calling the cops with a brick in there big enough to keep him locked up for his entire retirement."

Brittany reached into her jacket and dug around. She removed a retractable knife and pressed the mechanism. The blade shot out.

"What the fuck are you doing?!" Red asked.

Her body was shaking from the dope sickness. "I'm doing what I have to."

"We—we can't hurt him. He didn't do anything."

"I ain't gonna hurt him. Not if he listens."

"And what if he doesn't?"

"Then it's on him."

"No, you know that's not the truth—"

Brittany put the tip of the knife to her temple. "You know what it feels like cuz you feel it too. I'm about an hour away from losin' my fuckin' mind!"

Red shook his head. "If you do something to that guy, they'll put you in a cage for life. Then you'll really lose your mind. This isn't like you." He looked at the blade as it glimmered in the moonlight. "Where'd you even get that?"

"That doesn't matter." Brittany looked up at the window on the second floor and watched the lights go out. "Only thing that matters is, one way or another, I'm coming outta that house with that dope. And if you wanna have a home to go back to, you're comin' with me."

MACABRE MEMORIES: PART 3

Red and Brittany waited another hour and a half after the lights went out before they approached the back door. Using the handle of the knife, Brittany broke the glass as carefully as she could.

Gritting his teeth, Red looked up at the second floor anticipating the lights would come on.

They didn't.

Fuck, he thought.

Inside he was hoping that the house lit up and spooked Brittany. He'd much rather be running away from a crime scene than into one.

The door opened gently, and they both crept inside. Under the guise of darkness, Brittany guided Red.

"Where are we going?" Red whispered.

"It's somewhere in his upstairs office."

"Great, right near where he's fuckin' sleep—"

"Shhh." Brittany put her finger up to her lips.

Whether Red wanted to admit it or not, she was right. Complaints and critiques should be offered after they'd gotten out of there.

As Red approached the staircase, he held his breath. Every noise felt like it was coming out of a loudspeaker.

The narrow hallway at the top of the steps had three doors. The first was Francis' office, and the other two were presumably a bathroom and his bedroom. But as Brittany crossed the threshold, a cold barrel emerged from the darkness and pressed against the side of her head.

Red's instincts surprised him. He vaulted forward and grabbed the end of the revolver. They wrestled until the gun went off. Thankfully it was pointed at the ceiling, causing fragments of plaster to shower them.

The distraction was enough for Red to pull the gun from the old man's clutches. But before he could even consider pointing it at him, Brittany had already buried her long blade inside his abdomen.

Francis cried out. "You fuckin' bitch, you stabbed me!"

The panic in his voice was even more horrifying to Red than the blood gushing out of his stomach. He watched him fall to the floor clutching his gut. "Jesus, Britt! What… what the fuck?"

She ignored his question, instead dropping to her knees. When she hunched over Francis this time, it was for a far more nefarious reason than any prior meeting. She wrapped her fingers around the blade stuck in his gut and gritted her teeth. "Where's the shit?"

Red wanted to beg her to stop, but the shock of the situation had a hold on him. Things had gone from zero to a hundred. He gawked at a side of his girl that he'd never seen before. Even as he held the gun, she still terrified him.

"Please, I—I don't wanna…" Francis coughed up blood all over his nose and in his eyes. "I don't wanna die…"

"Then it's real easy." Brittany suddenly rotated her hand, pushing the blade deeper inside his stomach and twisted at the same time. Even more blood cascaded over his body. "Tell me where the fuckin' dope is!"

Red's eyes widened. He was aware he slept beside a monster, but the ruthlessness Brittany hid had so much more depth than he could've imagined.

Who the fuck are you?

Francis cried out. The strain on his voice and the look of terror in his eyes made him seem like he was on the verge of passing out. "It's in the closet, under—under the ceiling tile."

"Lie to me and I swear to fuckin' God I'll make another hole inside you that'll never get filled."

"I'm not fuckin' lying," he cried, tears and blood streaming down each side of his face.

Brittany turned to Red and nodded at the closet behind him. "Check it out."

It didn't take him long to find the brick. It was more dope than Red had ever seen before. Sure, they were both fiends, but at the same time, it was impossible for Red to ignore the monetary value of the stash. That much dope was easily worth over fifteen grand.

"Is that it?" Brittany asked.

"Yeah," Red whispered.

Brittany turned back to Francis. His body quaked as he clutched at his belly. His eyes pled for mercy.

When Brittany pulled the blade out of Francis, Red had no idea what the right next move was. The old man had seen their faces, and there was nothing they could do to change that. But he didn't expect Brittany to lose it. Before Red could blink, the knife had gone in and out of Francis' chest and through his hands a half-dozen times. As the old man tried to protect himself, the blood squirted all over Brittany. Thick cuts burrowed into his palms, chest, and fingers.

"This could've been easy!" she screamed, sending the point through his sliced open hand and momentarily pinning it to his sternum.

"You could've fucked me in the ass." She pulled the knife and reinserted it forcefully into the side of his ribcage. "I could've got my fix!" When she yanked the knife free again, Francis held his destroyed hand in front of his face and chest to try and defend himself. Brittany came around him, sinking the tip through the side of his head and deep into his brain. "And we could've both walked away happy!"

Red stood frozen and wholly stupefied. The devil inside Brittany had shown itself, and he had no idea how to react. Was his life over? What would become of Dessi if the two of them got bagged up on murder charges? These were both very real questions he now had to face.

Gotta get the fuck outta here. He felt like he might be sick, but Red looked away from the body and swallowed the burst of vomit that tried to come up.

An epiphany dawned on him—Red realized he should avoid touching anything. If he was going to find a way out of the mess he was in, they needed to cover their tracks.

"At least one thing's gone right," Brittany said.

Can't leave any evidence—

His thought was suddenly interrupted by the sound of a ringing telephone.

Red and Brittany both jumped at the same time. She stood up and took the gun from his hand. He couldn't help but notice how natural she seemed with a weapon. Walking down the hall, Brittany moved with a purpose and Red followed. As they entered the dark room, the phone continued to ring.

She looked at him. "What do we do?"

The way she'd taken control of the situation, Red was surprised she wanted any input from him at all. "I—I guess it'll stop on its own… eventually."

Brittany scratched the side of her head. "Who the fuck calls someone at this time of night?"

"They don't," Red said. "Not unless they're expecting them to answer. Which means we need to get the fuck outta here, now."

The ringing suddenly stopped.

Brittany looked at the king-size bed that she'd spread eagle in so many times and listened intently. "You're right about that." She paused listening carefully. "But I'm glad we came in here." She aimed the gun at the mattress, both sides of which looked slept in. "Because we can't have no witnesses."

When she fired the shot, Red jumped. A woman's screams filled the room.

On the other side of the bed, a panicked girl emerged. She held her arm as it bled all over her stomach and thigh, then made a mad dash for the hallway. But as she passed the dresser, the gun erupted again. The bullet went into her forehead and caused a heavy rain of brains and blood to paint the mirror behind her. The woman dropped to the ground, and Brittany unloaded another slug into her back for good measure.

"What the fuck are you doing?!" Red yelled. "What the fuck is wrong with you?!"

"What did you expect?" Brittany asked. "That we just let her walk? Where would we end up?"

"I—I don't know! But we've at least gotta talk about it! You can't just take me along on a fuckin' killing spree without warning! I didn't even wanna come here in the first place, I—"

"Well, you shoulda sacked up, been a man, and fuckin' said somethin' then! That doesn't matter now, anyhow! You're here! I'm here! Neither of us can change that or what's happened! But what we do have a say in is whether we let this be our undoing. If there's one thing I'm fuckin' sure of it's that I plan on making use of that dope!"

Red didn't want to argue. He thought about the caller. Maybe it had been someone looking for the girl. Or based on Francis' sex addiction, maybe there was another girl waiting. Either way, he didn't want to stick around and find out.

Gotta get back to Dessi.

"Let's get the fuck outta here then," Red said.

"Okay, but if we want this whole thing to go away, there's one thing we've gotta do first."

"Whatever it is, let's do it quickly."

Red followed Brittany into the bathroom where she grabbed a towel and a wet cloth.

"Be careful not to touch anything," Brittany said.

"Now you fuckin' tell me," Red replied.

As they returned to the room where Francis' lifeless body lay, she kneeled beside him again and pulled the knife out of the side of his head.

Red shuddered at the slurping noise the steel made as it vacated his skull.

He watched Brittany slip the gun into her coat and clean the gore and fingerprints off the knife. Red couldn't help but wonder if taking the gun with them was the right move. It was probably wise since they could ditch the piece—the less evidence the better.

Continuing to try and figure Brittany out, he watched her smear the knife with Francis' blood again. But she was careful to ensure that the raven symbol at the bottom handle of the murder weapon was visible.

"What the fuck are you doing?" Red asked.

"This blade belongs to Ronnie Wilks," she said.

"So what?"

"It's a gang blade. He rolls with the Ravens."

The explanation wasn't what Red had expected—he still wasn't catching on. "And?"

"So, only members have it. Cops are gonna recognize it right away. He was stupid enough to carve his fuckin' initials into it. Won't take long before they tie it to him. And maybe when he's in the clink, havin' to fuck guys up the ass to catch a nut, he'll wish he would've paid me properly for my services."

Red couldn't believe what he was hearing. He had no idea that such a petty, vindictive streak and penchant for extreme violence existed in her. There were so many things he wanted to say, but he blurted out the most obvious question first.

"Wait, you planned this whole fuckin' thing?!" Red yelled.

"Kinda."

The dread loomed. Red's eyes glossed over as he came to a gloomy realization. "You're not…"

"Not what?" she asked.

"You're not the person I remember."

Brittany pulled the gun back out of her jacket.

"Don't look at me like that. You're only as good as the company you keep. Actin' like you're on some high fuckin' horse! You are, and always will be a degenerate, junkie gambler."

"But I ain't a murderer," Red said.

She lifted the gun and pointed it at Red's face. "Yeah, well I am. And the way you're talkin' right now's makin' me nervous." She cocked the gun. "It's makin' me wonder if my work ain't done here yet."

Things had gone in a completely different direction. No matter what he morally felt about the events of that evening, the crime scene was no longer the place to discuss it if he didn't want to become a part of it. He tried to reroute his argument.

"Listen, I just wasn't expecting all this. It… it's a lot. Whatever happened, happened. I'm just not wantin' to get caught now so I'm gettin' a little hot."

"Well, you better fuckin' cool off."

"I'm cool now. I'm cool. But I'm just sayin', if you leave that blade on him, ain't the Ravens gonna figure that out? Don't that mean they'll be comin' for us?"

"No one knows I swiped it. And besides, Ronnie's got more serious beef he'd suspect first. No one would expect little old me—not even you, Red."

"Okay, I was wrong. Clearly you got all your bases covered. Can you just put the gun down so we can go?"

Brittany thought about his question and slowly lowered the gun. Gripping the knife with the towel, she bent over and jammed the blade back into Francis' brain. She straightened up and turned back to Red. "Alright, let's get outta here then."

MACABRE MEMORIES: PART 4

They'd taken the backstreets on their walk home to keep police contact minimal. When they came through the door, Dessi was already crying. She'd awoken from a nightmare, only to witness another walk in on her. Brittany hadn't had enough time to clean herself off. Red wrapped his jacket around her to cover the blood all over her clothes.

She was alone and scared, Red thought. *Then we bust in looking like a walking murder scene.*

"Mommy, what's wrong?" Dessi asked.

Brittany walked past her daughter and into the bathroom where she stripped down naked.

"What happened?" Dessi cried.

Brittany ignored her daughter. She pulled the brick of heroin out of the jacket, set it down on the sink, and closed the door.

She turned to Red. "Is… is mommy hurt?" Snot slid out of the little girl's nose, and she tried to sniff it up.

Red was still in a state of deep emotional disturbance after the entire ordeal. Seeing Brittany turn on him when he spoke against her abhorrent acts really messed his head up. After watching her in action, he didn't know if he was safe. He didn't know if *they* were safe.

Dessi's cries pulled him out of his stupor. He should've been thinking about her anyhow.

"Is Mommy dying?" she cried.

"No, no, no, baby," Red whispered. He dropped down to one knee and touched her face. "She's okay."

"What happened? She's bleeding."

"No, sweetie. That's not her blood—I mean, that's not blood. It's paint. That's why we were gone, we had to help a friend of ours paint their house."

It was probably the shittiest excuse he'd ever given, but it was a miracle he was able to manufacture anything in the state he was in.

"Why are you shaking, Daddy?"

"It's just—it's really cold outside. Why are you still up, baby? Shouldn't you be sleeping?"

"I had a bad dream that someone came inside the house again."

She was referring to a burglary that had occurred several months prior. They didn't live in the nicest part of town, but thankfully the break-in just ended up being all their things thrown out of order. Their drawers had been turned inside out and the place looked like a big mess.

But the general sight of such a disturbance had deeply bothered Dessi. The images and anxiety from the event had stuck with her. After the traumatic experience, it wasn't uncommon for her to have an occasional night terror. Usually, Red would just sit with her and whisper comforting words. Seeing his daughter in such a state made him feel like he'd failed as a father.

Even though he wanted to cry, he held himself together. "Well, I can promise you there's nothing to worry about anymore, sweetie," Red whispered. "Dad's here to protect you, okay?"

She nodded and used her sleeve to wipe the tears away from her face.

Red stood and grabbed Dessi by her hand. "C'mon, let's get you back to bed."

As the little girl slipped under the covers, Red sat in the chair by the side of her bed, gently caressing her with his trembling hand. "It's okay. Go to sleep."

While he continued to comfort her, many thoughts screamed inside his head. But the more important ones were pushed aside. Red's nerves were shot, and he was feeling the effects of his dope sickness. The only thing he could think about was going into the bathroom with Brittany and getting a fix for himself.

PRESENT DAY

TAKEN

As Red sat in the car, his uneasiness grew. The waiting game was the worst part. He was glad to not be an addict anymore. He was thankful to no longer be attached to Brittany in any way. But with that luxury came guilt. And that guilt had multiplied over time until it had dragged him into the gloomy parking space he currently sat in.

Can't fuckin' believe her, Red thought.

Brittany had turned his life upside down. It wasn't just the culmination of their horrible relationship—that one murderous night—it was the many years of abuse and psychological torture leading up to it. It was the everlasting aftereffects.

The way Brittany stabbed Francis and blew his lady friend's brains all over the dresser was a little too easy for her. When she'd held the revolver, she'd done it like she was comfortable shooting people. *She was up to more than just fuckin' when she was out on the streets.*

Brittany didn't have any kind of moral code. He'd seen her true form with his own eyes. She killed for powder. She killed out of spite. When it came to Brittany's underlying vindictiveness, she knew no bounds. So, naturally, Red couldn't help but wonder what she had in mind for him.

Was he an inconvenience? A loose end that eventually needed to get tied up? The paranoia in his head reached new heights. He couldn't fall asleep beside her. Whatever particles of trust they once possessed had been swept away in the wind. On the few occasions he did get to close his eyes, he saw their faces.

The bloody grimace.

The floppy scalp.

The eyes of death.

Red got to thinking, and sticking around to see how the chips fell didn't seem like the brightest idea. In fact, blowing town and never looking back was a constant thought for the first few days. Dessi was the only thing that kept him there. Red considered himself a fuck-up, but as fucked up as he was, he still didn't have the heart to let a psychopath be the girl's guardian.

For several days after the murders, he wrestled with the choice. Until he no longer had to. Brittany made it for him.

Red came home one night to an empty house. Brittany had taken Dessi and the dope and split. He didn't know whether to jump for joy or cry. But the moment he thought about Dessi, his natural reaction was the latter.

Apparently, Brittany didn't see him as much of a threat. It made sense to him; if she went down, so did Red. Even if she wasn't hanging around to make sure he kept his mouth shut, she probably figured it would behoove Red to do so if he valued his freedom. Plus, why would a fiend like her want to split the dope—or money that could potentially be made off it—with him?

In the days that followed the night of violence, Red was thinking clearly for once. Every time he tried to show his love for her, she turned her back. Every time he talked about their future, she wasn't listening. Every time he mentioned their daughter, there was a lack of interest. The relationship he believed they were in was a façade. But as a product of the gutter, Red didn't have too many other baskets to put his eggs in.

It had been easier to lie to himself. But when the falsehood rotted away, so did his reality. It was hard to admit how much time he wasted. As a man who'd isolated himself from everyone but his toxic love interest, there were few people who would even take his call. For the last several years, Red had been exclusively blowing his hustle money on underground gambling and heroin. The idea of starting over didn't exactly sound too promising. But after he'd seen lives ended, his perspective shifted.

He was relieved when Brittany left.

The hardest part was convincing himself that the little girl he'd protected for so many years wasn't his. The notion wasn't absolute, but he needed to believe Dessi wasn't his daughter to move on. So, Red packed a single suitcase and headed to the only person in the world that gave two shits about him—his ma.

Forever determined not to allow her son to end up like his father, Mrs. Blanchfield was forgiving. She had gotten him a bed at a rehab facility, where he'd officially commenced his pivot. It was the first of many steps taken to get his life back.

While he was riding out his time inside the facility, his demons resurfaced. But they were the type he could never talk about. The murders that transpired that night would follow him to the grave, the heavy weight on his soul that he imagined might eventually drag him to hell.

There was also the stress of it criminally coming back to him. They hadn't gone into the old man's house with the intention of murdering him—at least Red hadn't—so he wasn't exactly being extra careful not to leave any traces of himself. He tried to clean up as best he could on the scene, but while he was inside the rehab facility, the idea that he'd left something behind gnawed at him.

His fears were eventually dispelled. He'd watched the papers like a hawk for any details on the double murder case, and when his eyes one day came across the name Ronnie Wilks, Brittany's prophecy had manifested.

On the night of the murders, he'd thought planting the knife was her checkmate, but that was merely the setup. When he'd read the detail in the column about the police finding Francis' revolver at Ronnie Wilks' place, it became clear why Brittany had kept the gun.

Revelations like that made him grateful that Brittany remained out of his life. Yet, there he sat, chasing the ghost that was almost his downfall.

Red shivered and shook his head.

He had to remind himself, it wasn't about Brittany. It was about finding Dessi.

He looked down at his watch, not because he was curious about the time, but because he was curious about *his* time. Red wanted nothing more than to chuck the damned thing out the window, but he refused to lie to himself any longer. He wasn't ready yet. Since he'd gotten clean, the thought crossed his mind religiously.

Hopefully, I won't need a reminder someday. Hopefully, I'll get more time than you did, Pop—

A banging noise erupted just outside the car. It sounded like it was coming from behind his vehicle.

Red's heart thumped. Suddenly, all the memories were irrelevant. Was that who he was waiting for?

Afraid to get out of the car, Red convinced himself it was a better alternative than being ambushed. He opened the driver's door and stepped out.

The banging persisted, but now, it wasn't just banging. He could also hear what sounded like muffled cries. As he scanned the parking garage, it slowly dawned on him that the noises were coming from the trunk of the blue Caddy parked beside him.

"Lucky number seven," a voice echoed in the garage.

The interruption shocked Red. He was no longer focused on the trunk or his nightmarish memories. Part of him was grateful for the distraction, but another part was terrified. He had no idea how things were supposed to work out—no clue how much danger he was in.

"We've been waitin' on you, sweetheart," the sneering voice continued.

Red looked down the lane and saw a tall, dark figure standing several yards in the distance.

"Is this—"

Before Red could ask his question, the man cut him off. "No questions, just get away from the fuckin' car. *Now.*"

Another shorter figure appeared behind Red and slipped a black bag over his head.

Panic was setting in. His heart pumped with fury. "Hey! What the fuck is this?"

The sound of tires squealing and pulling closer approached, followed by a trunk popping. The ominous trio of men said nothing to Red. They rummaged through his pockets removing his wallet, keys, pager, and money from his jacket.

Red kept the cuff of his jacket over his father's watch, hoping they didn't key in on it.

"What are you doing?" Red asked.

"Assholes like you don't get to go inside with anything of value," one of them said with a laugh.

"You must've fucked up real good," the other man said. "Your boss requested the *VIP* treatment for you."

Several stiff shots blasted Red in the ribcage, and the air hissed out of his lungs. Before Red could catch his breath, the goons lifted him off the concrete, stuffed him into the trunk, and slammed it shut.

THE PATH OF DARKNESS

The ride was fast and bumpy. Red was grateful the men had pulled over for one of them to piss and at the same time removed him from the trunk. Since they'd taken the bag off his head, he assumed they were far enough along to maintain the secrecy of the route.

The car pulled around a massive cluster of rocks. The mountainous terrain dwarfed the vehicle, leaving them in obscurity—covered by the privacy of a hidden cove.

As the off-road excursion came to a halt, there wasn't a road in sight for miles. The abandoned mines illuminated by the car's headlights would've been undetectable had the men in the vehicle not been aware of the coordinates.

When they finally reached their destination, a black, compact shuttle bus approached the car. The drivers waved at each other as they passed.

After they came to a stop, the men immediately pulled Red out of the car. Twisting his arm behind his back, they ushered him up to the rocky edge of the massive shaft. The taller man lifted a misshapen slab of stone that overlapped the wall, revealing a keypad, and punched in a seven-digit code.

What the hell is this? Red wondered.

"Please, don't fuckin' kill me," Red begged. "I got a family. I got a little girl." Despite not knowing if the girl was his or not, Red couldn't help but think about Dessi. After all, she was the reason he'd embarked on his dark journey.

The men said nothing.

An oddly shaded patch of rock that looked slightly out of place started to rumble and slide. A seemingly impossible transformation took place as the side of the mine parted, exposing a hidden void.

The men promptly ushered Red into the darkness. Upon entry, they were greeted by a greasy, pimple-faced man in a bellhop uniform.

"Going down, I assume?" the bellhop asked.

The men nodded at him, and as he pressed the elevator button.

The elevator dinged.

"Is this it?" Red asked.

Again, the men remained mum.

A down arrow lit up in blacklight behind the bellhop. Just seconds later, the colossal steel doors behind him opened, displaying a huge elevator. The cell was so spacious that, despite the unoccupied, big rig box truck parked inside, there was still enough room to accommodate an entire football team.

The men stepped inside the elevator and dragged Red along. He was squirming desperately, but Red's actions were more out of fear and disorientation than outright disobedience.

While the purpose of the shaft appeared to be for cargo, the décor within it suggested otherwise. One of the men approached a series of regal buttons on the wall, sliding his finger past the one that read 'Cargo' down to another labeled 'Shadows.'

As soon as it lit up, Red could feel the momentum of the elevator's sluggish descent. His heartbeat accelerated more as the altitude dropped.

The elevator dinged again.

As the sound of the gliding doors found Red's ears, one of the men gripped his neck tightly.

"W—what's going on?" Red asked.

The burly fella in front of him held his hand out at his side. "Welcome to Shadows, scumbag. Good luck… you're gonna need it."

Red slowly turned around to face a thick black curtain. A garish, gray glitter was slathered across the lengthy cloth, forming the word: *SHADOWS*.

A meaty palm pushed hard against his spine, sending him stumbling out of the elevator. Red staggered forward through the split curtains before regaining his footing on the other side. When his eyes locked in on the monstrous sight, his jaw slacked.

"What the fuck?" he whispered.

The brightly lit glass encasement didn't answer all the questions for him, but it answered a lot of them. The ghastly and salacious stories he'd heard on the streets were true—Shadows was no ordinary casino.

There was a reason the location wasn't public.

Inside the glass, stapled to a black felt background, hung the dried husk of a man. The unfortunate man's beef jerky-like skin was stretched out like a trophy animal. It included his legs, torso, arms, and face. Every spectrum of the male anatomy—except for his genitals.

Red had seen a lot of shit on the streets and during his time with Brittany—robberies, stabbings, shootings—but the dehydrated and preserved shell of a skinned man wasn't one of them.

This was a different kind of evil.

The contents of his belly violently bubbled. As watery vomit crept up Red's throat, he noticed another particularly disturbing detail inside the encasement. The skin mask had thick stitching keeping the man's lips sealed while a single red and a single black poker chip—both bearing the letter S—occupied the space where each of his eyes should've resided.

Red needed to get away from the desecrated flesh. There was something extra mean-spirited about the entire thing. The image of the man was burned inside his head. He stepped past the disgusting case toward a much tamer sight.

Behind a barred cell and two inches of bulletproof glass sat a middle-aged woman smoking a cigarette. She seemed at ease, looking down at a glowing security monitor. The signage above her booth read: *Bank*.

THE BANK

To the left of the bank was a single door beside a massive wall of miniature lockboxes. A jacked black man in a security guard uniform with a buzzcut and shades stood in front of a metal detector. A glowing, neon-pink entrance sign burned bright above his head.

"Keys, watch, or wallet?" the banker asked, interrupting Red's study of the environment.

"W—what?" Red stammered.

The banker beckoned the security guard. "Pat him down."

"I don't have anything on me," Red said.

"It's just standard procedure," the banker replied.

The security guard retrieved a handheld detection device from the inside of his jacket. He noticed the silver watch around Red's wrist that the goons had missed.

"Time ain't allowed in here," the security guard said. "Gimmie the fuckin' watch."

"But that was my dad's—"

"Man, you think I give a fuck?" the security guard asked, slamming him into the wall.

The wind hissed out of Red, and the metallic timepiece slipped off his wrist and into the guard's clutches.

"Hold your arms out and spread your legs," the security guard demanded. After hovering the detector over Red's body, he found nothing else of note. He nodded his head and gestured to the woman. "You may approach."

"What about my watch?" Red asked. Despite the fear he felt, his father's timepiece was important enough to make him speak up.

"You'll get it when you come back out… well, *if* you come back out, I should say," the banker said. She snubbed out her cigarette in an ashtray and nodded.

Red turned his attention to the rectangular box that opened at the bottom of the window. The banker pushed a single white ticket stub forward. The paper had a series of numbers inked at the bottom.

"Just hold onto this," she continued.

"Okay."

Red remained flabbergasted by the surrealness of the entire situation. The dread and anxiety he felt could've brought him to his knees. He took a deep breath and forced himself to hold it together. Falling apart wasn't going to change anything. He'd have to deal with the situation one way or another.

"How much you lookin' to exchange?" the banker asked.

Red wasn't quite sure exactly what she meant, but he put two and two together when he saw the countless rows of chips stacked up behind her.

"I don't have any money," Red replied.

"I figured that much when you walked in here," she said turning back to the security guard and giving him a wink. "Hold his arm down."

"What?!" Red cried.

The guard took hold of him and muscled Red's arm through the bars and under the glass window.

"I plugged it in right when I saw you," she explained, lifting the electric soldering iron off its rest.

"Wait!" Red cried.

The red-hot tip of the device was custom-shaped to match the gothic curves of the 'S' that represented the underground establishment's name. It was there to brand those who entered with the emblem.

"I can get money! Please, don't hurt me!" Red begged, balling his hand into a fist. How many times had he said that in his life? It was becoming redundant.

"Just relax your hand, it'll be okay," the banker explained with a twisted grin. "You're already here, fella, so there's no turning back now. Besides, money's not everything. You might not realize it yet—most people don't—but everyone that walks in here has something much more valuable than money."

"What do you mean?!" Red cried.

"Meat," she said.

"Open your hand now, or I'll break your fuckin' arm!" the guard yelled.

Red continued to struggle and plead. "Please, I—I haven't done anything!"

As the security guard wrenched back on his joint, Red cried out and his blood-crusted hand loosened. The electric iron sizzled against the crispy crimson and a tiny plume of smoke arose from his flesh.

Red screamed as the scorching burn of the letter became everlasting. When the banker lifted the branding instrument off Red's skin, the abbreviated symbol instantly flared and puffed. The 'S' encompassed nearly his entire palm. The mark would undoubtedly cast a permanent shadow over his life—for however much longer that lasted.

THE BUFFET

When the door closed behind Red, he felt trapped. As he tried to shake the pain off from blistered hand, he wondered what the symbolism burned into his flesh meant for his future.

"Excuse me, sir. You look *hungry*. May I suggest a visit to our complimentary buffet before you play?"

Red looked in the direction of the voice. The initial agony of his burn distracted him from his surroundings, but he focused, pushing beyond the chatter and screaming in the background. When his eyes found the smiling man with the pencil mustache in the white collared shirt, he didn't know what to think.

Behind the grinning attendant stood armed security guards in black suits at each end of the buffet table. There were a half-dozen or so people looming over the sneeze guard and reviewing the party favors.

"Go ahead, have a little look-see," he said gesturing toward the countless trays. "Whatever you need to put you up to the task, I'm sure we have it."

Red didn't reply to the man, he just continued to grimace and stumbled closer, trying to get a look at the spread. As he moved in, he couldn't believe his eyes.

Holy shit, he thought.

Every drug under the rainbow had found a home. The flavors ranged in diversity from clinical prescription quality to the riskiest street shit. Each of the intense shades of vice were available in heaping doses and clearly labeled.

Red was in awe of the display—he'd never seen anything like it. Hundreds of thousands of dollars' worth of drugs just sitting out in the open, there for the taking. His eyes ran down the labeled trays:

Bath Salts.

Weed.

Acid.

Shrooms.

Cocaine.

Absinthe.

Ibuprofen.

OxyContin.

GBH.

Ketamine.

Benzos.

Salvia.

MDMA.

PCP.

Kratom.

Crack.

Speed.

Mescaline.

Roofies.

Spice.

Vicodin.

Heroin.

His eyes lingered on the heroin a few beats longer. *No, don't even think about it.*

He'd worked too hard to get his shit together, but at the same time, the stress was insane. He couldn't avoid thinking about how much relief came with a few sniffs. His ma and Dessi's horrified faces popped into his head.

I'll feel good, but what about them?

Red forced himself to ignore the tan but continued to review the rest of the area. At the very beginning and end of the buffet, occupying the area where one might normally find plates and cutlery, were several other buckets that were designated to assist with the administering of the various drugs. Joint papers, spoons, crack pipes, needles, blunt wraps, lighters, snort straws, and almost any other type of paraphernalia could be found.

"Jesus fucking Christ," Red whispered.

"Oh, don't let *him* catch you doing that stuff," a bald man in a collared shirt said with a cackle.

Farther beyond the unprescribed pick-me-ups and drug equipment, at the end of the case, sat a massive self-serve bar. It included beer, wine, and just about any other spirit under the sun. Additionally, swivel sticks, cigars, matches, and various brands of cigarettes were piled up on the side.

Despite his earlier efforts, Red found himself making his way back to the brown powder. He'd had a lot of fun with cocaine in his heyday too, but there was something extra special about the diesel that was rooted in his DNA. He remained mystified by the sight.

No. Can't go back down that road. Stop thinkin' about it.

He'd have killed for a snort, but at the same time, he knew the snort might very well get him killed. Red licked his lips. The dune of powder was beyond hypnotic, especially considering the circumstances. But if he was going to get out of Shadows in one piece, he needed to be on his A game.

Maybe I'm supposed to be here. Maybe I can get Mad Dog's money and Jack's in the same stroke.

For the first time, Red was thinking positive. Saving his mother and finding the whereabouts of Brittany and Dessi was within grasp. He just needed to get a handle on the situation. His entire life revolved around gambling. If all the things he'd heard about Shadows were true, then the house had to host a game that he had the edge on. But first, he was gonna need to take the edge off.

The throbbing pain spreading throughout his hand wasn't going away anytime soon. He'd need some kind of fix to get him through.

Red's eyes darted over to the Vicodin tray—*just a little something to take the edge off.*

He picked up a pair of pills and popped them in his mouth. It was too dry to summon enough spit to swallow them, so he looked to the bar to wash them down.

Red maneuvered around the man in the suit who had continued to linger. He approached him from behind. The balding bastard squinted through his wireframe glasses and stuck his fingernail directly into a pail of white powder.

"Ain't this fuckin' paradise!" the bald man exclaimed as the dust disappeared up his nostril.

Red hardly paid attention to him until he had no choice. "For some people, I suppose."

The bald man's forehead wrinkled. "Say, man, you look a little down on your luck. Is that fair to say?"

Red shifted the pills to the side of his mouth. "That's the understatement of my life."

"Well, it ain't much, but here's a little something to get you started. It sucks being broke in here." The bald man reached out, offering Red three five-dollar chips.

Red was beyond grateful and quickly snatched up the donation. But confusion contorted his face.

"How'd you know I was broke?" Red asked.

The man looked at the 'S' burned into Red's hand. "They make it pretty obvious in here." He eyed the three chips. "Lose those, and you'll be playing with house money. And let me tell you, that's a position you don't wanna be in. Unless you're a little fuckin' crazy, like me." He smirked in a devilish manner.

As the bald man reached into his mouth, the glimmer of the blue jewel in the center of his class ring caught Red's attention. But he was immediately distracted when the bald man popped out a dental plate that accounted for six of his front teeth.

"Trust me on that, bud," the bald man said.

Red winced at the gummy grin. "With any luck, I'll just have to take your word for it."

The bald man reinserted his teeth. "This is just one thing, I got plenty of other warts now, thanks to this fucking place."

Red zeroed in on the print on his ring.

"But sometimes I just gotta play with fire," he continued. "Sometimes, when I'm riding in on the shuttle with all them other nervous nellies, the thought just comes into my head. Even though I got money, I don't wanna play with it." He held up his finger and thumb an inch away from each other. "Sometimes I just want the rush of being that close to whatever comes next…"

The closer Red watched the man, the more unhinged his subtleties made him seem. He'd been around his fair share of whack jobs. Changing the subject was the best idea he could come up with.

"You went to Lincoln High School?" Red asked.

The bald man grinned. "It'd be weird if I wore the ring and didn't."

"No shit, I wasn't too far. I went to C.F. High."

The bald man chuckled. "I bet. I'm sure you were high every day, everyone who went to that ghetto ass school was. Heard that place looked a lot like this here buffet."

Red smirked. He wasn't wrong. "Yeah, not a lot of us got rings, if that's what you mean. We were more focused on the extracurricular."

"Yeah," the bald man replied. His face suddenly grew serious. The cocaine made his eyes flare. "I—I know what you're thinking; what's a middle-aged guy still wearing this for?"

Red shrugged his shoulders. "Hey, man, there ain't nothing wrong with it. To each his own."

"It's my lucky charm, I guess. When I was younger, a lotta things seemed to go right for me. Then I grew up, and not so much. I just wore it for nostalgia a few times at first.

But then I noticed every time I came here and didn't wear the ring, I got my fuckin' teeth knocked out, or ribs broken, or whatever."

Red nodded. "Well, I'm glad it's working for you."

There wasn't exactly anything 'lucky' about his father's watch—it was more of a comfort thing. But seeing the bald weirdo with his ring just made Red wish he had his dad's timepiece.

"It damn well better. Gotta pay these cocksuckers to even let me bring it in here." The bald man stopped like some kind of epiphany had struck. "Wait… shit, how long we been standing here talking?"

Red gazed into the bald man's eyes—they looked hellish. He had the kind of look you might find in the eyes of a cult member on a compound who let the leader fuck his wife.

"I, uh, I'm not really sure," Red said. "Five, or maybe ten minutes?"

"Okay, I gotta get going. I've gotta get my head right. I'm going to war a little later today." Sweat cascaded down the bald man's brow as he winked at Red. "But listen, I'll see you around."

The jittery, bald man scuttled away like a cockroach inside a crack house that was being raided. Where he had to be in a place like Shadows, Red could only wonder.

As he rubbed his fingers over the chips in one hand, Red examined the toasted tissue on the palm of his other. Despite the lack of a formal explanation, things were exactly as he'd suspected.

Red didn't stop to ponder it too much. He needed to figure out what he was doing next. The pair of goons at his mother's house were most likely not happy to be waiting around watching over her.

Plucking a highball glass from the bar, Red looked at the half-filled bottle of Maker's Mark. He tipped it sideways, pouring the poison until it reached capacity. He swallowed nearly a third of the whiskey in one shot, exhaling with a grimace of stiffness.

The sting of the alcohol was just the kick in the nuts he needed.

There we fuckin' go. Now I can think at least. He raised his eyebrows. *Just calm down.*

He would've loved another gulp of the drink—and even another after that. It would've allowed his mind to drift farther away from the frightening scenario. While the whiskey's bite had made him feel better, he knew that too much of a good thing would only dig his grave faster. His own history told him that much.

Slow the fuck down.

Red set the drink on the bar not planning to finish it. Instead, he reached inside the cooler for a beer. He wandered away from the growing line of degenerate gamblers at the buffet table, and for the first time, started to take in the other attractions that the room had to offer. But the moment he got a look at what lay ahead of him, Red wished he could run screaming out the door.

STRANGE GAMES

As Red investigated the room, it wasn't just the games that disturbed him, it was the people playing them. Many of them shared unsettling signature traits. He tried to register as many of the deformities as he could, and as the list in his head inflated, the terror in his belly grew.

Burned flesh.
Mangled limbs.
Dark bruises.
Deep cuts.
Skull knots.
Severed fingers.
Missing teeth.
Black eyes.
Snipped ears.
Eye patches.
Peg legs.
Canes and limps.
Wheelchairs.
Broken noses.
Wired jaws.
Skinned scalps.
Bullet holes.

Some of these horrors were fresh while others had either healed or were in the process of doing so. The rumors about the place were to that point still rumors, but such a scene of mass mutilation couldn't be ignored.

However, the crowd in the room was colossal. As he continued to scan, Red could see a decent amount of folks who were still all in one piece. His eyes might've just been drawn to the deformities first.

Thank fuckin' God, he thought. *Maybe there's still hope for me.*

He told himself such things for morale purposes. It wasn't that he truly believed them. From the moment he'd been stuffed into the trunk of that car, Red knew it was only a matter of time until he got his. The question wasn't so much whether he was going to get hurt but how badly.

The 'games' were like none that Red had ever seen. Well, that wasn't exactly true—he'd seen them all before in one form or another, but at Shadows they were severely warped. Perverse versions of many classic games he'd been introduced to throughout his years in the slums.

Across the hall, an overweight, female dealer ran a three-card-Monte table. The gist was the same as it ever was, but in place of bent playing cards, sat a trio of folded Maxi pads. As the dealer worked her gimmick, she periodically showed the undesirable underside that one of the pads bore—a vile absorption space saturated with a mixture of dry, jammy blood-stains and crusted pus.

"Find the red, find the red," the dealer barked in carnie fashion to the group of creeps in front of her.

A man standing at the center of the table pointed to the 'card' on the left. When the dealer flipped the pad, it was white as winter.

"Time to pay up!" She cackled.

A ghastly leer accompanied by a hiss of excitement pushed its way out of the obese dealer's mouth as she revealed the disgusting pad. She then reached into her black slacks and stuffed it between her legs.

"We'll get it freshened up for you, dear," she continued.

Biting down on her lip, she dug around like a dog trying to retrieve a bone buried in mud. After several moments of rubbing and scooping, she eventually produced a sweat-soaked rag saturated with an *extra* heavy flow.

The reluctant player took hold of the oozing cloth and elevated it over his mouth. He looked back at the dealer and then to the pad, seemingly concerned about the pieces of the woman that were now separated from her body. The grape-sized blood clot staring back at him was accompanied by a bouquet of wiry hairs.

"There's gotta be some other way," the man pleaded.

"There is," she replied. "But I'm not so sure you'd prefer it." The dealer looked at a gentleman wearing a black suit who stood beside her. He opened his coat, revealing his gun and holster.

"Al—alright," he said. "Just gimmie a second. Lemme work myself into it."

"You've got thirty seconds—just like everyone else."

As the man bumbled, trying to ready himself, he clasped onto each end of the gooey cushion. He moved it up to his mouth and a mixture of congealed and warm blood dollops dotted his chin. The terror in his eyes popped as he cranked the cloth in opposite directions, rolling the shiny blood clot into his mouth and juicing the rest of the ruby liquid like a blood orange on Sunday morning.

Red felt like he was going to be sick.

The man tried to swallow but gagged—his eyes watering as the blood trickled down his chin all over his shirt. He put one hand over his mouth as his cheeks puffed out.

"If that comes out of your mouth, your brains come out of your head," the dealer said.

The vomit that had puffed the man's chipmunk cheeks slowly started to deflate. He did his best to allow the soupy fluid to drain down his esophagus until he seemed to finish the task.

"Show me your tongue," the dealer demanded. "Open up!"

The man unhinged his jaw displaying a color palate on his tongue that was normal. But his teeth remained painted with her rancid expulsion.

She nodded at the man. "Well done. You're free to go."

Red was grateful the ordeal was over. He certainly wouldn't be playing that one anytime soon.

Gotta find some better options.

But when he turned his attention to the table beside the sickening sleight of hand, he realized that it wasn't any better. If it wasn't just as bad, then it was worse.

A pair of 'ladies' stood by a pool table, each with a cue in hand. The intensity in their eyes indicated they were in the midst of an argument. When one of them started screaming, Red's suspicion was confirmed.

"You knocked in the 8 ball!" the blonde with a southern twang yelled. "That means that you lose automatically, bitch!"

The goth girl's face that she was screaming into had several dozen piercings—a face that made Red wonder whose dick she sucked to get through the metal detector. She was every bit as red-eyed as her opponent. They both looked like they hadn't slept in days. While on the surface they appeared to be playing a simple game of pool, it soon became apparent there was far more at stake than just bragging rights.

One of the security guards at the pool table approached the hole the blonde was pointing at. After inspecting her claim, the guard extracted a black 8 ball.

Immediately another guard pounced on the goth girl, and together, they pinned her to the table bending her over in the process. As the guard lifted her black miniskirt, the blonde giggled and chalked up her pool cue.

"Let me go!" the goth girl begged.

The guards ignored her pleas, instead opting to rip off her orange thong and spread her pussy lips.

"You talked a lotta shit before," the blonde said. "What happened? You don't sound so tough anymore."

"Please, don't!" the goth girl cried.

"Hold still!" a security guard commanded, sliding his beefy fingers up from her dry pussy lips.

The goth girl's asshole flinched with unwillingness. "I had Mexican earlier—tamales!"

"You'd say anything," the blonde replied, gliding the pool cue between her fingers. The sadism flared in her pupils. When Red watched her mannerisms, he could tell she oozed with a lust for humiliation. The southern blonde had made it clear that she couldn't control her cruel nature.

Red watched as the chalky pool tip muscled its way into the girl's sphincter. It took some work, but as the blonde stabbed the stick in and out, the cavern started to loosen and leak. Yellow and transparent juices secreted from the goth girl's stink ring as more of the cue disappeared inside her. The flood of bowel liquid made Red believe her tale of woe about the tamales.

He winced in pain, almost forgetting about his hand as he watched the southern bell ram the stick in and out of her with increasing aggression. Her asshole gaped further as it stretched to accommodate the thick clumps of watery shit working their way around her rotten rim.

These are the kind of people in this fuckin' place? It's like it's only psychos in here.

Red forced himself to look away. Still, even while trying to ignore the chaos and calm himself, he couldn't escape the guttural screams.

Is this what she meant by meat? He thought back to the cryptic words of the banker, then to the array of deformities he'd seen afflicting the players around him. Not that Red was in a rush to play any of the gross games, but he wondered about the process. It seemed there were games where people played against the house, but strangely, unlike most other casinos, there were also games where people played against each other.

While he couldn't be sure he'd find something that struck his fancy, he hoped he would. Or, at the very least, a game that he had some type of experience with.

Times a-wastin'.

The urgency Red felt didn't waver. The idea of what could potentially happen to his mother continued to haunt him. Mrs. Blanchfield was getting up there in age, and Red didn't like leaving her by herself too long, never mind alone with a pair of bloodthirsty psychopaths like Buggs and Dane Fuller.

Red tried to block out the hysterical cries of the goth girl, who looked like she was now oozing bloody soft serve. He set his eyes on the only other game he could see in the entrance area. Just several feet away, a sizable group of men and women stood huddled around the table. There was too much traffic for him to see what the hustle was.

Gotta get moving.

Red took a swig of his beer and made his way through the crowd.

SICK STAKES

As Red penetrated the circle of degenerates, a collective cheer came from the audience. The craps table was hot. The croupier was a tubby, disheveled man wearing a rotten smile. On some areas of his face, the dirt clogging his pores was plainly visible. Using the rake, he pulled the pair of red dice toward him, scooped them up, and handed them to the high roller.

The middle-aged gentleman wearing a plum suit grabbed the dice and blew on them. His overly tanned skin made his teeth appear whiter than they were. He shook his head, causing his thin, feathery hair to flutter at the sides of his face. Dripping with jewelry his myriad of golden rings and chains sparkled as he elevated his pinky and adjusted his oversized shades.

"Good luck, Mr. Don," the croupier said.

"The Don don't need luck, baby," Mr. Don replied, closing his eyes and transitioning into a meditative state.

Red didn't play craps often, but he'd played enough to know the ropes. As he studied the table, it seemed relatively normal. But one thing stood out to him; the only chips on the table were all on the come bet. In a normal casino, a 7 or 11 created a winner when wagering on the come bet.

"Seven or eleven," the snaggle-toothed whore smoking the Camel beside Red mumbled to herself.

It appeared to be no different at the table.

But the fact that all the chips were stacked in the same place wasn't the strange part. That could've happened by chance. But the red lettering imprinted on the felt table wasn't by chance. The come section was misspelled. Instead of the traditional 'C-O-M-E' it read 'C-U-M.'

Additionally, what was normally known as the most common bet on the table—the pass line—had been relabeled to 'ASS LINE.'

"Daddy Don needs a new refrigerator," Mr. Don said, tossing the dice forward.

Snake eyes.

Red stared at the single dots on the dies, unsure what repulsive act might be next on the menu.

The croupier let out a phlegmy cough before speaking. "That's a shame," he said.

"Fuck," Mr. Don moaned.

Several people in the crowd cursed and dispersed from the muddle at the table.

"Do whatever you have to," the croupier replied.

Mr. Don unzipped his violet slacks and whipped out his pecker. He started to stroke his cock, but the sad, salty meat looked dead as ever. He looked to the crowd, staring at the wrinkly, snaggle-toothed whore beside Red.

Her torn fishnet stockings revealed a sexy, caramel skin tone. A thick ass crept out from her pink leather dress and a generous portion of her cleavage showed proudly. She pivoted her stance adjusting in her white high heels as she peeked over at Mr. Don's cock. Her face was a bit on the haggard side, but the heavy layers of make-up helped disguise the divots and acne scars. Despite her exaggerated features, there was something about her that Red found attractive.

Mr. Don firmly stroked his shlong but it was practically on life support. The visual of the whore wasn't enough.

"It—it ain't operational right now, damnit," Mr. Don crooned. "Too much fuckin' whiskey and Lexapro! I'm soft as egg salad!"

"Well, if I were you, I'd figure it out soon," the croupier said, gesturing toward the impatient-looking security guard with the handgun at his side.

Red was noticing a theme. Every single table inside the place had security. They always worked in unison with the dealers to ensure whatever nefarious outcome agreed upon went as planned.

Mr. Don was looking more concerned by the minute. He gazed back upon the whore beside Red.

"Hey Lilly, I've got a twenty-five-dollar chip if you suck my cock," Mr. Don said.

Red looked at the skank sucking hard on the cigarette beside him.

"Get fucked, Don," Lilly replied.

"That cost too much," Mr. Don quipped. "C'mon, baby, just help me out."

Lilly started to turn away.

"Time's running out," the croupier reminded.

"Okay! Fifty!" Mr. Don blurted out. "I'll put up fifty!"

Lilly turned back and smirked. She stuck her tongue out and extinguished the butt ember on it.

"Fine, just don't cum in my fuckin' mouth," she said.

"Fair enough," Mr. Don said, smiling as she approached him and dropped down on her scabby knees.

"Oh, baby, you know how to do it to me," he said, bridging himself up against the table.

As Lilly let his limp cock scrape the back of her throat, it got fatter. She slurped in air around the edges, and her saliva started to bubble around his prick. As she grabbed onto his balls, tugging downward, and backed away to suck in a full breath, Mr. Don's slimy rod doubled in size.

"Fuck my throat," she dared him.

Red furrowed his brow. *Either she likes it, or she's lookin' for the fastest way to the finish line.*

Mr. Don took a firm grip on Lilly's locks. "That what you want, bitch?"

Mr. Don rammed his glistening cock into her mouth. She wrapped her white fingernails around his thighs as Mr. Don thrust in and out as hard as he could. Tears streaked down her face. He went in harder on her, banging the back of her head into the craps table. As Lilly gurgled and gagged, Mr. Don cupped his hand under her leaky jaw and caught a bubbly rope of drool.

"Messy fuckin' whore," he said, smearing the translucent spit-wad over her face and nose. "But you like it messy, don't you?"

Red watched on as Lilly cried out with Mr. Don's cock deep in her throat, humming on his prick submissively. It didn't seem like it was the first time she'd had her face railed by him—she knew how to work him. Mr. Don's legs buckled inward, his thighs beginning to tremble.

"Oh, fuck," Mr. Don whispered.

He removed his throbbing prick from her mouth and aimed his dickhole between her eyes.

When Lilly tried to stand up, Mr. Don's grip on her hair remained firm. He wasn't about to let her leave before the fireworks.

"Hey, let go—ugh!"

A massive rope of hot nut splattered over her face. The semen stretched from Lilly's right eyebrow down to her nose.

"What the fuck!" She shrieked.

Several additional bursts went even higher, raining down on her hair before he angled his dick down and laid into her with more monster cumshots.

As Red watched Lilly continue to get blasted in the face, he was both disgusted and impressed. The countless vices and 'prescriptions' that Mr. Don was steadily overindulging in had apparently left a surplus of seed in his system. The Peter North specials were relentless.

"You piece of shit!" Lilly squawked.

Another girthy string of cum sprayed her in the eye then up her nose.

"What?" Mr. Don snickered. "Keep your mouth closed, and you'll be alright."

Once the load finally dwindled, Mr. Don slapped his oozing cock against the side of her gunky cheek for good measure then zipped up his drawers.

He retrieved a fifty-dollar chip from his inside pocket and flipped it at her.

"A deal's a deal," he said with a grin.

The croupier nodded at Mr. Don, letting him know he was free to go.

Red remained shocked by the outright perversion on full display, but also a little relieved. The fact that Mr. Don just had to rip one off publicly when he lost his roll didn't seem *that* bad. Sure, it was humiliating, but compared to the other shit he'd heard about, that was getting off light.

The croupier flipped the table marker from 'ON' to 'OFF' signifying the table was ready to take bets again.

Red looked around. Apparently, Mr. Don wasn't the only one who'd blown his load. Outside of Lilly wiping cum off her face, the buzzing crowd at the table dissipated.

Red let his fingers toy with the chips in his pocket, keeping his eyes on the 'CUM' box.

Doesn't seem like the worst thing.

If he was going to make any money with the charity chips, he had to go all in on something. It was the only way to get close to the amount needed.

The croupier looked at Red, seeing he had some interest in the game.

"Do we have a new shooter?" the croupier asked, toying with the dice rake.

Red didn't give him a straight answer, he just stared at the man.

What's the worst that could happen?

Red played with the chips inside his pocket.

If I lose, all I gotta do is be able to cum fast.

He thought back to his sex-starved days with Brittany. Back when she was fucking everyone but him.

That's never been a problem before I guess…

"Well?" the croupier persisted.

Red took a deep breath. "What's the bet with the highest payout?"

CRAPS

The croupier raised his eyebrows. "The rules here are a little different than your traditional casinos." When he glanced at the enflamed 'S' seared into the palm of Red's hand, the croupier smiled. "You have to build up to the high-stakes bets. *Everyone* starts out on the ass line."

"What happens if I lose?"

The croupier brandished his discolored gums and rotten teeth. "Nothing that'll hurt you… Well, except for your pride, maybe."

"You're not allowed to tell me?" Red asked.

"Why ruin the surprise? Either you're here to gamble or not."

Red thought about his mother alone in the apartment with that smelly piece of shit Buggs breathing down her neck. The anxiety in his gut grew. Still, Red required a little convincing.

"It's nothing worse than what you've seen in this room," the croupier added, trying his best to entice him to play. "This is about the lowest stakes a place like this can offer."

Fuck it, Red thought.

He retrieved the three five-dollar chips from his jacket and set them on the ass line.

The croupier handed Red the dice and flipped the marker over to 'ON.'

"Shooter coming out! Shooter coming out!" the croupier yelled.

No one in the area seemed to care—the table remained empty except for Lilly. She'd just finished wiping the nut off her face, then dropped her newly acquired fifty-dollar chip on the ass line.

"Something about you looks lucky to me," Lilly said, winking her gunky eyelashes at Red.

If you only fuckin' knew, lady.

Red didn't acknowledge the comment publicly, instead, he looked at the table, shaking the dice around in his hand. The toss was gentle. When the cubes settled on the felt, Red couldn't believe the roll.

Snake eyes.

"Craps!" the croupier yelled.

"Shit, mister!" Lilly said.

Red gritted his teeth in anger. With the run of terrible luck he was on, if someone was gonna be involved in back-to-back snake eyes, he knew it'd be him.

"Fuck," Red muttered.

The dread in his belly blossomed as he looked at the croupier.

"Dirty Ricky!" the croupier yelled, clapping his hands.

The strapped security guard behind the table pulled the curtain to his side revealing a barred cage front. He punched several digits into the numeric lock and the door popped open.

Red was afraid to see what grotesque sight lay in the darkness. Whatever it was, he knew it wasn't going to be good. Inside the cage was an animalistic man who resembled a Neanderthal. His dark, overgrown mane blended with his beard and the filth on his face.

"Bring your bowl, Ricky!" the croupier instructed. The cadence he addressed him with was one he might've used while calling his dog in the yard.

Hunched over in his fraying, dirty rags, Ricky snagged the rusted, metallic dish on the floor. In a flash, he exited his confines, vaulting up onto the craps table and setting the bowl atop it.

"That-a-boy," the croupier said. "Give us a craps."

Red watched on in disgust as Ricky slid his weathered pants down and squatted. He grimaced as his crusted asshole began to pucker. It was like he'd been trained to hold the turd inside him. The stench of age broke through the ring of stretching skin to accommodate the girthy yet mushy mass. The result of the filthy man's concentration was a piping-hot stool. While it ended up being a solo secretion, the plopper produced was sizable.

"Good boy!" the croupier said. As he reached under Ricky's rectum and slid the dish out, a bit of steam rose off the collapsed log. It looked more like a pile of melted fudge than a bowel movement.

"Here we are," the croupier said, handing the dish to Red. "Have at it."

"What do you mean?" Red asked.

"Eat it."

"No, I—I can't—"

"You can, and you will! The symbol on your hand tells me you have nothing left to bet but your body. We can take a carnal collection if you prefer. But I don't think either of us wants that, right?"

"I'll eat it for him," Lilly said.

"No!" the croupier yelled. "Shooter shoots, shooter eats. That's the rules."

Red looked down at the greasy turd. As disgusting as the shit was, he imagined that whatever they were feeding Dirty Ricky was probably just as bad. The peppering of moldy food particles created a vile crust around the log. He'd never seen another dish so unappetizing.

Red shook his head. "God."

"God isn't here," the croupier said. "Now eat up quick, or else..."

Red knew that if he didn't make his move on the turd, far worse bodily harm would be in the works. His stomach rumbled with disgust and dread. Flickers of his sweet ma invaded his mind again. He never imagined he'd associate a memory of her with a stranger's dump, but his life was just *that* fucked up.

Red set the dish back on the table, hesitant as ever. After working up the will, he finally plunged his fingers into the oily offering, feeling its unsettling warmth. The sickening scent smelled like something had crawled up Dirty Ricky's ass and died. As he pulled the pile apart and scooped, the rancid aroma broke free. A mixture of garbage, body rot, and feces swirled into his nostrils.

Do it for Ma. Do it for Dessi.

Red looked over to Lilly.

"Hold my beer," he said.

She giggled and accepted the drink. If there was ever a hold my beer moment, it was then.

He unhinged his jaws and dropped the excrement into his mouth. The gummy mush was slightly wet when it touched Red's tongue. The bile-laced nature of the movement tasted bitter, but also a lot like the vomit he'd swallowed back down at the entrance of Shadows.

"There you are," the croupier said, grinning with glee. "That's it."

Red gagged and coughed as the grainy chunks found their way between his teeth. The urge to regurgitate struck him again. His stomach rocked in and out.

"Eh, eh, eh, swallow," the croupier commanded.

Lilly watched Red with a crinkle of sadness in her brow. He didn't know why, but it seemed like there was something about him that intrigued her.

"You can do it, just have a sip of ya beer and swallow," Lilly said, handing the drink back to him.

Red snatched the bottle and put it to his lips, watering down the feces as best he could. He started to choke, and a little extra beer pissed out around the edges of his mouth.

The croupier watched Red with a judging eye, clearly not thrilled to see anything spilling out.

As Red felt the sandy streaks of feces drag down his esophagus, the beer helped wash it all down. Subduing the puke as best he could, he swallowed.

"Well, I'll be damned," the croupier said. He spoke like he hadn't quite believed Red had what it took, but he'd been proven wrong.

The nasty man snatched the bowl back from Red and reached under the table. He fished a smoked pig's ear out of a plastic bag and dropped the treat into the shit-smeared dish before returning it to the cage.

"Good boy. Go home now," the croupier commanded, pointing at the cage.

Dirty Ricky pounced on the dish like it was the only possession he had and got his teeth on the pig's ear.

Red gagged but continued to pour beer down his throat, shaking his head from side to side.

"Now what?" Red asked.

The croupier smirked. "Now, you figure out what to play next. Because no one leaves this place until they win a bet." He glanced back down at the burned insignia on Red's shit-caked hand. "And considering your situation, if I were you, I'd choose wisely."

THE MAN IN THE MIRROR

Red could've sat there all night washing the taste of shit and puke out of his mouth. He probably would've if his mother wasn't trapped at home with a pair of violent criminals.

Unlike any other venue he'd ever visited, the men's room in Shadows was quiet. With people shitting at the gaming tables and a drug buffet out in the open, there wasn't really any real reason for people to hide their demons. They were flying freely throughout the establishment. But Red wasn't like most of the people there; he hadn't come by choice.

He used a paper towel to wipe his face and looked at himself in the mirror. He didn't like what he saw. His blackened eye, strawberry birthmark, and crusted hand made him look like exactly what he was—a man on the ropes. He didn't want to think about what he'd become any longer.

Since he could still feel some of the gritty poo particles scraping against his teeth, he decided to rinse his mouth out one more time. As he turned on the faucet, the door to the men's room swung open.

The flamboyant attire and sparkling smile of Mr. Don brightened up the gloomy restroom. He eyed Red hunched over the sink. Slowly walking up, Mr. Don patted him on the back.

"I've been there, buddy," Mr. Don said. "Don't worry, the taste goes away eventually."

Red crinkled his nose—he didn't particularly care for the man after seeing how he treated Lilly, but he'd be a fool not to play his cards right. It was clear that Mr. Don had been around for a while and was smart enough to stay in one piece. If the rumors on the streets about Shadows were true, that was a feat in itself. He didn't have to be friends with the guy, but at the very least he could try and glean some knowledge from him.

"That nasty skid mark on your neck there..." Mr. Don said pointing at Red. "They do that to you here?"

Red spit out the water into the sink along with traces of the feces. "It's a port wine stain."

"Oh, wow. Never seen one in person. That's something else..." Mr. Don farted as he pushed open one of the stalls. "Man, she's ready *now.*"

After the stall door closed, Red heard Mr. Don's turds plop into the toilet. The sound made him grimace and think back to the obscene moment at the craps table.

Mr. Don sounded like he was still trying to push a little harder as he spoke. "So, what'd you think?" Mr. Don asked.

"About what?" Red replied.

Mr. Don laughed. "I been around here too long not to spot a rookie when I see one. That's the only reason you'd be at those shitty entry tables—no pun intended. I only do 'em to fuck around and kill time. But any fella who looks as desperate as you, doesn't waste their time on that shit. No sir, you've got a *real* urgent look about you. So, if you wanna stop fuckin' around and get to it, the big money's on the main floor."

Red wiped his mouth with another paper towel. "Oh, yeah? And what's out there?"

Another series of toots followed by a mass exodus of waste echoed inside the bathroom. Mr. Don grunted and exhaled before finally responding. "What—whatever you can imagine, pretty much."

"I've heard terrible things about the main floor," Red said. "Is what they say true?"

"To be honest, it's probably worse than whatever you've heard. Some things you've just gotta see to believe."

"So why are you here then?"

After some wiping sounds, the toilet flushed, and Mr. Don stepped out. There was a blankness on his face only amplified by his oversized sunglasses. "Because, this is who I am. You can get away with a lot of shit in here if you've got a decent bankroll." Mr. Don washed his hands and then checked his teeth in the mirror. "And if you're smart enough, you can get in and out of this place, at your leisure, unscathed."

Red took a good look at him. Mr. Don looked a lot different than most of the other patrons. He seemed calm, cool, and free of scars. Unlike so many of the people Red had seen at the entry tables, Mr. Don still had all his limbs and fingers. He was also making sure his teeth were clean, not popping them out of his skull like the bald man near the buffet table.

"So, what's the secret?" Red asked.

"You've gotta watch. Gotta take your time. The biggest difference between me and all the grifters coked out of their fuckin' minds in this place is, I ain't desperate."

While Mr. Don's method sounded logical, it required the one thing that Red didn't have: time.

It had taken him about a day to drive to the parking garage they'd kidnapped him from, and it would most likely take him about another day to return if he somehow obtained the money. By Red's estimation, he had forty-eight hours tops.

"In some ways, gambling's a lot like fuckin'. You're goin' in on something and not sure what you're gonna come out with. But it's only the desperate who get the diseases. Me, I'm fuckin' clean. I pick my spots. Sure, sometimes I play it risky. Some days I just need that—that little rush to feel alive. But I can't have too many days like that, and neither should you. You won't live long if you do."

Red thought back to the bald man at the buffet table. If there was one thing the jitterbug had made clear during their brief exchange, it was that he lived dangerously. But Mr. Don's approach was much more disciplined and refined.

That bald fella was going in too hard, Red thought. *But Mr. Don's not going hard enough. I need the best of both worlds. I gotta find a way to go fast while keepin' the risk low.*

Mr. Don wet his hair then ran a comb through it. "Now, on a more casual day—like today—I play the slots."

Red raised his eyebrow. "Why's that?"

"The slots allow you a chance at winning decent money while keeping the danger low. Them machines cost too damn much to destroy all the time. Of all the countless hours I've spent here, I've only seen one fella lose his life on the slots. So, for your casual gambling, you can't beat the slots room. Oh, and stay the fuck away from the blackjack tables."

Red wondered what exactly Mr. Don meant—why were the machines being destroyed while people were gambling? And what was the issue with blackjack? He needed to squeeze Mr. Don for whatever information he could. "What exactly do you—"

"Shit, speaking of the main floor, I'm supposed to be meeting a lady friend of mine over that way right about now. Maybe I'll see you later though. And if I do, hopefully, you're a hell of a lot richer. But more importantly, hopefully, you're in one piece."

With Mr. Don already heading for the door, Red didn't bother asking his question. He just nodded. "Thanks… I hope so too."

But just before Mr. Don opened the exit door, he turned back. Dropping his shades, he made direct eye contact with Red. "I forgot one thing. It's a lot more important than any of that other shit I just told you. Consider it the golden rule. The woman who runs this place—if you can call her a woman—they refer to her as The Black Widow. It would *strongly* behoove you not to find out why they call her that.

If you see her, stay clear."

As Mr. Don turned back to the door, Red couldn't help himself. "Wait, I've never been here before. I don't even know what she looks like."

"Trust me, you'll know her when you see her," Mr. Don replied.

As Mr. Don exited the restroom, exhaustion weighed Red down. He'd barely been inside the place, and already he felt defeated. It wasn't just from the stress of Shadows but from the grim totality of his circumstances. The gambling industry had a grip on him for a long time. It really got bad just after he'd been discharged from his toxic relationship with Brittany and gotten clean. After the heroin was gone from his life, the thrill of the bet was all he had left.

Red couldn't help but think about how he'd gotten into such a clusterfuck. The series of events wasn't anything he enjoyed remembering, but it seemed like his mind had been built to torture himself. Either that or he just hadn't mastered the art of self-control. Probably the latter.

Red knew from being around enough sinners that when people shook one vice, they tended to replace it with another. Once he'd disciplined himself enough to not crave a synthetic rush, he'd convinced himself that the dopamine hits he got while gambling were 'natural' and therefore okay.

And that's when all the trouble *really* started.

MONTHS PRIOR

THE BIG LOSS: PART 1

"Where are you going now?" Mrs. Blanchfield asked.

"Ma, I just gotta take care of a couple of things," Red said. He had the same surefire pep in his step like he did every time he was leaving the house.

"No crazy stuff, right?"

Red slipped his wallet into his pants and smiled. He'd have been lying to himself if he acted unhappy about his mother giving him a hard time about what he was up to. After everything that went down with Brittany and Dessi, and his battle to get off the heroin, he was grateful that someone still gave a shit about him.

"No crazy stuff." Red bent down to her as she rocked in her chair and sipped her iced tea. Puckering up, he kissed her on the cheek. "The only crazy stuff that ever happens is in here."

Mrs. Blanchfield furrowed her brow and tapped him on the arm. "What's that supposed to mean?"

He grinned. "It means I'm crazy about you."

She smiled back.

"Didn't you know?" Red asked.

"You were always a charmer," she said. "Even when you were a little boy."

Red looked down at his watch. He thought about his father momentarily and wondered if he was doing the right thing. He shrugged the idea off. While he'd been wearing the watch to keep himself in check, he still had a life to live.

"Shit, I gotta go," Red mumbled.

Mrs. Blanchfield glared at the vintage timepiece. "And you were always a handsome boy, just like your father. But that doesn't mean I want you to look the way he did when I last saw him…"

"Relax, Ma." Red pointed at the TV. "New episode's about to start. Why don't you focus on Columbo?"

"He used to say the same kind of thing."

"I'm not Dad, okay?" As he approached the hallway, he looked back. "But I do love you."

"I love you too, sweetie," she said.

Red smiled again and headed for the door. "I'll bring you a nice meatball sub on my way back."

"Bring me back some of that MD Sauce too, why don't you? I can use it on the leftover pasta tomorrow."

"Boy, you love that stuff, don't ya?"

Mrs. Blanchfield smiled and licked her lips. Just the thought of her favorite tomato sauce seemed to make her salivate. "It's made local and fresh. Unlike all that frozen food you try to feed me."

"Ha-ha, alright, alright. No problem, Ma."

After he made his way outside, Red hurried down the sidewalk, a little more eager than usual. He was excited to see if Buddy and Ernesto had any news on a certain situation they'd been trying to finagle for a while.

Red had always enjoyed the small-time hustles. Even when he got tangled up with the wrong people, took a loss, or caught the occasional beat-down, there was something he enjoyed about getting over in the streets. The people he was conning didn't even feel real. They were all just like Red—children of the ghetto. And in the city, some days you win big, while other days you lose everything. That was just the way it was.

He'd been hooked on heroin so damn long that he'd forgotten how good the grind felt, how high it got him. But it didn't take him long after he'd gotten clean to rekindle his oldest love. Red might've been off the dope, but he was still on the streets.

And as much as he loved small-time jobs, the more he thought about the proposed con, there was nothing small-time about it.

As he entered Rosie's, he was filled with nervousness and excitement.

Rosie stood beside the draft spouts. The bar was busy, but not too busy. The bartender's eyes met his as Red approached him, and he asked, "The usual?"

Red nodded.

"Bottle or draft?"

"Bottle."

He looked around and spotted Buddy and Ernesto. They were seated in the back of the joint at the darkest table. Buddy had a cigarette in his mouth. He took a final pull before snubbing it out. Ernesto remained emotionless, sipping his drink and staring at the maroon wallpaper.

Rosie set the bottle on the bar.

"Thanks," Red said, grabbing the beer.

He took a swig as he slid into the cozy, circular booth. It wasn't surprising that the fellas had chosen a space that was far detached from the rest of the commotion inside the bar. Not if they were about to tell him what he'd been waiting to hear.

"Ay, what the hell took ya so long?" Buddy asked.

Sitting with his pompadour haircut, Buddy never seemed to have a strand out of place. The several thin golden chains around his neck complimented the many rings on his fingers. His boxy sunglasses helped mask his emotions and true temperament.

"I was takin' care of my ma," Red said.

Buddy took another sip of his drink. "You never let family get in the way of business."

Buddy wasn't just saying that. Red knew for a fact he was living it. That was the entire reason for their meeting. While Red wasn't the type of fella to try and swindle his own family, he had no problem working with someone else who wanted to.

Ernesto stayed quiet, as usual. His tan complexion and wispy mustache made him seem out of place next to a fella like Buddy. Red also seemed out of place. But from the little he knew about the job Buddy was putting together, that was all by design.

"So, what's the story?" Red asked.

Buddy looked over at Ernesto and held out his hand. "E, give 'em the cards."

Ernesto reached inside his jacket and pulled out a deck. He handed them to Red.

"Shuffle 'em up real good, then lay the deck facedown on the table," Buddy said.

Once Red finished shuffling the cards a few times, he set the deck down. "And?"

Buddy took his shades off and let them hang on his V-neck tee. He looked Red in the eyes and grinned as he pointed at the top card. "Jack of clubs."

Red furrowed his brow. "Can we skip the magic tricks and just tell me what the deal is?"

Buddy looked at the big port wine stain on Red's cheek and neck. "Listen, period face, it ain't no fuckin' magic trick. This is the meal ticket."

"What?" Red asked.

"Don't talk. Just listen and flip," Buddy said.

He proceeded to rattle off every card in the deck. One by one, each of the fifty-two that Red laid on the table, Buddy called out before he flipped it.

"That's impossible," Red said. "What are you, fuckin' psychic or some shit?"

"Some shit."

Buddy looked around the bar, checking the faces of each patron carefully before leaning in to explain.

"How?" Red asked.

"My eyes look any different to you?"

"What?"

"Just fuckin' listen to me and answer quietly. Do my eyes look any different to you?"

"No."

"Okay, good."

Ernesto's stoic gaze fell over the room as he kept a lookout for anyone who might take interest in their conversation while Red and Buddy continued to talk.

"These ain't even available to the general public yet," Buddy whispered. "I got a guy… his pops was special ops or some shit. They're InfraRed contact lenses. I paid out the ass for 'em, but the amount we're gonna make back is gonna be stupid."

"I don't get it," Red said. "You can see through the cards with 'em?"

Buddy rolled his eyes. "No, dummy. I said InfraRed not X-ray. All the corners on the facedown sides of every card's marked with invisible ink."

Red's eyes widened. "So, you'll be able to see what everyone's holdin'?"

"Exactly."

"But wait, how you gonna get the cards on Mad Dog's table marked?"

"Let's just say I finally got the in." Buddy smirked. "You know that little cocktail waitress with the pierced tongue and nice ass?"

Red thought about it. "Gia?"

"That's her. But to get the in, I had to get it in, if you know what I'm sayin'. Her pussy's tighter than them tiny dresses she wears, and she's got a throat like a fuckin' vacuum cleaner."

It didn't take long for Red to feel uneasy. He didn't like it when new people got introduced to scams out of the blue—the more people involved, the more loose ends. His past told him most people weren't good at keeping secrets.

Furthermore, Red didn't sign on to jobs without talking to all the players in advance. And as he looked around the table, it was still just the three of them.

"So, if Gia's our girl, where is she?" Red asked.

Buddy scoffed like he'd asked a stupid question. "You ain't the brightest bulb on the runway, is you? What kinda mamaluke would I be to arrange for the three of us to be seen with her in public? How dumb is that?"

Red finished his beer as he tried to measure what he was about to say before unleashing it. "Buddy, you just got done tellin' me that you're railing the fuckin' broad. How dumb is *that?* How can we be sure after this is all said and done that she don't get her panties in a bunch if you stop pluggin' her? If she squeals to your uncle, then—"

Buddy turned stone faced. "She ain't gonna say shit."

"Well, if that's all fine and dandy for you fellas, then run with it. But I don't work with anybody that I ain't discussed matters with in person." Red put his hands on the tablecloth as if he was going to get up from the booth.

Ernesto pulled a switchblade out under the table and Buddy wrapped his hand around Red's wrist.

"Sit the fuck down," Buddy said.

Red said nothing and slid back into his seat.

"Relax, E," Buddy said. "Let me talk to him before we get all crazy." He turned to Red. "I think I can convince him to do the right thing."

Buddy leaned back and finished his beer, then stood. He looked at Ernesto and gestured toward the bar. "Why don't you grab us a few more beers while I straighten out our friend here… on me, of course."

Ernesto reluctantly put the switchblade back into his jacket and headed for the bar.

Taking his seat, Buddy exhaled. He nodded to Ernesto, who was still coldly staring at Red from a distance. "You see, now that's loyalty. That's trust. That's what I need from you, Red. Now, granted, I understand we haven't known each other forever, but I think it's been long enough."

Buddy lit another cigarette and took a puff. "You wanna know the reason that Gia ain't gonna say a fuckin' word?"

It was a rhetorical question so Red stayed quiet.

"Because she's scared of me. Same way *you* should be scared of me. So, newsflash—whether you like it or not, you're doing the fuckin' job. Because why would I allow you to keep breathing if you knew about this and didn't agree to participate? That's a lotta leverage for a little pissant like you. I don't wanna slow this whole thing down and look for another guy, but I will. Sure as the day is long, I'll put you in a fuckin' hole if I have to."

Red watched as Buddy leaned back and took another drag of smoke. There was no arguing about what he'd said. Buddy had the bodies on his resume to back the talk up. This type of threat was one of the reasons Red had been paranoid about getting involved when Buddy had initially approached him. Turns out it wasn't just paranoia after all.

"So, you're on board still, right?" Buddy asked.

Red nodded.

Buddy squinted his eyes. "Say it."

"Yeah, I'm in."

Red's reply came just as Ernesto returned to the table. Ernesto's expression didn't change despite hearing Red comply. He set the drinks down and slid back into his spot in the booth.

"Well, good." Buddy smiled. "Now that we're all on the same page again, for this thing to work, I need you two flanking me at the poker table. Keep betting small and losing to the other fellas over time. I'll be getting it all back anyway. But, with the two of you lettin' other players win a few of your chips here and there, it should be enough to keep the heat off me while I clean 'em out. And I'll intentionally drop a few rounds myself, so my wins don't seem too suspect."

"There's a lotta dangerous people that're gonna be sittin' at that table," Red said. "Wouldn't we be better off trying this at a casino or something?"

Ernesto turned to Buddy. He seemed interested in the answer to Red's question.

"No chance," Buddy said. "It took me months to get this in with Gia. There ain't no guarantees that we'd even be able to convince anyone at a legit gaming house to go along with this. Not only that, but if we get caught doing this in a casino, we're all going to the big house for a long time."

"Yeah, but if we get caught doing this on your uncle's table, we're fuckin' dead," Red said. "Which is worse? You know as well as I do, the biggest cutthroats in this city sit at that table every Saturday night. If one of them don't get us, the psychopaths representing your uncle will. They call him Mad Dog for a reason, and it ain't good—."

"Listen up," Buddy interrupted. "Don't tell me about my own uncle. You understand me, fuck stick? The reason they call him that ain't for the reason you think. Don't be a pussy. If we run this scam a few weeks, we'll clean 'em out over time, and that's gonna set us up for bigger things."

"Weeks!" Red exclaimed. "What the fuck are you talking about?"

"Well, I can't be cleaning them out all in one shot. We need to do it over several weeks and space it out. Make it look right. Each week a different guy wears the contacts. Otherwise, it'll look fishy if one of us keeps winning. But if we spread it out, it looks natural."

Taking about half of his beer down in one gulp, Red set the bottle back on the table. The stress was getting to him. He hated it, but in a sick way that he wouldn't admit, he also liked it.

"You want the safe way?" Buddy asked. "Well, this is it. If we take our time and do it right, no one gets dusted. We just get paid. Right?"

An awkward silence arose among the three of them.

"Fuck," Red mumbled.

Buddy had gotten him. He was right—elongating the job window made it safer. Red sighed, then grabbed his beer and chugged the other half. There was nothing left to say.

"Right?" Buddy asked again.

"Right," Red replied.

"I'm aware," Buddy said. "So is E."

Ernesto remained silent, staring at Red like he wanted to cut him into pieces.

"You're the only one I'm concerned about. I don't need to be concerned about you going into this fuckin' thing. I need to be a hundred percent locked in and making this thing play out as legit as possible."

The more Red thought about it, there was no need to fight any longer. Buddy wasn't going to budge on anything. Red was just along for the ride, and it was no longer a matter of choice. It would benefit Red if he allowed Buddy to focus on the job instead of worrying about him.

Buddy took another drag of his smoke. "So, Saturday night, when we go down there, if the inked cards are in play, Gia's gonna give us a signal. If things are a go, she's gonna bring me a scotch on the rocks. If shit isn't a go, it'll just be a bottle of beer. Got it?"

Red nodded. "Sounds easy enough."

"Good," Buddy said putting his cigarette out. "Let's get this fuckin' money then."

THE BIG LOSS: PART 2

"What'll it be?" Gia asked.

Red settled in, counting and stacking his chips beside Buddy. He did his best not to act nervous but wasn't sure if he was doing a good job. He looked at his watch.

This is about as much like my dad as I can get, he thought. *What the fuck have I gotten myself into?*

"Surprise me," Buddy said acting more focused on adjusting his chips than her.

Gia walked back to the bar. His was the last drink order she took. She wrote a little note on her pad, just like she had for everyone else.

Good. She's playin' the part at least.

The basement smelled moldy, and their surroundings weren't exactly what Red would've expected from a high-stakes poker game organized by Mad Dog. From what Red had heard, everything was usually grandiose with him. But the players sitting at the table made him quickly realize that, despite the glitz and glamour, the event had the crime boss' fingerprints all over it. Amid the mishmash of riffraff who'd arrived for the underground game, two faces of the thirteen were particularly concerning: Buggs and Dane Fuller.

Red tried not to fidget.

Anyone who knew anything about the criminal element in the city understood they were the right and left hand of Mad Dog. Red was never happy to see them. Mainly since usually if you saw them outside of a setting like he was in, that meant they were the last thing you'd ever see.

"Hey fellas," Buddy said, looking at Buggs and Dane. "How's things? My uncle treating you alright?"

The fly around Buggs' head landed on his shoulder. Red could smell him from across the table. Everybody could, but no one dared to say a word.

"Everything's movin' along," Dane said.

"It's been a good week," Buggs added. "But once your chips are sittin' on this side of the table, it's gonna be a hell of a lot better."

Buddy laughed. "I'd love to see you fellas have a little luck, just not at my expense."

Buggs and Dane furrowed their brows in unison.

Red's heart started to race. *Was that somehow a tell?* Red didn't think Buddy said anything that was out of order. He looked over at Ernesto who seemed as calm as ever. *Maybe it's just all in my head.*

"That's funny," Buggs said.

"Why's that?" Buddy asked.

A fly got stuck in the sweat on his face, but Buggs didn't bother swatting it. He just stared through Buddy like he was trying to read him. "Cuz, that's gotta be the first time I ever heard your cocky little ass wish anyone luck. You have a recent change of heart or somethin'? You find God, kid?"

"Yeah," Dane said, "cuz it ain't my fuckin' birthday for another three months."

"Fellas, fellas, take it easy," Buddy said. "You know how it is."

"How's that?" Buggs asked.

As the sound of Gia's heels approaching closed in on the table, Red started to sweat. He did everything he could to avoid shaking and did his best to seem like he wasn't paying attention to their conversation.

Buddy grinned. "Sometimes you gotta tell a girl a few nice words before you bend her over and stick it in her ass."

Laughter erupted at the table.

Relief struck Red when he heard the chuckles, followed by more panic as Buddy turned to Gia and looked into her eyes. She set the scotch on the rocks in front of him.

"Thanks, doll," Buddy said.

THE BIG LOSS: PART 3

Red stared at the shelf inside the grocery store. The sign taped to the edge read: *Fresh & Locally Produced!*

The MD Sauce was a big hit around the area with more people than just his mother. The fancy label and glass bottle made the sauce look like gourmet manufactured goods. Most people wouldn't have expected that 'MD' was an acronym for 'Mad Dog,' or that such an elegant-looking product was backed by an untouchable tyrant. Success like the sauce had only proved that Mad Dog's grip had slipped out of society's underbelly and onto the mainstream.

Red placed several different flavors of the sauce into his handbasket and headed for the twelve items or less lane. When the total came up on the screen, he opened his wallet. Money was plentiful at the moment—more so than at any other point in his life.

Five weeks had passed and the operation had been running so smoothly that they had to keep it going. While the table insisted on using a new deck each evening of play, Gia was still able to get access beforehand and mark the cards. Each week they played slow and safe—methodically draining the table. And since no individual kept winning, the goons were disgruntled but none the wiser.

But as Red walked out of the store holding his bag, the uneasiness that found him when he first signed up for the con remained. A nagging paranoia whispered in the back of his head, reminding him he was dealing with some very dangerous people—his partners included.

Buddy, true to his word, had gotten the scam on track. But he was also a violent criminal who wasn't afraid to flex his muscle. The original cuts everyone was supposed to get were equal. However, Buddy recently explained he'd be taking fifty percent moving forward. He claimed that he deserved extra for hatching the scheme and initially locating and investing in the InfraRed lenses.

While the new dividends revelation didn't shock Red, he hoped that it didn't piss off one of the other two parties. It felt like they were all in one big relationship, and Red was constantly walking on eggshells.

If Ernesto was pissed, he wasn't showing it. To Red, he seemed like he was always on edge. The way he'd drawn his knife on him at Rosie's left Red with little confidence that the psycho wouldn't stick it right in his back if the opportunity presented itself.

Gia was the wildcard. Red had no direct contact with her aside from the drink orders at the table. Whether she was disgruntled or not remained a mystery.

This is one job that I can't wait to be done with, he thought, pressing the button for the crosswalk.

It wasn't typical that he involved himself in a con as dangerous as their high-stakes poker games. Petty had always seemed to work just fine for him. If you got someone on a petty con, then you got a little extra scratch for yourself and the repercussions were low. But this job kept him up at night. This job was the kind of thing that could alter a life drastically, if not end it altogether.

Still, it wasn't just the repercussions that were on Red's mind. Red hadn't had decent money in years. Having such income at his disposal made him feel powerful. The first thing he did was take care of his ma.

He spoiled her with a brand-new television set—now Columbo looked twice as big—and took her to see Barry Manilow perform live. He'd bought her new comfy clothes and kept the apartment stocked with all her favorite things, hence why he was out late in the evening picking up more of that damn tomato sauce.

But there was one person who Red wished he could do something nice for that was no longer in his life. And he felt guilty as sin about it.

As the crosswalk signal changed, Red looked up at the full moon. The night that changed everything flashed in his mind. Brittany's blood-drenched body, Dessi's horrified reaction to the aftermath, the terrible feeling of failure burrowing inside him as she cried on his shoulder. Maybe the saddest part was that, by now, Red was sure Dessi had seen things far worse than some bloodstains. And it was all his fault.

What the fuck was I thinking? Maybe, now that I have some decent money, I can get enough together to try and find her—

The sound of squealing tires barreling around the intersection cut through the night. Before Red even realized what was happening to him, the door of the black van had opened. Buggs and Dane jumped out of the vehicle and slammed Red against the sliding door. His bag of groceries hit the ground and a bottle of MD Sauce smashed.

"What the fuck is goin' on?" Red asked.

"Going for a little ride is all," Dane said.

Buggs looked down at the broken label and the MD sauce that was spilled all over the ground. "Now ain't that a coincidence."

THE BIG LOSS: PART 4

When they arrived at the MD Sauce factory, Red thought he was having a heart attack. After the driver parked in the back of the building, Buggs and Dane led Red out of the van and through the loading dock.

"Fella's, what's this all about?" Red asked.

"Shut your fuckin' mouth," Buggs said. "You'll find out soon enough."

As they entered the factory, Dane locked the big wooden doors behind them. They walked past some forklifts and crates until Red saw who awaited them. Buddy, Ernesto, and Gia were all lined up in chairs. Each with their arms zip-tied behind their backs and gagged. Tomatoes had been placed in each of their mouths and clear packing tape was laid over their lips.

Watching over the three, in a dark, silver suit and thick glasses, stood Mad Dog. His gray and black hair was combed back with precision. In one hand he held a black cane with a steel ball for a handle, and in the other, a handkerchief. Maybe the oddest thing Red noticed was Mad Dog's lower jaw. It was frozen in place, keeping his mouth constantly agape. Drool continued to leak from its corner, forcing him to keep dabbing it with the cloth.

So that's what Buddy meant, Red thought. *That's why they call him Mad Dog.* He quickly moved on. *I'm so fucked.*

"So nice to see you," Mad Dog said. He spoke with a lisp and his lower jaw remained motionless. More saliva oozed, and he used the handkerchief to absorb it.

Buggs and Dane pushed him toward the older man. Red had only seen pictures of him. Standing face to face with a legend like Mad Dog made him experience a grade of terror he'd hoped he'd never feel again.

"H-hello, sir," Red stammered, unsure what else he should say.

"I want you to tell me exactly what happened, you little raspberry fuck," Mad Dog said. He aimed his cane at the port wine stain on Red's face and let the pointed tip rest on it. *"Exactly."*

There was no getting around it. They clearly knew what the deal was. They'd already rounded up all the major players involved—lying wasn't going to save Red or his accomplices.

Wide-eyed and with adrenaline rushing, Red tried to explain himself. "We ran a scam on your table, sir. Gia marked the cards, while me, Buddy, and E all took turns slowly cleaning out the room. We did it for exactly four weeks and planned on doing it again this week."

Buggs punched Red in the kidney from behind. He hit him so hard that he fell to the ground holding his side as he winced in agony.

"Fuckin' piece of shit, you wanna steal my money—"

Mad Dog raised his hand just as Buggs was lifting his foot to stomp him out "Not yet." He squatted down to Red's level and looked him in the eyes. "I want him to see what happens to the others first. And while he's watching, I want him to know that something much worse is going to happen to him once we're through with these other pieces of shit."

Drool leaked out of his face spilling onto the floorboards. He was like a rabid animal in a fit of rage.

Dane zip-tied Red's hands behind his back and sat him in a chair off to the side, facing his cohorts.

Mad Dog looked at Buggs and Dane then pointed his cane at Gia. "Let's start with the slut. I should've known better than to give a whore a job doing something besides suckin' dick."

Buggs and Dane took little time to pounce on her—they were excited to.

Gia begged them with her eyes, but Dane immediately slugged her in the face. A big gash opened up her cheekbone as Buggs approached with a pair of industrial-grade scissors. First, he snipped the zip tie holding her arms back, then opened the jaws of metal and inserted her pinky and ring fingers between them.

"You like drawin' bitch?" Buggs asked. "You like it so much, I figure we could do a nice little art project."

Dane held her in place while Buggs cut off her digits. The steel made short work of the tiny fingers. Blood poured out and quickly puddled on the floor as the lopped pieces of Gia were covered.

"Gimmie her other hand!" Buggs yelled.

She struggled a bit until Dane came across and smashed his elbow into the back of her skull. Gia went limp for a moment, and Dane put four fingers on her other hand into the crimson jaws of the scissors.

They cut through the woman like a knife through sausage. The mutilation brought her back to life in an agonizing fashion. Gia dropped to the ground and fell into the bloody pile of her fingers. She tried to scream, but it was muffled by the tomato stuffed inside her mouth.

"You like drawing, bitch?" Buggs repeated. "I know you like it, cuz I seen you markin' them fuckin' cards, didn't I? How about you draw us a fuckin' picture now?"

"Do it, and maybe we'll let ya live," Dane said.

Buggs picked up one of her fingers and held it out in front of the hand that had three fingers left. "You'd draw us something if you knew what was good for ya!"

With tears streaming down her face, Gia grabbed hold of her severed digit. She looked down at the massive pool of blood, traced a single long, curved line, and made two small circles above it.

Red's eyes glossed over. When he looked at the art, he unintentionally mimicked it.

A sad face.

A loud bang set off throughout the warehouse. The bullet went into Gia's forehead and her brains painted the wooden crates of tomato sauce behind her.

The sound just about made Red pass out. The extreme stress of the situation, along with knowing that what was coming to him was even worse, made him shake uncontrollably.

Mad Dog stood holding the smoking gun, spit raining down from his face. "Picture sucked."

"I kinda liked it," Buggs said.

"Tough shit," Mad Dog said. "On to this snake. Ernesto, my friend." He looked back at Red. "Did you know I gave this son-of-a-bitch his first paid hit? You get someone started on a path to success, and they got the fuckin' balls to try and put the squeeze on you. I mean, can you believe that?"

Red shook his head.

"Well, you ain't puttin' the squeeze on me, buddy boy. I'll show you how to squeeze." Mad Dog pointed his gun at a large, square device comprised of steel. "Put him on the press!"

Buggs and Dane dragged Ernesto out of his chair and over to the device. The remnants of a few dozen busted tomatoes lay on the press. They maneuvered past the barrels of tomatoes that surrounded the machine and laid him on top. Zip tying his legs together, they stripped Ernesto of the ability to fight back. Buggs wrapped his odorous armpit over Ernesto's head, holding him steady while forcing him to breathe in his nasty scent. Red could smell it from where he sat. The aroma of rotten bean burritos and moldy cheese filled the entire warehouse.

Holding Ernesto's body on the square, Buggs looked up at Dane. "Hit it!"

Dane turned the key on the control panel and pulled down on a lever.

As the square mass of metal above Ernesto's body descended, Red saw the delight on Mad Dog's face.

He's a fuckin' maniac.

The process of Ernesto's demise was gruesome and slow. The sounds of bones exploding, meat and muscle being vomited from the skin, and squishy gore oozing around the edges of the block were noises that would live on in Red's memory for eternity.

When the press mashed him flat enough to connect with the base, Ernesto's head came off in Buggs' arm. The big man stepped away from the device with the oozing trophy. He cackled to himself while holding the raining sphere up for Mad Dog to see.

Buddy started to throw up. A mixture of his saliva and the tomato flew from his mouth. "Wait—" The packing tape was suddenly only stuck to one side of his face as he pleaded. "Let me explain!"

Dane instantly lifted the tape gun and grabbed another tomato from one of the barrels.

"Please, Uncle!" Buddy cried. "Lemme—just lemme explain!"

"It's alright, Dane," Mad Dog said. "I was gonna let the kid talk anyhow. We're family after all. Gotta at least say our goodbyes."

"I can get the money back. I can… I can pay you back!" Buddy promised.

"It's not about the money, nephew. It's the principle. You think I built an empire letting little shits like you get over on me?"

"It wasn't even my idea!" Buddy nodded toward Red. "It was his! It was all him!"

The fear exploded inside Red. If there was ever a time to speak up it was then.

"That's fuckin' bullshit!" Red yelled.

Mad Dog snapped his head around and glared at Red. "Quiet, you! I don't need you to tell me what I already know." He turned back to Buddy. "After Buggs saw the whore markin' the fresh deck, it didn't take much to get her to spill her guts. She told us everything. I know about your little contact lenses. I know you betrayed me. And since you stabbed me in the back, I think it's time to return the favor." He looked at Dane and nodded.

"Wait! You can't fuckin' kill me! I'm family! I'm your nephew, for Christ's sake!"

Mad Dog laughed wildly while putting his gun away. He extracted the handkerchief from his suit and used it to wipe away a dollop of saliva on his face.

"Did you really think that alone was going to save you?" Mad Dog asked. "Just because you're blood don't make you indestructible. There's always a line. It's a shame that you had to find out this way. Out of respect for your father, I'll shed some crocodile tears at your service. But, afterward, make no mistake about it. I'm gonna piss on your empty grave."

Tears were running down Buddy's cheeks. "W-w-we can still fix—"

Before he could finish, Dane jammed his switchblade through Buddy's vertebrae. His face remained expressionless. Scraping around deep into his spine, Dane twisted the tip, elevating Buddy out of his chair.

As Mad Dog watched his nephew hit the floor face-first, he took a step closer to offer him some final words. "I wish I could've told you this instead of having to show you. But you can only be the top guy if you're willing to turn up the heat." He glared at Buggs. "Crank it."

Past the tomato press was another area of the factory with several massive vats. The large, metal tub that Buggs stood beside was taller than he was. Steam rose off the bubbling tomato sauce inside, but as Buggs turned the dial, the movement of the gravy grew more violent.

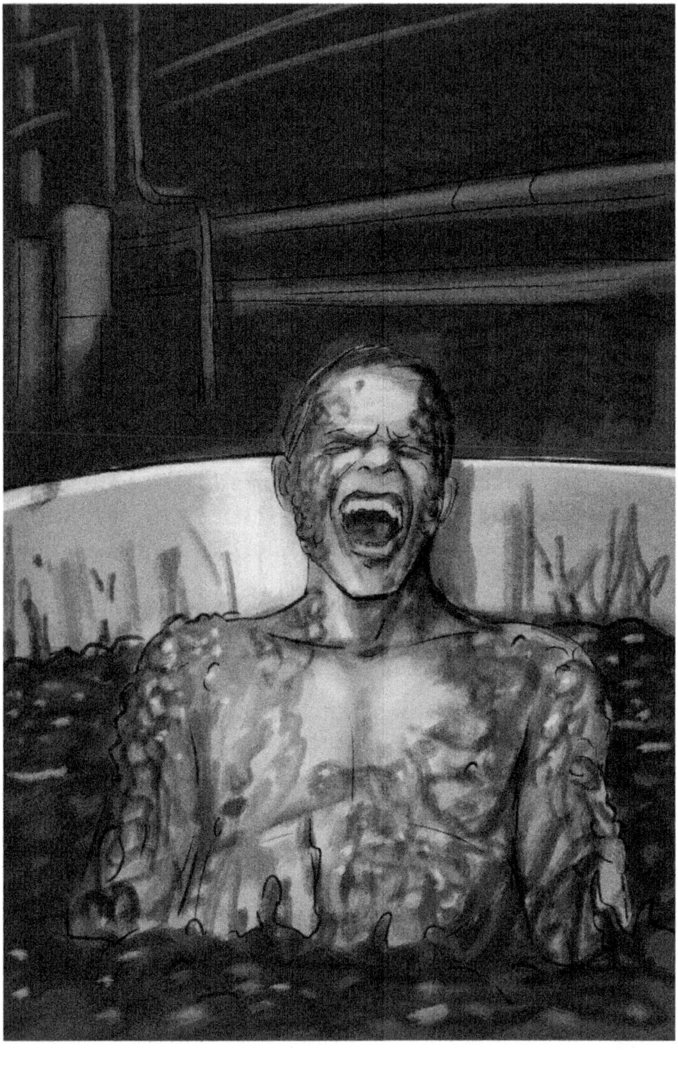

"I—I can't feel my fuckin' legs!" Buddy screamed. "You fuckin' paralyzed me!"

Mad Dog smirked. "That might be for the best. It's the parts of your body that you can feel that you should really be worried about."

Buggs took the bloody scissors he'd used to lop off Gia's fingers and cut through Buddy's fancy threads. Dane helped him strip all the clothing off Buddy's body, then dragged him to the boiling vat.

They used the step ladder inside the cook room to get Buddy high enough to dump him. Red watched in horror as he screamed and wailed. But he didn't have to deal with the crying for long. As his limp body disappeared into the pool of boiling gravy, Buddy's permanent silence began.

Red's tremors intensified. As he watched Mad Dog turn toward him and wipe away his drool, he knew that his punishment was about to be handed out. One that would be worse than the sick outcomes he'd just witnessed.

"I guess that brings us to you." Mad Dog turned to Red. "I don't know a whole lot about you—only what I've been told. But I do know of *you*. It's kind of ironic actually…"

He trailed off like he was holding something back, but Red was too shaken to probe him. It was best to let him talk first and just listen.

"Unlike Ernesto and that fuckhead nephew of mine, when I asked you to tell me what happened, you actually did. What you said matched up with everything the whore told us in private."

Red was grateful he looked at that favorably. "I told 'em, Mr. Mad Dog, I told 'em this was all a terrible idea—that w-we should be doin' this kinda scam at a casino, or somethin' not—"

"Shut the fuck up. I'm doing the talking." Mad Dog walked closer to him. "This is how it's gonna go down. You work for me now—indefinitely. You're on the clock twenty-four-seven, seven days a week." He looked at Dane. "Cut him loose."

Dane did as he was told and used the bloody switchblade to slash through the zip tie.

Red furrowed his brow and stood. It felt like a sick joke. Deep inside, he still believed he was going to die.

"One of my guys got clipped last week," Mad Dog continued, "and it just so happens that I need a warm body. You're gonna be my new book bitch. You'll be accounting for everything. Ball games, horse races, whatever the fuck it is, you're loggin' it. Not only will you log our bets, but you'll lay money down for me with other bookmakers across state lines. And you better do right by me, or it won't just be you who pays. I'll exterminate your whole fuckin' bloodline. I'll find the girl you fucked on prom night and cut her head off. I'll turn that mother of yours inside out. I'll dig up your dead daddy's bones. It wouldn't be too hard considering I'm the one who put him there."

It felt like a slug penetrated Red's chest and blew a hole in his heart. *He's just talkin' crazy. No way it was him. No one knows who it was…*

"They never did dust off the cold case on him, did they?" Mad Dog asked. "You see, the police only invest their time into people who are worth it. Hookers, junkies—people like your dad—they can't be bothered to waste much manpower on such pieces of shit."

Red knew his dad surely wasn't the best role model, but hearing Mad Dog continuously belittle him and tarnish his name was like getting hit with a series of gut punches. It dawned on Red just how little guidance he'd been granted. He was a man, yet he'd never been taught how to be one.

"I noticed you're wearing that same hunk of shit watch that he used to," Mad Dog said.

Red thought back to when his mother gave him the watch. From what she'd told him, his father always wore it. But just days before his death, the wristband had broken. Red's mother had been tasked with dropping it off at the repair shop. Little did she know that the timepiece, repaired or not, would never end up around her husband's wrist again.

"Life's strange," Mad Dog continued. "I mean, what's the odds of us crossing paths like this, under these circumstances? It's fate. Your scumbag father owed big—bigger than he could ever repay. So he had to take the *big* loss." He removed the chrome pistol from his pocket again and looked at it. "Therefore, it was only fitting that I plugged his ass. But now…" He grinned. "And now, it's like God himself dropped you into my lap to pay off his debts."

Red wanted to tell him to go fuck himself. He wanted to scramble forward, rip that pistol out of his hand, and beat Mad Dog's brains in or unload every damn bullet into his chest, the same way he'd done to his father.

He robbed me of our relationship. He took it all from me.

Mad Dog stomped his foot. "Because if you fuckin' don't, then *everyone* connected with your sorry ass will feel it: unimaginable pain, Hell on Earth type shit. And when they do, I'll be sure the last thing they know is that it was all compliments of your fuck-up. Understood?"

Red nodded, trying to control his emotions.

"Good. Cuz when I said you were gonna have a fate worse than them, I wanted you to use your imagination. To get yourself to feel fear like you never felt it before. And that's cuz I want you to wake up every day and remember that fuckin' feeling. And for every day that I allow you to walk this Earth, know that if you cross me, everyone you love is gonna feel that, followed by the real thing." He pointed back to the bubbling vat that contained his nephew. "So, are you gonna fuck it up?"

Red shook his head.

"Say it!" Mad Dog yelled.

"I ain't gonna fuck it up."

"You damn well better not." Mad Dog looked at Buggs and Dane. "There's a lotta clean up that needs to get done around here. You're all gonna have to stay late."

"We're on it, boss," Buggs said.

Dane nodded.

Mad Dog glared at Red.

"Make yourself useful," Mad Dog said. "Help them cut up the rest of the bodies and strip the meat off 'em. Then first thing tomorrow morning, the boys'll give you the run-down and the books."

Red nodded, still thunderstruck. He felt like he was on a rollercoaster that spanned the entire emotional spectrum. As he watched Mad Dog head to the exit, the feeling of being under the thumb of the man who murdered his father in cold blood was already gnawing at him. He'd accepted his father's death long ago. It wasn't difficult because he was already so detached from him.

But now, for the first time, knowing how it all went down, a fire burned inside his belly. But the rage quickly morphed into sadness and self-pity. What was he going to do about it? What could he do about it without destroying everyone he loved?

"Hey, asshole," Buggs said.

Red turned and looked at the foul men. They were suddenly his peers, and that said a lot about the path he'd chosen.

Dane was retrieving a hacksaw from behind one of the pallets.

Buggs lifted the bloody scissors. "It's time to cut up the bodies."

THE BIG LOSS: PART 5

The pager buzzed on Red's hip. With tired, bloodshot eyes, he looked down and pressed the button.

"What the fuck?" he grumbled.

"What'd you say?" Rosie asked.

"Oh, nothing." He tried to finish up his beer. "Say, do you think I could use your phone?"

Rosie frowned. "If I let one guy do it, then everyone'll ask. Just use the payphone in the back like everyone else."

Red set the bottle on the bar and stood. When you made as many calls as he did, the payphones got expensive. Still, it probably wasn't fair to have Rosie pick up the cost. But he didn't like doing his business at home. If he was on the phone constantly running numbers, his mother would catch on. He didn't want to cause her any more stress than he normally did.

Red hadn't even been on the job for a week and he'd been run ragged. He was maybe sleeping five hours a night, drinking like a fish between calls, and barely making enough to make ends meet. The days of him spoiling his ma with Barry Manilow tickets were long gone. Mad Dog wasn't lying. It was starting to feel like he'd have been better off getting thrown in the sauce with Buddy.

He dropped a coin into the slot, lifted the phone off the receiver, and punched in the numbers on his pager. As it rang, he pulled out a small black book and a pen.

"Hello?" a man's voice said.

"Who's this?" Red asked.

"Is that you, Red?"

"Yeah."

"It's Micky Skeggs. Put me down for the Giants to cover and the under."

"How much?"

"A grand."

"That it?"

"Yeah."

He hung up the phone.

Fuckin' idiot, Red thought. *They never cover.* He looked down at his watch. *Shit, it's gettin' late. Probably should get home now and make dinner for Ma.*

He stared at the watch for another minute, thinking about the man she married. The words that Mad Dog said still echoed in his head regularly. He couldn't stop thinking about them. He knew the man who murdered his father. And instead of putting an end to his homicidal threats and disrespect, he'd become his slave.

But the duality between his relationship with his father and his role as a father was complex. Every time he wanted to get mad at his dad, he didn't know if he was being too harsh. He couldn't pretend that he knew the man outside of a few foggy memories. Then the hypocritical thoughts crept in. How could he be upset at his old man when he'd let his own child be whisked away by a psychopath?

God only knows where the fuck Brittany's head is at now…

The more days that passed, the more Red's stress grew. Something had to give. He couldn't go on living a hollow life where he was crippled by fear and repetition, one where the face of his daughter appeared in his dreams and he woke up to a deadbeat nightmare every morning. Red knew he had to start looking for another angle.

He dropped a few dollars on the bar and wished Rosie a good night. When he got into his car, he decided to hit a burger drive-thru. He was buzzed, and after staying up for days, he didn't have the energy to cook for his ma anymore.

After parking in front of the building, he looked around the block. The feeling of extreme paranoia was always compounding. He never knew if Mad Dog was going to just wake up one day and decide it was time to snuff him out. He didn't trust their arrangement, despite everything going as promised.

When Red got inside the complex and opened the door to his apartment, he saw his mother seated at the table with a big grin on her face. A bowl of reheated pasta covered in an extra chunky sauce sat in front of her.

"I brought us burgers, but I guess you're already eating?" he asked.

She finished gobbling the rubbery bite so she could respond. "Someone sent a little case of my favorite, the MD Meat Sauce! I'm sorry, dear, I just couldn't wait for you. But there's more in the pot on the stove."

Red looked into the saucepan, mortified as she slurped up another mouthful. "This one tastes a little different, though. I can't quite put my finger on it."

Images flashed in his mind:

Gia's severed fingers and the skeletal nubs squirting copious amounts of blood.

Ernesto's body exploding like a carnal fireworks show on the tomato press.

Buddy's carcass boiled to the bone with all his meat and organs slipping off the framework.

Red dropped the bag of burgers. The horrific snapshots haunted him in his dreams, and now, also while he was awake. It had taken him some time to get his mind distracted from the double murder Brittany had sprung on him. With the more recent mother lode of horrors, Red would undoubtedly have enough trauma for a lifetime.

"What's the matter, dear?" Mrs. Blanchfield asked.

"N-nothin', Ma."

Red walked over to the counter and examined the case. He spotted a note folded inside between two of the glass jars and slowly slipped it out. As he unfolded the sheet, he put his hand over his mouth.

The note read: *Never forget.*

PRESENT DAY

A PRETTY FACE

When Red exited the restroom, he was surprised to see Lilly waiting. She let the tiniest grin curl the corner of her face. Her crooked teeth didn't bother him—he thought they were cute. But the globs of Mr. Don's dried cum in her hair did.

"You wanna get a drink?" Lilly asked.

Red's brow furrowed. He wasn't sure what her angle was, but he still remembered, back at the craps table, when she offered to eat shit for him. In a *very* weird way, she was trying to help him, but why?

"Sure, why not," Red replied.

He didn't know why he agreed. Maybe it was because he was still overwhelmed by the situation. Or maybe it was because she seemed different than the other savages inside Shadows. There was a certain humanity to her—her face was pretty, but even more than that, caring.

"Okay, then," she said with a smile. "Follow me."

Lilly led Red forward, strutting beside him sexily. There was something about her white high heels that drove him crazy. *Damn, she looks so good in heels.*

He thought about Brittany. He didn't have many good memories of her, but the long, pointy heels that she wore before hitting the block were burned in his mind.

She looks a helluva lot better in 'em than Britt.

Red walked side by side with her, but as he veered off to the buffet area with the self-serve bar, he noticed Lilly was heading in the other direction.

As they passed the initial gambling tables, Red scratched at his head. "Um, I thought that you said we were getting drinks?"

"I did."

Red pointed toward the buffet. "But isn't the bar over there?"

"We're gonna get some real drinks, not that poison." Lilly extended her hand, fingers first in a ladylike fashion. "And I don't think we've had a formal introduction yet. I'm Lilly, Lilly Marlene."

"It's a pleasure." He took her hand. It was soft and gentle—the same as her personality. "I'm Red."

As they moved toward the back of the room, they approached the comforting sound of flowing water. Just ahead a gigantic waterfall stood. It was made of beautiful marble and had several black spotlights angled down, eerily illuminating the carved structure. While purple lights glowed in the water beneath the bubbles, at the top of the waterfall loomed stone letters that spelled: *Shadows.*

Beyond the fountain, also carved out of the rigid rock, were four separate paths. From left to right they read:

The Doll House.

The Main Floor.

The Theater.

Mystery Parlay.

"When you look at the signs, it makes the place seem kinda small, but it's a lot bigger than it looks," Lilly said. "Big enough to get lost in forever."

When she said the last part, there was a somber weight to her voice. She said it like she knew from experience.

"Forever seems like a word that's a little too permanent for a place like this," Red replied. "This place… these people… they just give me the creeps."

Lilly furrowed her brow and exhaled. "Do *I* give you the creeps?"

"No, I didn't mean you. Sorry if it came off that way. You seem like the best thing about this place. I know I just met you, but coming from where I did, I'd like to think I'm a pretty good judge of character. I can tell you're not like these animals. I can tell you're different."

There was a stirring of emotion when he peeked over at her. She turned to the side, trying to hide it. After Lilly composed herself, she tried to change the subject.

"Thanks. So, what kinda drink you want?"

"Something sweet, I suppose. Anything to get this taste out of my mouth."

As they walked under a neon pink sign that read *The Doll House*, Lilly giggled. "I think I know just the thing."

THE DOLL HOUSE

"Thanks, Clyde," Lilly said as the bartender set a Shirley Temple down in front of her. Red had already started sipping his Lime Rickey, trying to wash the taste of Dirty Ricky out of his mouth.

"Thanks," Red whispered.

He was lost in the bad thoughts brewing in his brain. Red hadn't been able to get comfortable since they entered The Doll House. Black lights covered the entire room, making the bright attire of the promiscuously dressed workers pop. The darkness served them well, but the smoky room and dim atmosphere couldn't mask their horrors.

The lavender light shined down on the girl on stage. Her body was an amalgamation of discolored and warped scar tissue. As she rubbed her ass against the pole with her droopy cunt hanging out, she showed off her history.

Her meat curtain comprised the most abused lips on her body, but only because the ones that were supposed to be attached to her face had been cut off. The unnatural and wrinkly flatness on her face made Red shudder. One of her tits looked like it had several globs of breast meat pulled out of it with an ice cream scooper. She bridged herself against the pole with one arm since the other had been lopped off just past her elbow.

Red couldn't look at her any longer. He shifted his gaze to another girl who looked to be about twenty-five years old. She sat on a man's lap rubbing her tits in his face. She looked completely normal outside of the fact that all her teeth had been knocked out. Most of them were missing completely, but there were enough broken ones remaining to confirm that she wasn't just bad at brushing and flossing. Despite her two black eyes, she smiled. Her grin was oddly sharp, giving her appearance a certain demonic quality.

Each girl Red's eyes landed on had their own issue.

A plus-sized woman covered in burns, craters, and sweat shimmered all by her lonesome under the eerie lighting.

An Asian girl rolling around in a wheelchair, missing both of her legs, slowed in front of a man. Leaning over the armrest, she bent over to reveal a butt plug. She pulled the hunk of metal out and offered up her warped asshole.

A toned, black girl propped up on crutches chatted with a man at the bar. Both of her ears had been clipped off and an eyepatch rested over her left socket.

The Doll House was a living, breathing nightmare. One that Red hadn't properly prepared himself for.

"Everything alright?" Lilly asked.

It was a silly question considering the circumstances, but Red found himself distracted by the damaged girls.

"What happened to them?" Red asked.

"When you've been around this place as long as we have, I guess you're always looking for a way out. They all risked a little too much."

"You can't leave?"

Lilly shook her head. "Not unless we earn our way out. But that's just a pipe dream."

"What do you mean?"

"I mean we satisfy johns and janes all day and all night, but every penny we earn goes to the house. They give us a few dollars a day, so most of us bet it. It's not enough to save. We'd be long dead before we ever saw the outside of this place if we tried to save our way out. So, just like all the crooks and creeps in here, we're looking for the best wager. Sometimes bets that are worth more than we earn, and when that happens—well, you know."

"Actually, I don't. This is my first time. I'm not here by choice. Well, I… I guess it was my choice, but…" Red trailed off, unsure of how to explain himself.

"What do you mean?" Lilly asked.

He took a moment to rethink what he was trying to say and sipped his drink. "I guess it wasn't my choice, but I'm here because of my choices, if that makes any sense. All I know is things… things weren't supposed to turn out this way." Red looked at Lilly's reflection in the mirror behind the bar. "Why don't you look like them? You're still so… beautiful. N-not that they ain't but, ah, you know what I mean."

Red felt a little blush hit his cheeks and took another drink of his Lime Rickey to try and make it feel less awkward. Why he was embarrassed then but not when Lilly had watched him house a hunk of shit was beyond him.

Lilly grinned with pure glee. It seemed the sappy line was about the best thing she'd heard a man say to her in years. "I knew there was something about you. When I saw you standing next to me at that table, it was like I was just drawn to you."

"Was it the black eye or this nasty-ass birthmark that drew you in?" Red pointed to the port wine stain on his neck and face.

"I like your birthmark. It distinguishes you. The black eye I could do without."

"Why's that?"

"No reason for such a sweet fella like you to be gettin' hurt."

Red squinted his eyes in the darkness as he let out a huff. The stress was audible.

"What?" Lilly asked.

"It's my, ma. She's in a bit of trouble right now," Red confessed.

He hadn't been able to talk to anyone about the sticky situation, and it was wearing on him. Red didn't know why exactly, but it felt like Lilly was the perfect person to tell. There was a kindness about her that was special.

"What kinda trouble?"

"Well, let's just say if I don't leave this place in the next couple days with at least six figures, something really bad is gonna happen to her."

Lilly grew quiet.

Red banged his fist on the bar. "How did this all get so fucked up?!"

When his eyes returned to Lilly, there was a despondent look on her face. He wondered if she thought less of him. Was he just like all the other scumbags that showed up at Shadows? The dregs of society that selfishly involved their loved ones in their own unsavory affairs. The ones who came in swinging by the end of their rope, staring through the eyes of desperation. The ones who suddenly started praying to a god they never acknowledged nor believed in before they stepped into this hellhole?

"How'd your mom get wrapped up in it?" Lilly asked.

Her voice was still tender and caring, but Red wasn't sure how she'd feel about what came next.

"It's a long story."

"Shit, all I've got is time."

"My ex, Brittany, a few years back, she was in a bad way. We were in a bad way. It was our dependence on heroin that started everything. Things went downhill and kinda snowballed from there. Anyway, long story short, I saw her do something terrible. Something that disturbed me in a way that I can't forget. When I saw that side of her, it made me question everything. Then, she ran away…"

Red pulled the lime out of his drink and sucked the juice from it. It was hard for him to continue.

"There are times when that can be for the best," Lilly said. "If ya put a pair of firecrackers together, sometimes the pop's too loud."

Red looked down. "It would've been fine if she'd just left. That's what I was hopin' for. But she took our daughter with her."

"Shit, how long has she been gone?"

"Little under a year now. I just tried to forget about that part of my life for a while. You see, Brittany was hookin' the whole time she was with me, and even outside of her job, she wasn't exactly the faithful type. After she left, I tried to convince myself that my daughter Dessi wasn't *my* daughter. I put enough powder up my nose to where I actually started to believe it. Then I took a bunch more to forget what it was I'd convinced myself of. I eventually forgot everything... but you can only forget for so long. It wasn't until after I got clean that I realized it."

"Realized what?" she asked.

"That I never knew what guilt was."

Lilly's brow furrowed as Red unwound the tragic tale layer by layer. Her pity only seemed to swell more with each word he spoke.

"And then it just happened. One morning, I woke up, and I just had to see her. Even if I wasn't sure she was mine, and even though I had no clue where the fuck they were, I had to know."

"But I don't get it. How'd you end up here? Oh, fuck, do you think she brought Dessi here?"

"No, it wasn't that... thank God. I didn't have the first clue about how to track them down, so I hired a PI. Problem is, that cocksucker's expensive. The kind of money he wanted to continue the search wasn't the kind of scratch I just have layin' under the mattress."

Lilly leaned in. His story had sunken its fangs into her. "So, what'd you do?"

"The type of people I work for are dangerous. I'd seen the kinds of things they did to people and it wasn't anything I ever wanted to see again. I was a bookie—I organized and took bets, but they also gave me the bets to lay down with other bookmakers."

Red wondered if Lilly had heard stories like his before. If she had, she wasn't showing her hand. She made him feel comfortable enough to continue.

"But then I noticed my boss was making the same shitty parlays every week. Impossible bets if you knew anything about football… or so I thought. Anyway, the scam worked smoothly for a few months: instead of placing the bets, I kept the money and rolled it over to my PI so he could keep looking for Britt and Dessi. Until last Sunday."

"What happened Sunday?" Lilly asked.

"The impossible bet hit. They would've won big—and I mean *big*—if I'd laid the money down like I was supposed to. Now, I'm in the fuckin' hole, deeper than deep. Now, it's all or nothing for me."

Lilly reached out and placed her hand over Red's blood-stained palm. "How much money do you have?" Lilly asked.

"Nothing," Red grumbled.

She turned his hand over slightly and looked down at the freshly cauterized 'S' burn.

"I see. We have more in common than I thought."

"What do you mean?"

"I mean we both got dealt shit hands." She smiled, seemingly grateful to have someone that she could relate to.

"How'd you end up here?"

Lilly looked like she wanted to tell him but brushed off the question. "That's a story for another night, love. We'll definitely need a *stiff* drink for that one. Let's just focus on one problem at a time, okay?"

Red nodded. *She sure is a sweet thing.*

He checked out Lilly again—she was too attractive not to. She had a perfect complement of beauty and personality. When he looked at her hair, he felt saddened. When she turned, Red could still see Mr. Don's sperm crusted in her locks—it glowed under the black lights. Suddenly, Red realized the radiant globs and splotches that peppered every inch of the seedy establishment were jizz stains. The entire place looked like a motel exposé.

Lilly deserves a lot better than The Doll House.

But as the jizz stared back at him, another thought arrived. Maybe Lilly had more details about what Mr. Don had mentioned to him in the men's room. The urgent way the high roller had talked about The Black Widow made any specifics about her seem extra pertinent.

"You know anything about The Black Widow?" Red asked.

When that name came out of his mouth it was like a switch inside of Lilly flipped. Her mood shifted from melancholic to agitated. She peeked back at the stage behind the bar and looked at an oxygen tank on wheels that seemed oddly out of place.

"What is it?" he asked.

"I'm familiar with her—too familiar," Lilly said.

"I been told it's best to stay clear of her."

"You been told right."

Red sipped his drink. "Why does everybody call her that?"

"Because she's fatal. Like a spider sucks the life out of its prey, she sucks the life out of the people in this place."

"Shit," Red said.

"She was never put in charge of this place—she *took* charge. Actually," Lilly shook her head, "I could probably learn a thing or two from her. I guess taking freedom's the only way to truly have it."

"What do you mean?"

Lilly looked around like she wasn't even comfortable telling Red what she was about to say. "The way I heard it, when she was a little girl, her daddy lost her here on a bet. And the fella that ended up winnin' her, he was the previous owner—the creator—of Shadows."

"And what happened to him?" Red asked.

"You should've seen him already, or at least what's left of him. His skin's pinned up in a glass box at the entrance."

"She did that to him?"

"That and a whole lot more. I haven't seen it myself or anything, but I know some girls who have."

"Seen what?"

"She kept his cock and balls, like a trophy, on her desk."

"Christ."

"She thinks cuz she had it hard and went through some things that everyone else deserves to take it up the ass along with her." Tears welled up in Lilly's eyes as she continued to gawk at the oxygen tank. "She's gettin' revenge on the wrong people, and it ain't right."

Red rubbed her back. "Jeeze, I'm sorry. Sounds like you've been through hell."

"It wasn't just me."

Red couldn't help but think about Dessi. He hoped that whatever shit she was going through didn't turn her sour. He hoped that Brittany hadn't tainted her. It was hard to imagine the sweet girl he'd known doing terrible things to people. Lilly's words resonated with his own situation. He hoped Dessi didn't think that he'd abandoned her.

"She's probably all fucked up from what her daddy done to her," Red said. "Now she's just mad at the world. Few things in life hurt worse than abandonment."

Lilly snapped sideways. "Don't try and fuckin' justify her actions. You didn't see what I saw, okay?"

"I didn't mean nothin' by it. I'm sorry. I ain't saying it's right. I just try to look at both sides of the coin sometimes."

"Yeah, well, both sides are black. It's all death and darkness. Trust me, I've been through my fair share of it, but never even considered the unspeakable things she's done."

"I believe you, I'm just—"

"Listen, I like you, Red," Lilly said. "I wanna see you stay alive and find your little girl. Maybe we should just talk about that instead."

"Fair enough," Red replied. "But I just want you to know... Hey, look at me, please."

Lilly turned to him.

"I'm on your side, okay?" he whispered.

Lilly nodded and seemed calmed by his statement.

"You're about the only normal person I've met in this shithole. I'd be a dumb fuck not to be grateful that you're even talkin' to me."

"You think I'm normal?"

"Better than normal." Red smiled, unable to not look at the glowing cum in her hair again. "You're the cream of the crop."

"You know, you ain't so bad yourself." She took another swig of her drink. "So, you said you've got a six-figure problem, right?"

He sighed. "Right."

"Well, there's only *one* bet in this place that can haul in that much. But it's a risky bet—the riskiest. I don't think I have to tell you what's at stake."

Red swallowed hard. "What's the bet?" He asked the question, but truthfully, he would've preferred not to know the answer.

"That's the thing, it's kind of a mystery—"

"Hey, *puta,* you got two minutes," a stern, male voice said. "Better move that fuckin' ass quick."

"Okay, okay," Lilly said. "Just relax, Day Day."

The Colombian club manager was decked out in an all-white suit and shiny black shoes. He removed the lollipop from his mouth and licked his lips, his quick tongue tagging the wispy mustache that rested under his nose.

"You spend too much fuckin' time running your mouth when you should be poppin' that pussy. Then you wonder why you don't make shit. You keep your head in the wrong place, and eventually, it'll get knocked off those pretty little shoulders."

Day Day's eyes shifted from Lilly to Red. He squinted at him and held his arms out. "The fuck you looking at? Got something to say, *pelirrojo malparido?*"

As Red started to open his mouth, Lilly squeezed his burned hand. "Ouch."

Lilly leaned into him. "Sorry, just ignore him," she whispered. "Trust me, it's for the best."

"That new *puta* Star is in the casino for the magic show tonight," Day Day said. "She's had an eye on the buffet since she walked in. Keep her fuckin' nose clean until show-time. The boss has big plans for her. Understood?"

"Where is she?" Lilly asked.

"She should be in the locker room." Day Day turned, letting the candy clack against his teeth again. "Now get movin'."

Lilly nodded then turned to Red. "I've gotta start my shift, and apparently, I'm babysitting now, too. But it's only a few hours until the show starts. Come and meet me back here later, and we'll figure things out, okay?"

Red's forehead remained wrinkled. He didn't like the way Day Day spoke to Lilly, but if she was telling him to keep cool then he needed to heed her warning. He was thankful for her. In the frightening world of Shadows, he was grateful to have a friend—and maybe something more. There weren't many people who had shown him kindness as of late. He also hadn't exactly had time to explore his options much since Mad Dog enslaved him.

Am I just desperate or do I feel something?

"Okay," Red said. As she stood, he gently squeezed her hand and she pulled away slowly with the look of a puppy dog.

Red's eyes were glossy when they met hers. Even though he could still see Mr. Don's encrusted cum in her hair, he wanted to kiss her. But they both had their warts. He figured his mouth probably still tasted like Dirty Ricky's asshole. If their first kiss was going to happen, better that it did when they were both a bit more removed from their sins.

His world was a dark place. It had been a long time since anyone besides his ma had been decent to him. The feeling made Red nervous. A strange sensation swelled within—the feeling that, if their paths had somehow crossed outside of Shadows, they might've held onto each other and never let go. She might've been exactly what he'd needed.

Red decided not to share those thoughts and restrained his emotions. He didn't want to dump all that on her out of the blue. But he did show his gratitude. "Thank you," he whispered. "Thank you so much."

Lilly smiled again.

Something about seeing the girl's teeth made Red warm inside. The agony that lay ahead felt a little more manageable.

It was all he could've asked for.

THE MAIN FLOOR

In spite of the fear festering in Red's mind, curiosity had gotten the best of him. He knew he needed to hit the main floor to see if he could glean any tips or strategies from his observations. Those would assist him when he decided it was time to put it all on the line.

As he exited The Doll House and proceeded past the annex, the digital language of the various machines blurted out over the sound of wheels spinning and people screaming. If Shadows was a storm of depravity, then Red was now outside the eye of the hurricane. While the room itself looked like any other casino he'd been comped free drinks at, the ghastly events transpiring within were unimaginable.

"Domino!" a female voice yelled.

He barely had time to register the automatic going off. Two women sat at a small table with submachine guns staked up on steel rods. Sheets of bulletproof glass were erected behind them. Their legs and waists were shackled to their chairs as they stared at each other across the table. The touchscreen tabletop showed a long, snaking trail of dominos that had been laid out during their play. The brown-haired cougar grinned as she watched the younger blonde competitor struggle in her chair.

As the five digital dominos flipped on the young lady's side of the screen, the computer system calculated the sum of the tiles. Twenty-three displayed in red on the screen, and just as the total appeared, that number of rounds ripped out of the barrel fixed across from the blonde.

The blonde's wails were quickly cut short.

Blood and brains exploded out of her cranium as the bullets knocked her face in. The caliber of the rounds was enough to ricochet wads of her head off the glass and cast bits of the dead girl all over Red's face. Speckles of gore painted him as he released a feminine shriek.

"Domino! Domino!" the cougar cried with joy.

She stretched her freckled arms out and reeled in dozens of chips that the young blonde had stacked on her side of the table.

Red tried to wipe the fluid off his face and staggered backward. The abrupt violence was a wake-up call. The game tables near the entrance suddenly looked like child's play compared to The Main Floor. The people that lurked inside Shadows were comfortable with death. At first glimpse, the atmosphere felt inhuman.

Jogging away from the woman's hole-riddled, twitching body, Red was soon confronted with another face-off scenario. And at the new station sat a familiar face.

It was the bald man from the buffet that had thrown him a bone. While Red had lost the chips almost immediately, he still appreciated the gesture.

The bald man looked zooted past the stars. High off the free fuel and the daredevil nature of the games, he grinned manically in his chair. Looking at the expression on the bald man's face, it almost seemed like he was enjoying himself.

What the hell's his deal? Red wondered. *Gotta be some kind of psycho adrenaline junkie or somethin'.*

Across from him sat a woman who was also strapped into her chair. Like her counterpart, the woman's legs and arms were restricted. The devilish font above both of their heads read: *WAR*.

A dealer sat beside each player, drawing the cards that would be pitted against each other. Behind each of the players stood two stoic security guards.

As the dealers flipped, they each called out the card.

"Ten!" the first dealer said.

"Four!" the second dealer followed.

The wheezing woman cried. She tried to suck in some air but looked on the verge of losing consciousness. She was barely able to plead for her life. "Wait, w—"

The hulking guard behind the woman cut her plea short. Lifting a plastic bag, he held it tight over her head, cutting off her oxygen. She gyrated violently in her seat.

"One Mississippi, two Mississippi," the dealer said.

As the plastic sucked in, she struggled. Red suddenly realized that he was observing a sadistic game. One that meshed cards and suffocation. The loser would be deprived of air for the difference in the numbers drawn.

Ten minus four is six. When Red saw the bag finally come off, the woman was desperately gasping for air. It seemed like they'd been going at each other for a while already. But just as she snuck a quick breath, another set of cards had already hit the felt.

The bald man had taken off his Lincoln class ring. He bit his lip and began superstitiously rubbing the blue jewel with his thumb.

"King!" the first dealer said.

"Two!" the second dealer said.

The security guard put the bag over the woman's face again and counted.

What the fuck kind of nightmare is this?

"Yesssss!" the bald man wailed, slipping his lucky ring back on his finger. "Count it slow!" He let out a disturbing laugh as his eyes connected with Red. "This is what it's all about, fella! This is how it's done!"

Red was speechless as he watched the woman struggle, the bag sucked against her face, mirroring the terror as she stopped moving and made the final transition.

"That's the problem with this place," the bald man said. "Once you leave, nothing's the same. Sex, music, work, family, movies, personal achievements—it's all fucked! Diluted! Because the only truth in life is, you'll never feel as alive as you do when you think you're about to die."

As the suffocation completed, Red figured they'd been playing awhile already. As he watched the woman's shoulders slack and her body lose its fight, he knew she'd pushed her luck one time too many.

"But a win or two is never enough," the bald man said. "You always end up needing something bigger. But I think it's finally happening for me. My moment has arrived. Today is *my* day." A sickening grin swarmed his face as he turned his attention to the dealer. "Now, where's my fucking money?"

He ain't gonna stop until it's too late.

The crazed look in the bald man's eyes was familiar. Red had seen it when he looked into the mirror while he was under the spell of addiction. While their vices might've differed, the results were the same: the destruction of normalcy, a way of life predicated on chaos.

Red was still trying to get past the trauma of the brains that had just smacked him in the face at the dominos table. Now the shocking image of the woman's final grimace at the war table left another awful stain in his head.

They looked to be untying the bald man, and Red wanted nothing to do with him. The way he thought was frightening and had the potential to stall his mission. The last thing he needed was a psychopath taking a liking to him.

"Hey, buddy, hang on a second, I wanna ask you something," the bald man said.

He did give you money before… Maybe it'd be worth it for me to stick around for a few minutes and at least hear what he has to say? But glancing at the psychosis swirling in his eyes instantly changed his mind. *Fuck that. Just act like you didn't hear him.*

Red turned away from the war table, distancing himself from the bald man as fast as possible.

"Hey!" The bald man struggled in the chair, trying to free himself quicker. He looked like a lunatic trying to get out of his cell. "Hey! I'm fuckin' talkin' to you!"

There was no doubt that he was ignoring him now, but Red didn't care. His only objective was getting away from him. He needed to find an out from the situation as soon as possible. Slipping into the sea of people, Red picked up his pace as he scanned his surroundings.

It didn't take long for him to spot the black and red sign in the distance. The huge dark curtain that separated the space from the main floor gave Red the chills.

The sign read: *BLACKJACK.*

While he didn't know why Mr. Don had suggested that he stay clear of the blackjack tables, it no longer mattered. He needed to disappear. Breaking away from the bald man was a priority.

Red headed for the dark fabric and approached the sign, reassuring himself that he was just going in to throw the bald man off his trail.

It'll be fine. It ain't like I gotta place a bet or anything.

BLACKJACK

The giant black curtain that segregated the blackjack tables from the rest of the casino was heavy. Once Red pushed his way inside, the black light made various areas in the room pop. He was looking at a layout that was unlike any other gambling establishment.

A dozen shadowy signs were posted throughout the spacious room. The white paint applied to them glowed eerily. The font indicated the table numbers, but the strangest part was the ebony curtains that encompassed each of the stations. They reached to the tall ceiling space—bolted into the mountainous terrain—creating an intimate circle of privacy for each table.

They look like big ass shadows, Red thought.

The creepy drapes tied in perfectly with the casino's name. The room was relatively quiet, except for the oldies tunes that rang out with a slight echo and what sounded like a faint thudding noise.

What the hell is that?

Red could see white teeth bouncing vividly in the black light. A few stragglers walked around in the distance, but there wasn't much doing. He imagined that all the action was going down inside the tents.

I guess I can just check it out, and at least see how they work it here. Scope the place out a little.

As soon as the thought crossed his mind, the thudding in the distance ceased. A feeling of dread hit him as the curtains at table number six parted and a tall, ominous figure stepped out.

The highlights of his mask became clearer when he elevated his head. His face was familiar. The slight curl of a grin, the golden blond hair, the pencil-thin mustache.

He was the jack of spades.

Dressed from head to toe like the Bicycle personality inside any deck, there he stood. But he wasn't alone. His hand was wrapped around the white collar of what Red imagined to be a player. The mass of gore flapping and oozing from the man's cracked cranium made him gawk in horror.

He tried to close his eyes, but Red saw flashes from his past. That night inside Francis' house when the bullet exploded from the revolver in Brittany's hand. The gore from the girl's head coming apart and painting the dresser, leaving a massive crater full of crimson tissue spilling over when her lifeless head smacked against the floor.

The guilt was raging inside him again. How could he have allowed himself to be part of such a horrible deed?

He recalled Brittany pulling the knife outside the house. While he never expected her to use it, Red still battled with his culpability in the murder.

I should've known. Maybe I deserve to be here…

That dark voice in his head spoke again. The one that chastised him on the topics he couldn't delve into outside of his own mind.

He turned away from the jack of spades and the dead man to face a sign that read: *Table 5.*

"Fuck it," he mumbled.

"Yeah, that's what I say," a voice from behind him said.

When Red turned around, he was confronted by a black man with short hair. He was smoking a cigarette in a way that was less about enjoyment and more about relief.

The man took a big puff and the orange ember flared. "You seem a little bit hesitant. Oh, sorry." He stuck his hand out. "The name's Lane Stewart."

"Red," he replied with a nod. Red imagined it would behoove him to avoid giving his Christian name out in such an environment.

Shaking his hand, Red winced slightly. His palm was still tender from the house branding.

"Ah, say no more," Lane said. "I see we're in the same boat. I don't wanna go in there either." Lane lifted his hand and showed off the 'S' branding on his palm.

"What's it like in there?" Red asked.

"I'd be lying if I said I knew for sure. I only know what I've heard. A lady back at the buffet told me that if you lose, whatever the difference between your cards and the dealers' cards is, is the number of times they hit you."

"What do they hit you with?"

"She didn't really go into much detail. I asked, but she was rambling, all coked up."

Coke. That would be a godsend right now.

The beautiful buffet table at the entrance butted into his thoughts. A little taste might help extinguish his fear, get him in the mindset he needed for any task. That's how he felt whenever he snorted. He knew just a line or two would get him feeling invincible. Confidence was something he was severely lacking.

Red pointed back to the puddle of blood and brains just outside the curtains of table six. "Looks like they beat the brains right out of that guy's fuckin' head."

Lane took his last puff and exhaled. "I think that's what they call a 'bust.' You bust on the table, they bust your head."

Red closed his eyes, trying not to picture the violence. "Glad she told you that much. Was there anything else?"

"I wish," Lane said. He snubbed out his butt in the nearby ashtray and immediately reached for the pack in his pants. "You want one?"

Red hesitated, then snatched one out of the box. "When in Rome."

"So, what brings you here?" Lane asked. He flicked the match, lit his cigarette, then lit Red's.

"I'm in deep with some very bad people." Red took a series of drags. "It was either this or a fuckin' dirt nap. What about you?"

Red truthfully didn't care about his story. He was too wrapped up in his own damn problems. But the man had been helpful, so the least he could do was show some decency.

"Oh…" Lane paused. "Honestly, it's hard to even say it out loud." His eyes glossed over. "I lost it all."

Red wished that was his biggest problem. "That happens to a lot of people. You don't have to put your goddamn life on the line. You can build back slowly."

Lane's eyes beamed with rage. "You don't understand. I didn't just lose it for me, I lost it for everyone around me. I've been lying for eight years now. The weight of the lies—it feels like it's suffocating me. And now, there's nothing left to use as collateral anymore."

Red exhaled a cloud of smoke. "What do you mean?"

"I mean every single penny I have. I mean my wife's retirement. I mean the kids' college funds. I mean the forty grand I borrowed from my brother-in-law." Lane locked eyes with Red, a look of despondency dominating him. "I haven't made a mortgage payment in almost a year. My wife thinks we're selling, but we're foreclosing."

"Shit," Red said.

"That's not even the worst of it. I'm a contractor, so often clients leave me large deposits for jobs. I've gambled away hundreds of thousands of other people's money. If I don't leave this place a winner, I'm losing everything. My family, my kids, my freedom. I looked at the charges. I'd go to prison for at least five years—probably more. I—I got nowhere left to hide." He looked up at the curtain. "This goddamn game took everything from me."

As he scratched the side of his face, Red was starting to understand. The situation wasn't life or death, but to Lane, it was. "I'm sorry to hear it. That's fuckin' heavy, man."

"Yeah, but maybe today's when I turn it around," Lane said. "After all, I figure I'm due."

Red took another pull of his smoke. "Don't take this the wrong way, but player to player, can I ask you something?"

Lane nodded.

"When you were just talkin', said blackjack took everything from you—is that right?"

"Yeah," Lane said.

"Then why the fuck would you gamble with your life on the game you're prone to losin'?"

"Because, blackjack's the best odds in any casino," Lane said. "The house edge is just under one percent."

As a man who had been around gambling for the better part of his life, Red knew that already. Maybe he was more superstitious than the next player, but if he was getting his dick kicked in the way that Lane had, best odds or not, he'd be looking for a new angle. Still, being reminded of the game with the best odds made Red curious to, at the very least, see how the game was played in Shadows.

Lane nervously cracked his knuckles. "The fact that blackjack pays three to two doesn't hurt either. With the hole I'm sitting inside of, it's still the most realistic way for me to build a bankroll."

"You sure they pay three to two here? That usually varies from casino to casino." Red looked back at the gore on the floor again. "With the way this fuckin' place operates, I wouldn't be so sure."

"That coked-up broad back at the bar said so, but I'm not sure I'd trust it unless I seen it with my own eyes."

Red was still debating what to suggest. Like Lane, he'd also gotten some advice from random players. But it was still up for debate how much any of the information was actually worth. The bald man, Lilly, and Mr. Don had all provided him with pieces of intel. And Mr. Don had specifically told him to stay clear of the blackjack tables, but he still didn't know why.

"I've gotten a few suggestions from players around here too," Red explained.

"Did you?" Lane asked.

"Yeah, this one guy, he's kind of out there, but he told me to stay clear of the blackjack tables."

Lane lit up another cigarette and widened his eyes. He couldn't stop chain-smoking. Just existing seemed to stress him out. "Interesting. Why's that?"

"I don't know," Red replied. "Didn't get to ask him." His eyes found the bright, golden sign at the other end of the blackjack area that read: *SLOTS*.

"That's too bad," Lane said.

"But he told me the slots were the safest bet in here."

"Is that so?"

"Yeah. The guy didn't have no cuts or scars neither. He was a weirdo, but he definitely had his shit together."

Lane nodded. "That might be true, but I don't have the luxury of playing it safe. And the odds on the slots are shit. Besides, they're cash only. We'd need to build up some kind of capital before even thinking about that."

Red wasn't really sure if he liked the comradery he was building with Lane or not. The way the guy was saying *we'd* need to build up capital first made it sound like they were poker partners or something. While it felt good to have someone with a decent head on his shoulders to talk to, Red knew what partners meant.

Splitting the earnings.

If there was one thing Red couldn't afford, it was that. And the way Lane was talking, he needed even more than him. The situation was an undesirable one, but Lane had also been useful with the information he'd offered.

What's this fuckin' guy's angle exactly?

The constant shiver in Lane's body language made Red think he was just scared shitless.

Probably thinking about death and just a little chatty.

"You get what I'm sayin', right?" Lane persisted.

"Yeah, I hear you."

Lane exhaled deeply—the nerves seemed like they were starting to get to him.

Red took a pull that brought his cigarette down to the filter. As he blew the smoke down, he snubbed out the butt. "Well, if that's the case, then what are you suggesting?"

"I… I don't know."

Red rubbed his eyes. "Shit, I don't know either. But I've gotta figure something out, fast."

Lane stepped up to the curtain and listened. He waved Red over.

"What?" Red asked.

Lane hushed him. "Listen."

They both put their ears to the curtain.

"Hit," said a female player.

"Twenty-one," the female dealer replied. "Wow, congratulations. You're on quite the streak. Wanna go again?"

"I wouldn't dream of stopping now," the player said.

"Someone's winning in there," Lane said. "What if we just take a look inside? Watched a bit to kind of get a feel for it?"

The same idea had been on Red's mind, but he hadn't been sure if he wanted to say it out loud. He looked at Lane and nodded. "Yeah, I guess it couldn't hurt."

TABLE 5

When Red and Lane stepped through the curtain, the scene inside was unnerving. While the dark-haired blackjack dealer with oversized glasses and a fresh perm wasn't anything out of the ordinary, the several menacing figures placed around the room were.

The jack of spades Red had seen dragging the man with the broken skull out from table 6 was doubled inside table 5. Two of them, towering over Red and Lane, stood at each side of the entrance. Their creepy masks and overall stillness were highly worrisome.

But that wasn't the most alarming aspect of the setup. Beside the blackjack table stood a third jack. His indolent but pleased expression was creepily aimed at them. His hat was a different style and so was his hair. It remained blonde but was shoulder-length and curled at the bottom.

He was the jack of clubs.

Besides the various suit symbols imprinted onto his costume, there was one other item that clarified that he was the jack of clubs. The tightly wound leather around the lead bar in his hand attracted Red's eyes. The mini, steel studs that covered the outside of the instrument were short but stiff. The modified blackjack club suddenly made sense.

The dead man from table 6's mashed brains flashed in Red's mind. He looked at the hanging chains that dangled beside the jack of clubs. There was also a closed, coffin-shaped box behind him.

Red's heart raced but there was nothing he could do to calm himself. And his anxiety only further blossomed when the dealer spoke.

She slapped her hands together twice. "New players, welcome." She gestured to the table.

"No, ah, we just wanted to have a look is all." Red tried to turn around, but the jack of spades grabbed him by the throat and squeezed.

The second jack of spades snatched up Lane.

"Wait, this is a mistake," Lane pleaded.

"We'll see about that," the dealer replied.

Red scrambled to explain their intent again. "W-we just wanted to watch how it works—"

"Everyone who enters plays at least one round," the dealer replied sternly. "Minimum bet is a hundred."

"That's why we didn't wanna bet, we don't have anything," Lane said.

"Ah, I see," the dealer said. "That sucks."

The jacks pushed Lane and Red against the table. As they squirmed with discomfort, the frightening card caricatures attached ankle shackles to the men to hold them in place.

"What the hell is this?" Lane asked, angrily jingling the chain around his ankle.

Red looked at the other player that they were seated at the table with. The woman was in the same predicament except for the chips that sat in front of her. She was the middle-aged soccer mom type—not a person who Red would've expected to be in such a place. She seemed to have kind eyes and looked at them like she wanted to help. But then she spoke.

"Chains shouldn't be that unfamiliar to you," the soccer mom said.

"Excuse me?" Lane replied.

The dealer dropped cards in front of them, as well as the female player at the far side of the table.

Despite what he thought he'd heard the woman say, it didn't take long for Lane to ask. He took one look at the stack of chips in front of her and begged. "Miss, please, can you spare a chip? I-I-I can find a way to pay you back, I swear it!"

The soccer mom shook her head in disgust and let out a chuckle. "If I had a dollar for every time I heard that one, then I might have enough to spare. But I got no interest in helping you or your friend."

"C'mon, lady! We… this could kill us!" Lane yelled.

"Guess you boys should've known better," the soccer mom replied.

Lane narrowed his eyes at her. "Is my life not worth a measly hundred dollars to you?"

"You really wanna know?" she asked.

"Just forget about her, Lane," Red said.

"The moment you walked in here, I pictured you tied to the back of my daddy's pick-up. That's what I think about *all* of you."

"Shut your goddamn mouth!" Red yelled pointing his finger at her.

"Well, you shouldn't have asked then." The soccer mom bellowed with laughter.

As Lane continued to cuss her out, the other jack of spades restrained Red.

"Enough!" the dealer yelled.

All three of them piped down.

"No one in this room says another word! You don't make the rules. The house makes the rules! The Black Widow makes the rules! Any more talk out of you three, and I'll call up to her right now!" The dealer pointed up to the black sphere in the corner of the room. "She's always watching, always listening, and whether you're a winner or a loser," she looked from the soccer mom, to Lane, to Red, "you're not untouchable."

An uncomfortable silence filled the room.

You've really done it now. Red's knee began to bounce.

Based on what Lilly and Mr. Don had said, Red hoped they hadn't given The Black Widow a reason to visit them. Due to the current blackjack dilemma and another bone-chilling reference to the head of the house, Red was starting to believe that Mr. Don really knew his shit. He should've listened to his advice in the men's room and never walked through that curtain.

The dealer pushed her bulky glasses up from the tip of her nose. "Now, let's play."

THE DEAL

When the cards dropped on the table, they revealed the following:

Red's hand: king, ten.

Lane's hand: ten, five.

Soccer mom's hand: ace, ace.

Dealer's hand: one card facedown, seven.

"Two aces!" the soccer mom screamed. "Split!"

"Oh, wow," the dealer said. "Most people don't have the nerve to do that."

"Wait, what do you mean?!" the soccer mom asked.

But before she could dispute her decision, a card was already en route.

The dealer grinned. "I'm afraid there's no waiting." She set down a four beside the first ace and a three atop the second. "But what that means is, you'd better not lose both of your hands."

"Shit," the soccer mom said, glaring at her cards. She looked back up at the dealer. "That's not fair! No one told me that there were special rules with splits!"

The dealer's grin widened. "Well, I guess you should've known better."

"What happens if I lose both?" She chewed her nail.

"You'll just have to wait and see. I'm assuming you wanna hit on each of these, right?"

The soccer mom was shaking.

"Yes or no?" the dealer persisted.

The soccer mom put her hands together. "Yeah."

The dealer dropped another card on each hand.

Soccer mom's first hand: ace, four, queen.

Soccer mom's second hand: ace, three, nine.

Her eyes darted back to the dealer's hand.

Dealer's hand: one card facedown, seven.

"No!" the soccer mom screamed. Her hands quickly broke prayer and she slammed both of her fists on the table. Her brown ponytail bobbed with fury.

"Again?" the dealer asked.

"Just… give me a second!"

Red looked on, grateful to be in a much better position. He wasn't out of the woods yet, but he was in far better shape than the soccer mom or even poor Lane. He could see the beads of sweat forming around the crown of the man's head, while the soccer mom looked like hers was about to explode.

A loud thud made all three players jump. They turned around in unison.

Red saw the jack of clubs had smashed the wooden box next to him with his weapon, as if demanding that the soccer mom expedite her decision.

"I need an answer," the dealer persisted.

"Hit me!" the soccer mom yelled, tears now running down her face.

"For both?" the dealer asked.

"Yes."

When the first card dropped, so did the soccer mom's jaw. As the second card fell, the screaming started.

Red didn't like the mean woman or her racist remarks, but even he was afraid for her after the reveal.

Soccer mom's first hand: ace, four, queen, jack.

Soccer mom's second hand: ace, three, nine, jack.

The jack of spades and jack of clubs staring up at the soccer mom no doubt bothered her, but not as much as the ones staring at her from behind would.

"Please, I can pay. I've got plenty of money! I didn't know this—"

One jack clamped his hand around her mouth while the other removed her leg shackle.

"I'm afraid money isn't everything in this place," the dealer said. "If you want to win big, you've got to bet big. And trust me, it doesn't get any bigger than this."

"Jesus," Red whispered.

He and Lane looked back as the two spades dragged the soccer mom over to the jack of clubs. He reared the spiked weapon back and smashed the soccer mom in the knee with all his might.

She wailed in horror as her leg collapsed on itself and her light blue jeans ripped at the point of impact. A surge of blood rained out of the wound as a bouquet of bloody bone, mangled meat, torn tendon, and lacerated ligament came to light. One side of the soccer mom's jeans now looked like the port wine stain on Red's face.

"I can give you more than I have here," the soccer mom cried as the two spades each grabbed hold of an arm.

The jack of clubs returned to the coffin-shaped box and opened it. He set his blackjack club inside and removed another item Red had never seen before. One end of the item was pear-shaped and affixed to a screw-threaded shaft while the other side was connected to a key-like handle.

"We're satisfied with our winnings," the dealer said.

"But I can—"

The soccer mom's bartering was cut short by the steel pear that the jack of clubs rammed into her mouth. He held it firm and deep, and as she choked on the device, he twisted the key.

Red watched on, terrified as his eyes expanded along with the soccer mom's. When the key turned, they both figured out what the device's purpose was.

The steel pear that filled her mouth was not a single piece, but four fractions brought together. And as the jack of clubs continued to rotate the key, those portions separated further from each other. Drool poured out of her jaws as the device expanded wider.

Red watched as her eyes bugged out and grew inflamed. Her tears trickled, and he cringed when he heard her jawline cracking. The soccer mom's mouth enlarged to hallucinogenic dimensions. The saliva draining over her lips transitioned to red. She gagged and cried, but that didn't stop her molars from exploding. Fragments of ruby enamel leaped out of her mouth as her tongue flailed wildly.

The jack of clubs seemed satisfied with the extent of the damage, allowing the device to unfold just short of ripping her lower mandible off. When he returned to the coffin box, the jack removed a new piece of equipment.

The apparatus he held resembled a jump rope, except each of the handles was made of solid wood and the 'rope' that connected them together was a steel cable. The jack handled it carefully as if it was incredibly sharp.

Red's suspicions proved true when the jack of clubs slipped the handle past the soccer mom's groin and into the grips of his counterpart. As the jacks lifted her off the ground, the unforgiving cable saw gave her a sickening case of cameltoe that there was no recovering from. The cutting pain caused her to wail and shriek.

As the third jack steadied her, the weight of the soccer mom's body pushed down on the razor cable. The wire cut through her clothing with ease and quickly burrowed deep into her vaginal lips and rectum. Blood rained generously as the sadistic jacks elevated the cable higher, splicing into her bowels as they feverishly worked it back and forth.

The shocking cut continued to part her like the red sea, spilling the contents of her intestinal tract and stomach all over the floor. As her entrails vacated, the smell of partially processed dairy and bitter bile filled the room and her eyes rolled. The smack of the gore hitting the floor echoed.

A raw sewage scent wafted toward Red, causing him to vomit in his mouth. He was so shaken by the display that he lost control of his bladder. A bit of urine leaked through his boxers and the front of his pants grew moist while he shook uncontrollably.

He'd seen terrible things before—cold-blooded murder and torture—but what he was watching was something else entirely. As horrible as those violent acts were, there were at least reasons behind the depravity. Not that it justified the acts, but it allowed him to at least process it. This was violence for the sake of violence. This was hell.

"The fuck are we gonna do?" Lane whispered.

Sweat dripped down Red's neck. "What can we do?"

Red watched aghast as the jacks yanked up. The cut was no longer perfectly aligned to the center of the soccer mom's body. As the cut ascended, the destructive wire dug through the left side of her ribcage.

The look in the soccer mom's eyes was like she'd been set on fire. Drool and blood now poured like a waterfall from her mouth and nose as she emitted death gurgles. The hideous hole in her face looked like some kind of horror CGI gone wrong.

As the jacks continued upward, it became clear that the wire saw was not on track to split her in half equally but was headed to exit around her collarbone. Her shaking body showered the ground with a mixture of organs and meat as the division continued.

When the cable made its way out of her shoulder, the two shredded puzzle pieces of the soccer mom smacked onto the ground. The expulsion of bodily fluid commenced a smell of iron and fecal matter that permeated the air.

The player that once looked to have a leg up on both Red and Lane sat in a heap. She was torn in a way that was beyond the comprehension of any moral man.

Red found himself wondering if he was in store for a similar fate.

A GAME OF DEATH

"A split for a split," the dealer said.

Red looked at Lane. A gawk of fear dominated the man's face as he watched a woman in a queen of spades outfit continue to clean up the mess the jacks had made. She used a tether-free, Bissell vacuum cleaner to suck the blood and bits of body off the carpeting.

The once clear water inside the device looked like cherry juice. After the queen sucked what was left of the sludge up, the jacks placed the destroyed pieces of the soccer mom's body into a plastic-lined bin that sat atop the dolly the queen had wheeled in. She remained silent, nodding to thank the jacks before setting the vacuum inside the cart and pushing it out of the tent.

"Hopefully, you gentlemen have better luck than she did," the dealer said. She glared at Lane, already asking the question with her eyes. "Anyway, clean-up's over now. What'll it be?"

As he continued to perspire, Lane looked at his hand, then back to the dealer's.

Lane's hand: ten, five.

Dealer's hand: one card facedown, seven.

"Quickly, please," the dealer said.

"I'm-I'm thinking!" Lane yelled.

Red could see he was panicking but didn't know how he could help. He was busy doing the same as he thought about his own hand.

"What the fuck do I do?" Lane asked.

"I wish I knew," Red said. "If she's got ten under there, you're fucked."

"Yeah," Lane whispered. "I-I gotta hit, right?"

"Hit it is!" the dealer said dropping a card down.

"Wait!" Lane screamed.

It was too late. The card fell beside his hand.

King.

"Bust!" the dealer yelled.

"But I didn't even—"

The spiked blackjack club slammed into the back of Lane's skull before he could finish his protest. The jack of clubs held his neck against the table as he raised his weapon again.

Instantly, Red saw the tiny holes the spiked blackjack had made in Lane's cranium. The back of his head was warped from the blow. Blood pissed down his neck and all over the table.

"No!" Red yelled, trying to pull Lane away from the murderous figure. But one jack took hold of his arms. He continued to plead but was forced to watch the graphic onslaught.

The other jack of spades removed a miniature sword from under his garb. He jammed the point of the instrument violently into Lane's lower back. The spade tip penetrated and cut into his spine, rendering his limbs inoperable.

The studded blackjack found the back of his skull a dozen more times. With each blow, the steel studs pulled more flesh away until the tissue and hair once attached to the back of his head had devolved into a disgusting mush.

As the club slammed into the wet brains, more broken bone became exposed. Transparent juice was forced out of the organ, and blood sprayed all over Red.

Red screamed, watching the jack of spades remove the blade out of Lane's spinal column. His brain retreated to the last time he'd seen such a thing.

He recalled Buddy's blood-soaked body oozing as Dane stood over him twisting his switchblade in his backbone. The horror ingrained on his accomplice's face was a reminder of the profound fear that Mad Dog would never let him forget.

The imagery of the current and past back stabbings intertwined with the metaphorical one. Glimpses of Brittany poking Francis' bloody hands and chest. The murder that was never supposed to happen. The haunting woman he'd allowed to walk out of his life.

At that moment, a new realization suddenly dawned on him: his entire life had been a long series of nightmares. And it only seemed to be getting worse.

Red didn't want to watch the grueling display, but at the same time, he was so terrified that he couldn't take his eyes off it. He had hoped that Lane would somehow find a way to make it back to his family. Red had his own hopes of such things that now felt much less realistic.

When the jack of clubs pulled Lane's body up by the neck, it looked as though a panful of bloody, scrambled eggs was falling out of the hole in his cranium. With his leg still shackled in place, Lane fell onto the floor.

He had busted.

STAND OR FALL?

"It's better to decide quickly," the dealer said.

Red looked down at his blood-soaked cards and then at the dealer's.

Red's hand: king, ten.

Dealer's hand: one card facedown, seven.

This is a no-brainer, he thought. *Don't overthink it.*

He couldn't help but look at the clumps of brain on the table. The gore made him shudder.

"You're running out of time—"

"Stand," Red replied. "Stay."

He said the command twice just to make sure there was no confusion.

"Alright then," the dealer said pushing her oversized glasses up from the tip of her nose again. She flipped the card in her hand that was facedown.

Dealer's hand: ten, seven.

Red exhaled a deep sigh and tears rolled down his face. It was much more than just his own life that he'd been thinking about. He was grateful not to have to go out like Lane or the soccer mom, but he was much more grateful to be given another chance to fix all the countless things he'd screwed up.

"Winner!" the dealer yelled.

Red shook in his seat. The jacks unshackled his leg and promptly returned to their places.

The dealer took a hundred-dollar chip and placed it in front of him. "Congratulations."

"A-a hundred dollars?" He was stupefied. The amount of the winnings was not what he'd expected, but he was too frightened to further complain.

The dealer leaned in closer to Red. "I don't do this for everyone," she whispered, "but there's something about you. Might just be that awful stain on your face, but I feel bad for you. So, a little friendly advice. Most players inside this place aren't walking around broke. If you're broke, you're betting with your body, and the payouts aren't going to be in your favor. It's a last resort, desperation move."

Red gulped and nervously fidgeted. "Why's that?"

"Let's just say ownership doesn't value life the same way people outside this place do. If you *have* less, you *are* less—at least under this regime. And if you are less, you earn less. The people who come in here with nothing are always the ones who will truly lose everything. But unlike anywhere else, they're still afforded an opportunity."

"What would you do if you were me then?"

"Well, you've already won a bet. House rules are, that as long as you have something to cash in, then you're free to leave. I'd suggest that you get the hell out of this place and never look back."

More tears streamed down Red's face. "I wish I could. But I can't leave this place until I get enough money to save my family."

"Oh," the dealer said. "You're one of those… Then, mister, for your family's sake, I would head over to the roulette table and lay this chip on red or black. It's almost fifty-fifty odds. Then you can try to work your way up from there. Maybe check out Underground Alley and get a little traction to build your bankroll."

Red nodded, absorbing whatever knowledge the dealer was willing to give him. He wasn't about to squander the opportunity, squeezing in one last question.

"And if I lose?"

The dealer narrowed her eyes and tapped her nails against the table. "How much do you need?"

"Over six figures."

She motorboated her lips in shock. "Then, I hate to say it, but your only hope would be the mystery parlay—"

"Hey, buddy!" a voice yelled from behind Red.

When he turned around, he saw the bald man rubbing his high school ring like some kind of supervillain.

"Shit," Red mumbled.

The bald man's eyes were bloodshot while his body remained drug-fueled. The madness swirling in his pupils startled Red. It reminded him of the horrible person he used to be. The sad man who watched Dessi get kidnapped and turned his back on her.

The dealer slapped her hands together twice. "New player, welcome." She gestured to the table that was covered in blood and brains.

The bald man grinned. "Well, I wasn't really planning on playing—"

The jacks took hold of him and dragged him to where the soccer mom had been sitting.

"But what the hell!" the bald man screamed. "When you're hot, you're hot!" He glared at Red. "Ain't that right?"

Red's eyes widened. The man seemed fearless. *Maybe the buffet* is *the right move.*

The jacks shoved him into the seat and shackled his leg in place. As the bald man looked down at the glistening brain matter resting on the table, he scooped up a few globs. He was so drugged out that, as he squeezed the gore with his fingers, his pupils looked like they might launch out of his face.

"Looks like someone else already did all the losing here!" the bald man yelled. "But I'm not losing… not today!" He opened his hand and dropped the slimy brains into his mouth.

"I fuckin' eat losers!" the bald man screamed, gnawing on the mushy organ like a savage. "You understand me?!"

Red watched in horror as the madman continued to rant. Grabbing his chip, he rose from his chair. He stumbled backward, tripping over Lane's motionless body.

The queen hadn't yet returned for her second clean-up. Feeling like he was trapped inside a night terror, Red scrambled back to his feet again. Rolling around in Lane's blood, he finally made his way to the exit of the tent. As Red ran through the curtains, the last thing he heard was the bald man's screaming.

"No one can stop me! I'm on a roll! The roll of my fuckin' life! You hear me, buddy? Where you going?! I still got somethin' to tell you!"

When Red escaped the tent, the chaos was finally getting to him. He needed to get away from the blackjack tables right away. As he turned his head, he saw the massive golden sign that read: *SLOTS*.

Red gritted his teeth.

Hopefully what Mr. Don said was true.

THE SLOTS

When Red rounded the corner, he expected the slot parlor to be filled with a sea of machines. He imagined rows of computer-based terminals that were nestled up against each other with very little breathing room. But the slot room couldn't have been further from his expectations.

While the room was every bit as large as the massive slot halls he was accustomed to, the machines were spread out several yards apart from each other. In addition to the separation, the devices were vintage—not the computerized, futuristic stuff in most modern casinos. Each had a classic pull lever with a ball at the end and between three and five motorized reels with a variety of insignias. They also had one odd feature: a clear, rectangular cell encompassed each of the devices. They looked like cases that you might see in a museum protecting a rare artifact.

What the hell's that for? Red thought. Back in the shitter, Mr. Don had said something about them getting destroyed. He wondered if the casing had something to do with that.

While the machines were spaced out, there were still quite a few of them. Red passed by several people who all seemed relatively at ease. In comparison to the disturbing games he'd just passed, the slots seemed almost relaxing.

While the contrast was strange, as Red watched the people feed coins into their slots, he noticed a lot of them were winning. They were collecting smaller increments, but as the money rolled out, Red saw a lot of smiles on the haggard faces of the risk-takers.

Maybe Mr. Don was right. Despite his rude actions at the craps table, he seemed a lot more level-headed than the psychotic bald man.

The only problem was, Red didn't have the luxury of winning slow. He'd already burned through all the bald man's charity chips. If he did the same with his blackjack winnings, his next bet might be his last.

He wondered how the slots worked. As he continued to study the people, he noticed it wasn't like the other tables. No one was betting with their bodies—just coins.

Red noticed a man passing by him and figured he'd shoot his shot. "Hey, man, do you know what the deal with these machines is? Just was wondering if you could tell me how it—"

"Fuck off," the man said without hesitation.

Jesus, what an asshole…

Red continued past the man until he noticed a familiar hue through the glass of one machine. The pressed, plum suit, oversized shades, and jewelry were unmistakable. Through the glass door of the encasement, Red spotted Mr. Don. A slender lady with a pair of monster breast implants, excessive makeup, and a fresh perm rubbed his shoulder seductively.

Mr. Don fed a coin from his bucket into the slot and let his hand rest on the pull handle while the other rested on the ass of the girl's glittery dress. She stuffed her tits in his face like she was ready to bring home a winner.

"Oh, baby, you wanna go home with Daddy Don and fuck around in the jacuzzi?" Mr. Don asked.

The woman giggled. "You know it, Daddy." She held her hand up and wiggled her fingers beside her absurd cleavage. "Just as soon as you win enough to put a ring on it."

Mr. Don winked at her. "Well, sounds like I better get to work then."

He pulled down on the lever.

Red looked at the spinning grid. As the first machine reel landed, he narrowed his sights. The emblem was clear as day and didn't look promising: a bomb with a lit fuse burning away at the end.

"Shit," the girl mumbled.

"Don't you worry, baby," Mr. Don replied. "The odds of even getting two are—"

When the second bomb landed, Red believed he knew what the purpose of the encasement was.

"No!" Mr. Don yelled. "The odds of bombing are almost as low as hitting the fuckin' jackpot!"

"This isn't happening!" the girl shrieked. "We've gotta get the fuck outta here!"

Mr. Don and his lady turned away from the machine and attempted to exit the chamber, but it appeared the locking mechanism on the door didn't allow a player to bail out while the machine was active.

When the third bomb hit, the trifecta validated Red's sneaking suspicion.

Mr. Don's lady screamed at the top of her lungs while he pounded on the door, "Lemme out! Lemme, the fuck out!"

When the machine exploded, Red jumped, nearly losing his footing. While the unexpected detonation caught him off guard, somehow the magical glass cell contained the violent blast in its entirety. The loud boom echoed and the space rumbled, drawing the attention of others.

How the explosion that came from the machine didn't harm anyone outside of the encasement shocked him, but not as much as what he saw inside. The old-school steel shell of the slot machine turned into nasty shrapnel. The metal flew so fast that Red couldn't even keep track of it. But that was primarily because Mr. Don's entire body had just erupted like an over-ripened whitehead.

His well-endowed lady-friend suffered a similar fate. A flood of gore, bone, and twisted metal splattered all over the entire cell, blurring the glass' transparency.

"Jesus fucking Christ," Red mumbled.

The series of vicious gut punches was getting to him—four sickening games in a row. Even though he considered Mr. Don to be a perverted piece of shit, he didn't think he deserved to die.

As the blood ran, Red could see their disfigured bodies. The woman was semi-hollowed—her destroyed torso lay on the ground with a mangled arm and missing leg. Many organs had vacated her husk or been torn to pieces. Her dress was partially on fire and one of her gigantic breast implants had exploded. The other was covered in blood and streaking down the wall. It oozed a foggy, gray fluid as it smeared blood down the encasement.

Mr. Don's cheeks and lower jaw were blown off his head completely. His exposed slick, muscle poured red, while the top of his face looked like a banana that had been peeled from the bottom up. The explosion had also warped his limbs, but the main point of impact was his abdominal region. Mr. Don's upper and lower halves had been separated. The ripping point was just above his waist, and a slimy tangle of entrails twitched in the pool of garbled gore.

This *is the safest fuckin' game in here?*

The way that Mr. Don had spouted off his seemingly impressive experience in the men's room, Red figured him for a fella that was going to stick around. But the violence had opened his eyes. It reaffirmed the rumor that Red had heard on the streets; once you stepped inside Shadows, there were *no* safe bets.

Mr. Don might not have had all the angles covered, but Red could tell, at the very least, that the man was a veteran of the deadly casino. The fact that a big-time player like him was laying there with his liver hanging out and his lady-friend's implants blown all over the walls was a lesson that he wouldn't soon forget.

If even the big-timers are going night-night, I gotta stay on my toes.

"Shit, a twofer," a woman said as she passed Red. She smiled at him. "Don't see that every day."

Red didn't reply. She passed him and peered through the glass to get a better look at the smoking corpses.

Everyone was so desensitized. It was like blood was as ordinary as orange juice to them. Red wasn't at Shadows by choice, but based on the casual attitude of other players, it seemed many were. Whether it was desperation, the adrenaline rush, the drugs, criminal circumstances, or just a dark craving for utter depravity they all had their own reasons. A frightening thought crept into his mind.

All these people are fuckin' whacked.

The atmosphere was starting to get to him. Red felt like he'd transitioned from amateur hour to the pros. The tremble in his body was intensifying, and he was struggling to hide it. But more than the physical aspects, the biggest step he needed to take was in his mind. He was going to have to get his stones up.

He looked at the 'S' branded into his palm while his heart pumped wildly. With his other hand, he squeezed the hundred-dollar chip.

At some point, I gotta bet, and I gotta do it soon if I wanna see Ma in one piece again. Lilly had said there was only one bet that could set a guy in his position straight. *Hope she wasn't talkin' about the slots…*

Red's legs started to move again. His brain wasn't even processing his surroundings any longer, just the fears that produced his panic.

After speedwalking his way out of the slot parlor, he stood below a massive sign that read: *ROULETTE.*

Red was still holding the hundred-dollar chip the blackjack dealer had given him as he stared at the sign. Out of everyone he'd tried to gather guidance from, did he dare trust the house? He couldn't be sure, but he liked to think he was a pretty good judge of character, and the woman seemed genuine to him.

I should at least take a look.

The last time he had that thought Red was forced into a game of death. But as he studied the area from a distance, that didn't appear to be the case with roulette.

That's probably why Mr. Don told me to stay clear of blackjack. It's the fuckin' Wild West over there.

The lights flickered and flashed on the enormous, neon roulette wheel and lettering. The signage was hung above a dozen tables, but there only seemed to be one table people were interested in.

The blacks and reds were a blur as the wheel at the table swirled with great speed. It was hypnotic but Red couldn't allow himself to be enticed. Truthfully, the last thing he desired to see was another lethal game. He would've been content hanging out near the buffet and just waiting for Lilly so they could figure out what came next.

The buffet.

The notion returned to his head. After seeing a series of gruesome tortures and slayings, Red couldn't help but think about escape. Since he couldn't escape physically, why not mentally? The big pile of tan powder that brought back memories of his selfish bliss pushed its way back into his mind. Or maybe he could have just a little bit of the white to take the edge off?

When he was sticking stuff up his nose on the daily, it helped him forget about his problems. The broken friends that disappeared from the streets because they couldn't pay up. The threat of violence that always loomed for a grifter. The woman he once believed loved him, even though she sold her pussy. The screaming cries of a newborn that drove him mad. He pictured Dessi back in that infantile state. She always seemed in a state of discomfort around him at that age.

Is this all for someone else?

While he couldn't be sure about Dessi's exact origin, there was something inside that made him feel a connection. He wouldn't have thrown so much damn money at Jack Tunney if he hadn't.

Red had chased the dragon for years before realizing that he could only hide within its scales for so long. The heroin worked while he was on it, but between doses, during those tiny windows of sobriety, he couldn't help but see their faces: the love he never found and the seed he wasn't sure he'd planted.

They would haunt him until he put it to rest.

It was the questions that helped him get straight. But the problems that came into his life because of his change in character were far more daunting than his solitary demons. Either way, he was in too deep to turn back.

ROULETTE

From just outside the slots area, a scream ripped through the casino. Red was no longer stuck on his pity party or desire to sniff dust at the buffet. He'd decided to see what the fuss was about and joined those loitering at roulette table 6.

A well-dressed ball of stress stood at the table by himself. The reason for his screams became obvious—the man had his index finger jammed around the back of his right eyeball. The tension he pressed against it with was enough to lift the orb out of the socket and allow him to work the switchblade into his nerve and blood vessels.

As he severed the slimy cord, his wails amplified to an inhuman pitch. The disturbed man in the suit had a look on his gushing face like he couldn't believe he'd done it. He let go of the switchblade. As it fell on the rug, he reached into his suit and retrieved a white handkerchief.

As blood oozed from the hollow cove in the man's head, Red saw some of the drippy, pulsating meat in the socket along with the nerve nub. Red's guts swirled as cool sweat pooled on his forehead. Stomach bucking, he raised his branded palm over his mouth but couldn't look away. Keeping his composure, Red watched the man ball up his handkerchief and shove it into the runny void in his face.

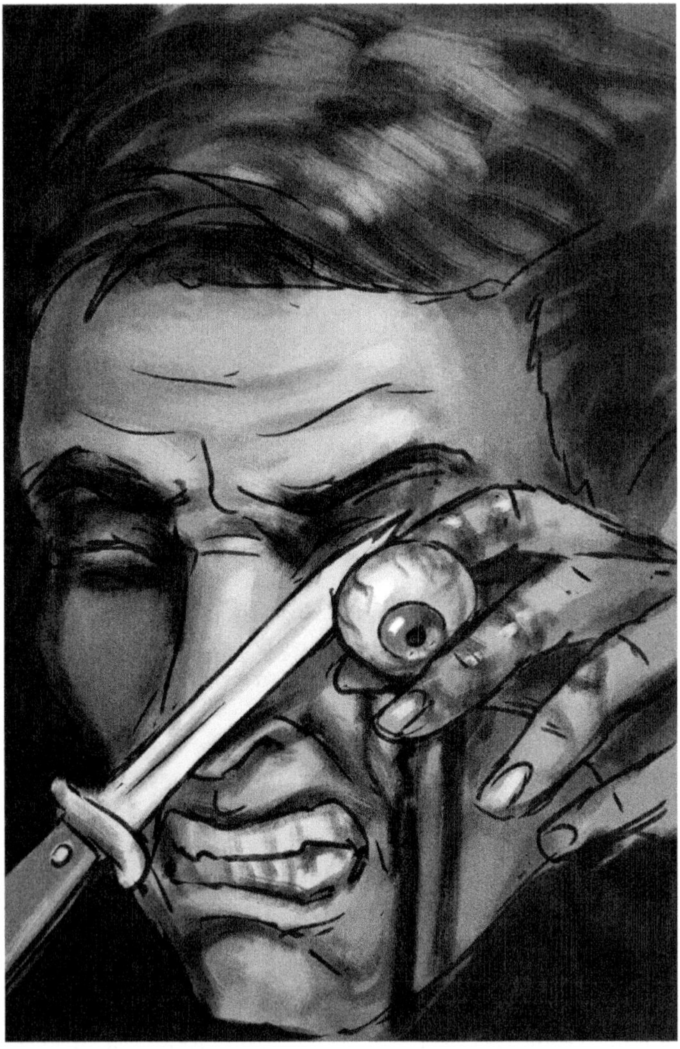

Red was glad he didn't have to see the gory chasm any longer; just looking at it hurt. Trying to control his tremble, his gaze dropped from the one-eyed man to the marker on the table—the bet was on red.

It's now or never, Red thought. *That blackjack dealer don't got a reason to lie to me.*

"Change a hundred," Red said to the dealer.

"Any more bets?" the dealer asked the rest of the table before giving Red four blue, twenty-five-dollar chips.

The other men stayed quiet.

Red slid all his chips beside the one-eyed man's outside bet, going all-in on the color he was nicknamed after.

The dealer smirked as he took the maimed man's eyeball, pinching the squishy sphere like someone would a filter when casually bumming a smoke.

As the one-eyed man screamed in agony, the croupier raised his free hand to his earpiece. He listened intently and looked up at the black camera mounted to the uneven stone wall. He nodded and yelled, "Stand by."

Red had no idea what any of it meant, but it appeared that the pause made members of the crowd uneasy. The men rocked with anxiety for several minutes as the drama dragged on until the bystander next to Red snapped his head sideways as if he'd caught something out of the corner of his eye. When the color abandoned the bystander's once rosy cheeks, a frightened whisper escaped him. "That's… that's The Black Widow…"

The bystander no longer cared about the macabre wager unfolding before him. He scurried away like a mouse when the lights came on.

Red got nervous. After what Mr. Don and Lilly had said about her, he needed to proceed with extreme caution.

That's gotta be her. A firm, athletic woman in an elegant black dress walked toward the roulette table. She was flanked by three security guards clad in black suit jackets with sleek button-ups underneath. Their dark pants and shoes completed their uniforms.

The two guards farthest behind The Black Widow were all business—a mean-mugged woman with advanced cauliflower ear and a stocky, black male. The pair broke away from the group, creating a perimeter around the roulette table. The Caucasian man who was the most grizzled of the three guards remained beside The Black Widow. His weathered flesh made him seem older than he probably was. He looked like a man with military experience, the type of person Red would prefer to stay clear of. All of them were, really.

As Red watched the grunt usher The Black Widow to the table, he noticed discomfort growing in most of the men around him. The sudden shift in atmosphere left many of them looking away, unwilling to make eye contact.

One gentleman dressed like a high roller with a scar on his face didn't seem too affected by her presence. The bearded man wore garish boots, aviators, and a cowboy hat. He could've pretended he didn't see The Black Widow but chose to tip his cap and give her a nod.

The only person who didn't hush was the poor bastard who'd just plucked his eye out in front of the roulette wheel. The throbbing cavity in his head remained leaking blood, the once white handkerchief now red.

The Black Widow looked at the dealer.

"Give it a spin," she said.

As the dealer hovered his hand at the top of the wheel, Red watched the eye hit the track. The rubbery sclera rolled around, leaving a juicy trail of blood-dotted, translucent fluid behind. Red didn't even know what the stakes were for the one-eyed man, but he imagined they were every bit as serious as his own. The terror swelling inside Red caused his burned hand to tremble again.

He turned his attention back to The Black Widow. She was looking over the table, utterly enthralled by the gory drama unfolding. Along with Red, she watched the wet orb slide onto the wheel. It tumbled over the dividers countless times. The oversized ball hit both consecutive and different colors, not yet ready to relinquish its momentum.

Red.
Black.
Black.
Red.
Black.
Red.
Red.
Black.
Red.
Black.
Red.
Black.
Red.
Black.
Red.
Red.
Red.
Double-Zero.
Red.
Black.
Red.
Black.
Red.
Black.
Red.
Black.
Red.
Black.
Black.
Red.
Black.
Black.
Red.
Black.
Red.
Black
Single-Zero.

Black

The one-eyed man howled like a wounded wolf when his lone peeper confirmed his worst fear. "No, please," he moaned. His legs suddenly weakened as he almost lost consciousness. The one-eyed man fell forward, putting both of his hands on the table to bridge himself.

The blood-saturated glob of handkerchief fell out of his eye hole and plopped down, soiling the once pristine felt. Blood rained out of the tender pit in his face, pissing all over the outside bets. Tears of terror joined the blood but were quickly dominated by the crimson sludge.

The two guards on the perimeter rejoined The Black Widow.

"I guess you should've bet on black," The Black Widow said. "Take him to the Red Room."

"With pleasure," the grunt beside her said, nodding at his peers.

Red wanted to scream. As the dealer cleared the bloody chips away, he realized he'd just lost the opportunity to continue gambling without risking his body and life. And as he watched the one-eyed man panic, Red wondered how many bets removed he was from such behavior.

The one-eyed man attempted to flee but the black guard slammed his fist dead into his nose, then extended his baton. The impact of the blow shattered the bone and cast it crooked. Blood and snot flew out of the one-eyed man's nostrils and dribbled into his mouth. Before he hit the floor, the female guard stepped in and hooked him under his armpits, and they all worked together to drag him away.

The anxiety in Red was overflowing. Was he looking at his future? What came next for the one-eyed man?

"Show's over," The Black Widow said, smacking her palms against each other. "Time is money, so get those bets in, and enjoy the night."

Just as Red thought she might walk away, she curled her head back. "Oh, and don't forget, the buffet is open. I encourage you all to do whatever it takes."

The buffet.

Images of the powder flickered in his mind. Maybe just a little bit of tan would calm him and get him back on track. If not the tan, then surely the white. If he was going to pull this off, he needed to find a way to loosen up.

Gotta be cool, gotta be—

"Hey, Red," The Black Widow said.

Fuck, how does she know my name? He couldn't decide if the woman knowing him was a good or bad thing. But judging by the story Lilly had told him, it was probably the latter.

He tried to wet his throat. "Ah, yes, Ma'am."

"How far are you willing to go?"

Red was afraid to answer. "I'm, uh, I'm not exactly sure what you mean."

She pointed at the one-eyed man. "I mean exactly what I said. Would you be willing to go that far for Dessi? Do you want it enough to pull your own fucking eye out of your head… or worse?"

His mouth hung slacked open. *How does she know about Dessi?* Red moved on from his own question, battling with hers in his head. How much did the girl truly matter to him? *Fuck…*

When he said her name in his head it brought him back. He was the one who'd given it to her. After Red started calling her Dessi, that was all she wanted to be called.

Red wasn't a perfect role model, but he'd done what he could for the girl. He remembered all those somber nights that Dessi stayed awake, moistening his tee shirt with her tears. He could never tell her what her mother was out doing. He could never tell her that the drugs and dick were more important than she was. But he tried his best to make up some comforting lies. There was a certain comradery between the two of them that didn't happen in most broken homes. He'd used his heart to cultivate it.

Good or bad, we had some moments.

"I suppose you don't have to answer just yet," The Black Widow continued. "But I only ask because you need to be prepared to go the distance if you ever want to have a chance at seeing her again. The road out of this place is bumpy and littered with bodies. So, start thinking about it."

After the explosion of memories, he realized he and the girl had something. Whether or not he should've wasted so much money and risked his life trying to solve the mystery of her disappearance was another question.

"I'd do whatever I needed in order to find her," Red replied firmly.

The Black Widow grinned wide and looked back at her muscle as they collected the one-eyed man. "We'll see about that."

Red tried to digest what she was telling him, but it all seemed so heavy. As she turned her back on him, Red looked beyond the room, at the signage that hung on the wall and read: *UNDERGROUND ALLEY.*

As Red watched them drag the screaming man through a set of double doors, the jitters and emotions in his system left him in a frenzy.

The deadly dominos.

The wicked war.

The barbaric blackjack.

The sickening slots.

The repugnant roulette.

All the images of violence swirled in Red's head, a gory mess littered with the faces of the dead and intermingled with people whose lives hinged on his success. Would they soon be interchangeable?

Red stared at the nefarious sign for Underground Alley.

I can't handle anymore right now.

He couldn't be certain, but the stress and proximity of the horror made one thing clear; if he was going to work up the sac to go gamble with his life, he was going to need a little something to get him on the level first.

BUMPS ON THE ROAD

Red lowered his nose to the small pile of brown. He sniffed hard, ensuring when he raised his head away from the marble rim of the fountain, it was dust-free. Glossy-eyed, he looked up at the big letters within the water that read: *SHADOWS*.

He got the sniffles almost immediately and sat down on the bench near some fake plants. No matter how brief, he hated the dead time between the sniff and when the dope hit, but it was *always* worth the wait.

Red found himself scratching at his arms again, just like he used to. There was a part of him that regretted breaking down and succumbing to his demons, but then there was his dark side. His dark side was excited. His dark side was ready to take it even further.

For a moment, he entertained the selfish thought of just wandering around inside Shadows for eternity. Becoming a casino zombie wasn't that bad of an idea. He could tell that some of the stiffs inside had been stewing in there for a while. Sniffing dust didn't seem like such a bad day job. He could just inhale and try to forget about his past life. The endless supply of drugs would keep him numb, 'happy,' and distracted until his body finally went.

But deep down, Red knew he couldn't hang his mother out to dry. She was the only person who ever gave a fuck about him. Back when she was still working and Red owed money to the loan sharks, she'd paid them off. When he'd gotten thrown in jail for fighting at the bar, she'd bailed him out. After showing up at her house withdrawing from heroin, she'd found him a bed at rehab. And through all his fuck ups, she never judged him. She always saw the good side of her son. Was she happy with all his decisions?

No.

Did she make him aware that he could've been doing much more productive things than running around the streets and causing trouble?

Yes.

But now, the tables had finally turned. His mother was too old to bail him out any longer. After a life of selflessly shelling out to save his ass, she needed her son's help. *He* was supposed to be taking care of *her*. Red was supposed to have gotten his shit together. And nothing hurt him more than failing in that regard.

The truth of the matter was that Red would've been dead long ago without her—swallowed up by the gutter dwellers and the repercussions of his failures. In retrospect, he wondered if death would've been a blessing in disguise.

No, he thought. *This ain't about me anymore. I gotta save Ma. Gotta find Dessi, too.*

Red couldn't fault her for allotting him more time. He should've been able to figure things out already. But then there were other problems that, no matter how long the calendar was, there was never enough time to resolve.

Time's a funny thing.

A euphoric rush crept up inside him as he stared at the flashing sign above The Doll House entrance. When the next thought came to Red, his mind clouded, and his pupils pinned out.

Speakin' of time, where's the hell is Lilly? I wonder how… how long it's been.

Red looked down at the watch he no longer had.

I kinda, really miss her. She was sweet. The sweetest damn thing in this place.

Fishing around in his jacket, Red took out a fingernail worth of white powder. The tan got him in gear, and the white would help him peel out. As he sniffed the coke, he felt a chill run down his spine. In case he needed a little extra fuel along the way, Red had filled his entire pocket with cocaine back at the buffet.

He would've liked to have taken more of the tan, but he needed to be able to function. Keeping just a bit in his other pocket was the most rational thing he could think of.

Her beautiful, crooked smile came into his mind again.

Lilly…

A strange excitement spread throughout his entire body. His eyelids became heavier with each blink until he was no longer able to open them.

THE NOTE

When Red's eyes came back open, his heart thrashed in his chest. He was sweating and itchy all over. The feeling wasn't foreign—he felt like he was dying. Maybe he'd done too much. Even during the time he'd been straight, part of him felt like he was dying every day. The confusion spinning his head overwhelmed him. But regardless of his bodily chaos, Lilly Marlene was the first thing on his mind.

Fuck me, what time is it?! he thought. *Did I miss her?!*

The thought terrified him.

He suddenly felt like he was trapped in a timeless tomb, the restrictive measures that Shadows had in place leaving him in the dark. It was the same shtick every casino had, but there, it seemed even more nefarious.

Where the hell is she?

The feeling of something rough against his fingers confused him. Red looked down and saw a folded piece of paper had been placed inside his hand.

"What the fuck?" Red mumbled.

He immediately scanned the surrounding area of the annex, but there was no one in sight. Not sure what to think about the mysterious offering, Red carefully pried open the note. His eyes widened as he took in the scribbles.

The note read:

You weren't awake, or I would've told you in person. I wanted to say it before, but we didn't have time. I hope this doesn't sound weird, but I've been feeling luckier every time I see you! I can't wait until we meet again!

The odd note was unsigned, but in Red's mind, it didn't take a rocket scientist to figure it out. There weren't many people he knew in the godforsaken establishment.

Damn it! I missed Lilly!

When he read that she'd been feeling luckier every time she saw him, his heart started to race.

Maybe she's back at work!

The simple idea had solved his problem and addressed his fears. But before he put it into motion, Red needed another pick-me-up.

When he'd awoken, alcohol was suddenly on his mind. Rushing back to the bar, he pushed a woman aside. She said nothing as he grabbed the entire bottle of whiskey and took several gulps. When he burped, he nearly threw up. But that didn't stop him from polishing off nearly a third of the bottle with his next few sips. Still, the liquor wasn't enough.

The buzz suddenly smashed him over the head like a fucking sledgehammer.

Red grinned and reached into the pocket filled with cocaine. *Gotta balance out.* He pulled out a pinch. *This'll do the trick—nothing to worry about. Everything's gonna be just fine.* Elevating a clump with his fingers, he pushed it into his nose and snorted like a pig.

LOOKING FOR LOVE

When Red got to The Doll House, it was like his brain kept turning on and off. When he spoke, the words were fractured, and particles of brown and white dust fell from the tip of his nose.

"We—we were with Rickey Lime before," Red rambled. And Shirley's always nice. But Lilly's my favorite."

The bartender, Clyde, appeared annoyed. He looked like he was used to dealing with tweaked-out scum, but the sight of Red's face just seemed to bother him. Not to mention the nonsense he was speaking.

"What the fuck do you want?" Clyde asked.

"I—I wanna see my Lilly pad."

It was a miracle he was able to speak with enough structure for Clyde to understand.

"She ain't gonna be here the rest of the night."

"The fuck do you mean?"

Clyde gritted his teeth. It seemed like he was losing his patience with him, but then his demeanor shifted. His clenched jaw transformed into a smirk. "I mean her shift got swapped. She's actually performing at the theater in just a few minutes. She's part of the magic show tonight. If you go now, you'll still be able to catch her."

Red didn't know if he was just paranoid, but there was something about the way Clyde delivered the message that bothered him. Was he just trying to get another drugged-out dumb fuck away from his bar, or was it something else?

"Wait, wasn't she watching the girl for the magic show?" Red asked.

"She was, but it looks like she got promoted to performer," Clyde said, a wider grin stretching across his face.

He's a real smug fucker, Red thought.

While he didn't like the way Clyde explained it, the paranoia dissipated. When Red thought about seeing Lilly again, his peepers lit up. A big grin found his face and drool bled out.

Magic, she certainly is.

The moment they'd had was magic. He'd never opened up to a stranger about his familial and drug problems before. He still wasn't even sure why he'd chosen her, but he was glad he had. At the end of his rope, Red had to tell someone. But it wasn't even so much that he'd chosen to share his dark secrets with Lilly, it was how she reacted.

The care in her eyes.

The lack of judgment.

The genuine concern for his future.

She was a diamond lost in a mountain of malevolence. But even in the darkest of places, she still shined bright. She gave him hope.

Red wanted nothing more than to repay that kindness to her. He wanted to show Lilly that he cared for her enough to accept the sins of her past as well. It might've been the heroin enhancing some of the feelings he normally wouldn't have been comfortable acting on, but he still felt things he hadn't felt for as long as he could remember—maybe ever. At that moment, learning her story was not only important to him, it was a priority.

"I'd love to see my Lilly perform, that-that's why I came here," Red confessed, removing another pinch of powder from inside his jacket.

Clyde frowned.

As Red sniffed up more of the white, his glossy gaze settled on the bartender again.

"C-can Rickey Lime come with me too?" he asked, pointing at a glass behind the bar.

Red asked him like he was a five-year-old pitching a sleepover to his mother.

Clyde rolled his eyes and turned back to the bar. Grabbing a smudged glass, it looked like he aimed to fix Red the mocktail. He quickly set the fizzing drink down on the bar. "Anything to get you the fuck out of here."

THE THEATER

The Lime Rickey crashed onto the floor just outside of the entrance of The Theater. As Red staggered through the black curtain, the darkness didn't help his already shaky vision. The deafening roar of the crowd sounded like a Roman Colosseum.

There were several vacant seats near the doors, which was perfect since Red was starting to lose his legs. He slumped into the raggedy seat and struggled to hold his head up. But when he reminded himself that Lilly was about to take the stage, somehow his chin rose.

The dark performance space was illuminated. Several blue stage lights were angled upward at a rectangular, see-through chamber. The wavy, colored lighting made the skull-faced woman inside look like she was floating in pool water. The rows of dense chains that circled her body not only restricted her but weighed her down.

Fear bit Red in the gut like a cobra.

Is that Lilly?! he thought. With so many mini waves of dope and coke rushing through his drunken system, his perception was beyond warped.

To the right of the water tank stood an entrancing magician in a bizarre mask.

The massive eyes on his devil mask swirled with madness like two pinwheels melting in the wind. The wicked magician whipped his cape and gestured to the tank, while the skull-faced woman continued to struggle with the heavy chains.

Oh no! Red tried to digest the intense scene through blurry vision. But as the bubbles near the skull-faced woman dwindled, so did Red's consciousness.

***

Darkness enveloped the theater. Red didn't remember waking up. He was suddenly just awake. He found his fingernail filled with more powder and looming under his nose. He took another whiff, this time of the tan, unsure how many he'd ingested while drifting in and out of the dream state.

Wicked imagery flashed on the stage. The devil man projected strange lights, while the skeleton woman danced in the smoke. But it wasn't the stage that caught Red's eye, it was the insidious woman on the balcony.

The Black Widow grinned as she watched the show. Red's vision rotated between blurry and sharp with each blink of his eyelids. The stark transitions forced him to take notice of the new nightmarish features The Black Widow projected every few seconds.

Her eyes dimmed dark as the abyss.

Her teeth grew long and demonic.

Her mouth glistened, hungry for the souls of evil men.

Red could hear her words echoing in his head. *How far are you willing to go?* He shuddered uncontrollably as everything went dark again.

***

The sound of the chainsaw coming to life forced Red's eyelids back open. The first thing he saw was the devilish magician squatting under the table, driving the long, spinning blade into the wooden plank.

The saw blade shredded through several inches on the underside of the assistant's table. Red's heart dropped as the curly hair and snaggletooth caught his eye. His worst fear manifested as he realized his only friend in Shadows was in grave danger.

Resting above the maniac magician, screaming in a black and red leotard, lay Lilly. Each of her limbs were firmly shackled in place on the table. She struggled desperately but couldn't move an inch. As he watched helplessly, Red felt like he was choking. The drugs confused his mind. All he could think as she bellowed was that Lilly still looked beautiful.

Red wanted to stand up and rush over to her rescue. He didn't know if it was part of the show or not; it felt so real. Still, even if he wanted to get up, the fat doses of heroin left him paralyzed. He could only watch and hope. But as the chainsaw blade found Lilly's snatch, the horrifying wails amplified.

The blood sprayed all over the devil-man's mask as he eagerly forced the saw forward. His wicked, spiraling eyes were painted with tiny particles of her meat. The meat that Red had seen a future with. The meat that understood him.

Has the trick gone wrong?! Red thought.

Panic exploded inside him. He'd seen the tricks where people get cut in half before, but he'd never seen bloodshed at a magic show. While the theater was of course a place of theatrics, it still didn't feel right to him.

The unforgiving cycle of the steel continued to rip into her pussy and asshole. As the devil-man pulled away momentarily, Red could see several dangling ribbons of gore within the garble of mutilation. The leaking lips of her pussy and the rubbery shine of blood and fecal matter oozed all over her torn rectum.

After looking at his handiwork, the twisted magician resumed the assault. Burrowing even deeper this time, the gaping slice carved through Lilly's flesh entirely. The muddy sound of the saw on the meat and blood changed abruptly when it met with Lilly's pubic bone.

As the extreme violence increased, a foul expulsion occurred. The russet tone of bodily waste exited Lilly's body, splattering with the blood. Under the bright, white spotlight the mixture of juices oozed all over the table and leaked underneath.

While Lilly voided her bowels, her body shook. Straining her muscles, she struggled but moved very little. The shrieks increased in volume.

Amid his stupor, Red felt like even from the back of the theater, they were locking eyes. Just like she lay chained to the table, he might as well have been chained to his chair.

Red struggled to keep his eyes open but had zero control over his body. Sweating profusely, he faded again. The horrifying world he saw left him confused. He couldn't be sure what was real. But whether it was part of the show or not, it was still real to him.

THE TRUTH HURTS

When Red awoke, his brain was still buzzing. The clothing on his body was sodden, and beads of sweat rolled down his face. He was still high but not over the moon. He felt closer in touch with reality.

As he looked around the room, he noticed the non-show lights in the theater were on and every seat was vacant. The bright room was empty, except for a Hispanic janitor. The shorter man with a goatee rolled a mop bucket around the stage. As he pushed the cloth into the ringer, blackened, reddish water bled out of the holes on the strainer. A series of flashes invaded Red's head.

The devilish magician.

The woman with the skull face.

The chainsaw buzzing through the wooden table.

The blood and feces shooting up from between Lilly's legs and splashing all over her horrified face.

It was just a show, Red told himself.

Red wanted to believe it but felt like he was lying to himself. Red rose from the fraying seat. Struggling get his legs under him, he staggered down the aisle until he reached the front of the stage.

It can't be.

The janitor slung the mop into a puddle of blood, shit, teeth, and various entrails. He pushed it side to side, sopping up as much of the mess as possible.

Red's lips quivered as he examined the pile. The severed large intestine had a stream of partially-digested food leaking out, and just beside the glistening tube, lay a blood-speckled, white high heel. The eye-catching shoes he thought looked so sexy on Lilly's feet would be of little use to her now.

A tear welled up in Red's eye. "It was real."

The janitor looked up from his mop bucket at Red. "You bet your fuckin' ass it is. Smells like shit over here."

ALL IN

Red pulled another pinch of white out of his jacket and raised it to his nose. As he looked at the sign to The Mystery Parlay entrance, he needed another bump or two to help him find the testicular fortitude to go all in.

It didn't take him long to figure out what the bet that Lilly never got to tell him about in The Doll House was. And especially after what the blackjack dealer had told him, it made total sense. Red stared at a small sign at the entrance of The Mystery Parlay that read: *Become a millionaire in thirty minutes or less with three back-to-back bets!*

In a strange way, the mystery element of the bet comforted him. Red had checked with the croupiers at the gross game tables back near the entrance. He'd have eaten shit all day if it meant saving his mother and getting enough scratch for Jack Tunney to finish the job, but the payouts at the low-level tables weren't enough to fix his problems.

And even if he was bartering with his life on The Main Floor, after crunching the numbers, Red had realized that he'd have to win dozens of times to even get close to the amount he needed. Winning dozens of times didn't seem like something that happened at Shadows. Winning The Mystery Parlay was his only hope.

And if the odds weren't enough, on top of them, there was the issue of time. Red had no idea how much he had left. Never mind the lack of clocks, but the drugs kept his thoughts and senses jumbled. While he couldn't be certain, his instincts told him that his time was almost up.

Hope Ma's alright, Red thought.

He shook his head from side to side. The best help he could give his mother was focusing on the task at hand. Lilly was right. There was only one bet that could earn him enough to right his wrongs.

Red didn't want to know what kind of creative sadism he was in for—knowing would've been worse. Going in loose and blind gave him the best chance. But even in his drugged-out state, with such a high payout being offered, Red understood that the mystery parlay would most likely be his final bet. He was just thankful the drugs made him more accepting of his fate.

I'll do what I can. I'll make the best of it. A tear beaded down his face. *This mess started with a parlay. I guess it's only fitting that it ends with one.*

Taking a deep breath, Red rubbed his finger under his nose and sniffed before stepping through the black curtain.

MYSTERY PARLAY: BET 1

Beyond the curtain stood a door. And as it closed behind Red, it locked automatically. The space was tight but not claustrophobic. It contained a large table full of almost every sharp instrument or blunt object imaginable: knives, scissors, needles, razors, hammers, pliers, saws, weights, paddles, and more.

At the front of the room, a massive wheel stood with many horrific acts scribbled on the divided sections. A countdown clock hung above the wheel stuck at thirty seconds. There was an exit door to the right of the wheel with another digital readout that read: *Locked*.

The floor was covered in bloodstains. But it wasn't just the bloodstains that were concerning—something had been left behind. While whatever body the blood came from had been removed, a lone arm lay on the floor. The edges of the suit jacket near the shoulder area were frayed. The joint had clearly been cut in a crude fashion.

Within the puddle of blood that surrounded the limb, a sparkle caught Red's attention. The blue jewel implanted in the Lincoln High School ring didn't seem so lucky anymore. The individual Red knew only as the bald man had pushed it too far. At the war and blackjack tables, he'd claimed that today was his day.

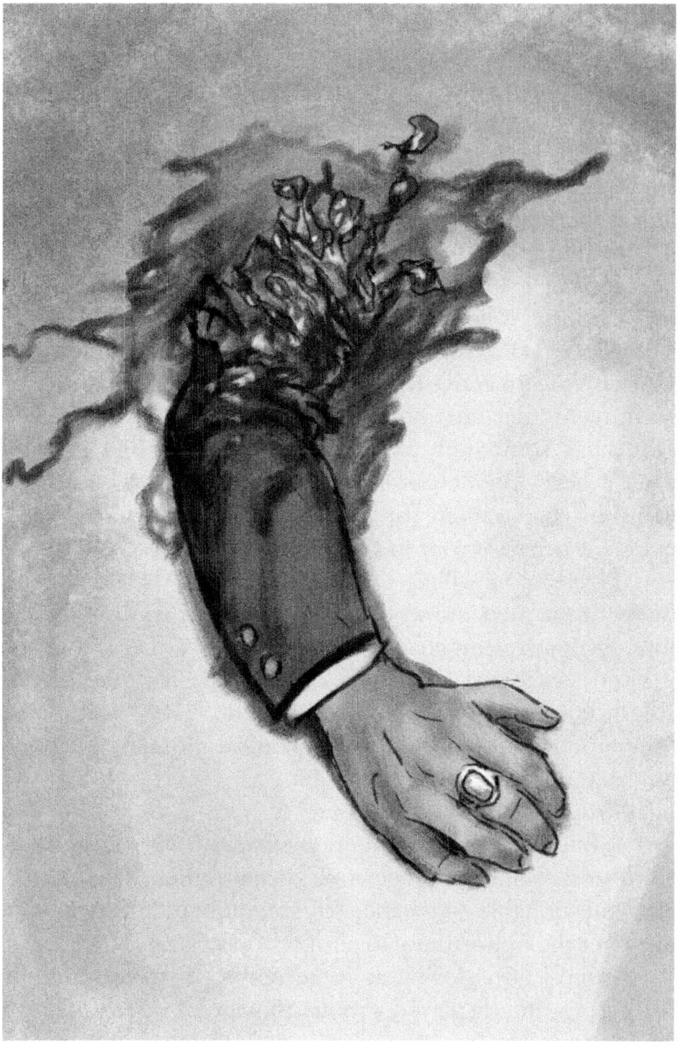

Guess he was right, Red thought.

When the widescreen TV monitor mounted in the left corner of the room suddenly activated, it caught Red off guard. "Shit!"

A thin, well-dressed, Italian gentleman appeared on the screen, grinning ear-to-ear. The handsome, clean-shaven man ran a comb through his slicked-back hair. The silver locks were perfectly positioned above his cool blue eyes. While his pupils were calming, they were somehow insidious at the same time.

"Bonjourno, high roller. Thank you for offering up the *ultimate* wager. I'm Gianni Lito, owner and creator of Shadows Casino. I'd like to begin by officially welcoming you to The Mystery Parlay. When I first established Shadows, it was with the objective to create a space where society's most wealthy and destitute could stand side by side. Where everyone has something to wager, be it money or blood. A place where anyone can step up to the table and not only win, but change their fortune *forever*. The one caveat is, of course, to change your life into what you've always desired, you'd have to be willing to risk it. And why shouldn't you? Many of the men and women who find their way into Shadows don't just want change, they *need* it."

Red swallowed a big gulp of spit. The icy gaze of the elderly owner sent a chill down his spine. There was something about him that Red found familiar. Something about him that made him uncomfortable.

Where have I seen that face before?

"While some may frown upon what unfolds within these cold, stone walls, we give people a chance here. That much is unquestionable—a chance so rare, most people wouldn't even get the opportunity to sniff it otherwise."

Gianni's grin glowed as he turned to a smaller box on the screen that displayed various footage of different areas in the casino before stopping at the entrance. "Since you have chosen the ultimate wager, I will afford you a brief glimpse into the spirit of Shadows."

Gianni pointed at the box that showed the bank. "Like any respectable gaming house, we have a bank."

The video transitioned to a sexy woman squatting off the edge of a craps table and pissing into a man's mouth. The man gulped mouthfuls of the dehydrated fluid quickly while a security guard aimed a gun to his head.

"The entrance tables are designed to break and humiliate the player upon admission—to shatter their spirit. Remind them they are less than human. That they are worthless. And once they are reminded, it doesn't take them long to make their way out to the main floor."

The cut in the footage changed to a man's testicle bouncing around on a roulette wheel. Red winced but forced himself to continue watching and listening.

"The Main Floor is, of course, where all the real magic happens. But if a player needs more convincing, we have all the amenities one could ask for."

The camera ran the entire length of the drug buffet spread, then showed the entrance to The Doll House.

"Forbidden desires," Gianni continued.

The movie showed a woman dancing under the darkness of the strip club while wearing an oxygen mask. A throbbing cock was in the frame, unleashing a massive cumshot that coated her face and mask.

"And if all that's not enough, we also have top-notch entertainment."

The camera changed to a band with a female lead singer. She screamed into the microphone and the band name, A Gift of Death, hung behind the trio.

Red raised his eyebrow.

Gianni scrunched his face as if what he was about to say was difficult for him. "But I suppose it would be dishonest for me to say this isn't a little about me, too. Maybe it's not all about a level playing field. Maybe I like seeing people tear themselves apart. Maybe sometimes we all should have to eat shit and learn to like it. Maybe I know something that you—and everyone else—doesn't."

Red didn't know what to make of the confession. The entire speech had a contrived, over-produced feeling to it.

"It's a fact of life that most people ignore," Gianni continued. "Because, let's face it, most people would rather be kind than candid. But I won't ignore it—never have."

Red's eyes left the screen for a moment and looked at the weapons on the table. His heartbeat accelerated.

"Not *everyone* deserves to live," Gianni whispered. "The elite members and high rollers that come to Shadows aren't without skeletons in their closet. To make it to the top, they stepped on a few anthills. And the very same can be said for their counterparts. The penniless, lost souls who make their way here were already familiar with the darkness long before we cast it over them. And dare I say that *everyone* who's made a wager here has *earned* the outcome of their bet."

The tremble in Red's body was impossible to control. While the drugs and alcohol clouded his head, he was still functional enough to think about what Gianni was saying.

Do I deserve *to be here?*

As Red felt his heart banging, he thought hard about the question. In some ways, he did. Sure, his boss, Mad Dog had consistently put money on some of the worst parlay bets he'd ever seen. But just because Red thought he was throwing money away, it hadn't give him the right to siphon it for his own causes. He should've known that could lead to violence against him, especially since he'd tried ripping him off in the past.

But his mother?

What about his father?

Those were the ones that really ate at him. Mad Dog stole Red's relationship with his father and was ready to sever the one with his mother too. Red could find a way to blame himself for the latter, but there was a good chance his downward spiral was predicated on the former.

The old mobster with the drool leaking out the side of his face appeared in his mind.

Red gritted his teeth.

If I get out of this place, he's gonna feel it. I fuckin' swear it.

Payback might've seemed like a pipe dream, but it didn't stop there. He needed closure on the pain he'd caused on himself. Red was willing to sacrifice whatever he needed to get Jack Tunney his payment and extinguish the familial anguish that haunted him. He needed the question marks that his demons presented to be put to rest. How could he move on from the past when he didn't understand it? But was wanting to know a selfish act in itself? Had he done more harm than good?

From where he stood, he couldn't be sure. The events of the evening and the odds he faced seemed to indicate that he'd made another shit decision.

"But enough about why and how you're here, it's time to talk about what happens next." Gianni grinned devilishly on the screen. "A parlay, at its core, has a low probability of landing. Depending on the odds of each bet within the parlay, the chance of success only gets grimmer. So, if you've entered this room, it's safe to say you're at the end of your rope. I'm not here to lie to you, there's a very good chance you're not walking away from this a winner."

Red swallowed, his discomfort only growing.

"But if you do," Gianni continued, "then rest assured, your remaining days will be golden."

The sweat beaded off Red's face. The tension alone felt like it was enough to cause a stroke.

"I'm sure by now you've noticed the big wheel in front of you. In total, it contains twenty-five possible outcomes. Only the lone, green advance space will allow you to move on to the second part of the parlay. But spin carefully, because each time you don't win, you'll be forced to complete a task. The tasks vary in difficulty and degeneracy, but each *must* be completed within thirty seconds of the wheel coming to a stop. If you should require an item that is not in the room, the dumbwaiter behind the curtain under this screen will deliver it to you. Once you complete the task, you will then spin again until you're either too inoperable to continue or until you advance to the second stage of the parlay. If you're unable to complete any of the tasks, you will quickly notice an almond smell seeping out of the vents above your head. That's Zyklon B—the same gas used by the Nazis."

Red looked at the grid above, his dread and discomfort expanding inside him. He didn't enjoy thinking about dying, but it was unavoidable. At least the gas seemed like a decent exit plan if things became more than he could handle.

It doesn't seem like the worst way to go.

"And trust me, it's not an easy out. It's one of the absolute worst ways to die," Gianni said.

Damn it! Red frowned. *Doesn't matter anyway. I should be thinking about getting through this, not giving up.*

"Lastly, should you choose not to or become physically unable, to complete a task, be ready for the gas."

The terror surged inside Red. Despite his own life being on the line, he couldn't help but wonder where Dessi was. Would he ever get to find out where she'd been taken, or understand what the true nature of their relationship was?

"Well then," Gianni said, "before we begin, I'll afford you a minute to review the wheel."

Red turned away from the screen and looked at the circle of horror. The frightening possibilities read:

Advance to the next room.

Hold an M80 in your mouth and light the fuse.

Snort broken glass.

Chop off one finger.

Rupture your eardrum with a nail.

Balls or Boobs in acid.

Light your hair on fire.

Fishhook in your pee-hole and reel.

Shoot yourself in the foot.

Drink a shot of diseased pig cum.

Slit both of your wrists vertically.

Chug a jug of garbage water.

Remove both front teeth with the pliers.

Eat a pail of rat poison pellets.

Insert a pipe cleaner into your urethra.

Bite off an entire fingernail.
Saw off your arm.
Use a short sword and perform hara-kiri.
Run a razor through all your toe webbings.
Blow your chin off with a shotgun.
Eat a Doll House mini (aborted fetus).
Melt your tongue with the blowtorch.
Use a melon baller to extract your eyeball.
Consume a plate of geriatric foot fungus.
Inject the contents of a mystery needle into your arm.

"Apologies, high roller, but I'm afraid that's all the time I can afford you. If somehow, you're able to make it to the next room, you'll be provided with a new set of instructions for the second part of the parlay. Good luck. You're most definitely going to need it."

Red couldn't control his body. His trembling bounced his arms back and forth as Gianni vanished from the screen and was replaced by red letters that said *Spin Now!*

As the green bulbs around the edge of the wheel lit up, Red took hold of one of the divider pins. It looked like it had been modeled after Wheel of Fortune but a bit smaller and elevated vertically.

In that moment he wanted nothing more than to walk away, but he was trapped. There was no way out of the sick game. He tried to prepare himself mentally.

I can do this. Maybe it won't even land on something. Maybe I'll move forward on the first shot.

He was lying of course but urged himself to believe. The drugs helped him just enough to muster the courage to move forward. As Red took hold of the edge of the wheel, he tried to gauge its resistance and weight. It seemed like when he would spin, the momentum would guide it smoothly. Since Gianni hadn't given any specific directions around how he could or couldn't spin the wheel, Red's strategy was to give it a modest turn. Depending on where it stopped, he could estimate how far he landed from the advance space and how much force might be appropriate for the next attempt.

Red didn't want to spin the wheel, but looking up at the gridded vent on the ceiling motivated him. If he just kept procrastinating, the gas surely wasn't far off.

Here goes nothing.

As the wheel began its rotation, the triangular pointer at the top flapped with each bar that passed. Red was satisfied with the speed. When the momentum started to slow, it looked like it might stop on the advance space.

C'mon! You're almost there!

But Red's hope transitioned to dismay when the wheel moved past it.

Bite off an entire fingernail!

"Fuck!" Red yelled.

The screen lit up again and Gianni Lito returned with a big smile creasing his handsome face.

"Well, if you're a nervous nail biter, this isn't what you're thinking. We're not talking about nibbling on a nail. You're going to need to get your teeth under the whole nail and uproot it."

Red winced at the thought.

Gianni held up his hand and pointed to his index finger. "The process is not done until the entire nail is detached from your finger, which must be accomplished using only your mouth. Remember, we're watching. And should you complete the task in any other manner, the gas awaits you."

Gianni disappeared off the screen again, replaced by red letters that reminded Red of the sick task.

Bite off an entire fingernail.

Red's eyes fell upon his pinky nail—the smallest of the lot—then back to the clock above the wheel just as the number transitioned to *29*.

Opening his jaws, he forced himself to begin the gruesome task. From the top down, with Red's front and bottom teeth, he bit firmly on each side of the tiny nail plate. He started out gently, but as the clock dwindled, he knew he'd have to move past his fears sooner than later.

As drool leaked out of his mouth, he intensified the pressure. He felt pain in his finger where the nail was starting to bow. His teeth drove harder until blood surged out around the keratin as it ripped away from the tender flesh below.

Just bite hard! Fuckin' bite it!

Red grimaced and screeched.

The nail plate popped, and he dug his teeth into the gummy flesh below. The taste of iron intruded on his palate. He looked at the clock as the throbbing pain caused Red to cringe and elevated his cries to a higher pitch.

Only a few seconds remained.

While the nail was uprooted, Red was still going to need to bend it all the way back if he was going to tear it free before the time was up. He approached the floppy nail from the front and used his tongue to lift it. Hooking underneath, he clamped his front teeth down. In a single, quick motion, like ripping off a Band-Aid, Red bit down as hard as he could, bending the nail plate backward. It detached from the skin and stood straight up at the cuticle. With tears now streaming from his eyes, Red yanked upward, ripping the entire pinky nail away from his finger. When he looked up at the clock with blood all over his lips, only two seconds remained.

Red spit the nail out onto the floor and covered the raw flesh with his other hand. As he clamped down on his pinky, the green lights around the wheel lit up and flashed. He looked back at the screen which now read: *Spin Again!*

The agony in his hand was unignorable. There was no way to block it out and focus. With the clock pushing him toward the finger-biting so quickly, he hadn't thought about which hand to gnaw on. He suddenly regretted his decision when he raised his drippy right hand to spin the wheel again. He'd picked the right hand because he'd already had several gashes around his palm from breaking the beer bottle at Rosie's. But this time when he grabbed the wheel, his grip felt different. The data measured from the rotation he'd given it last round seemed tainted by the distraction of his mangled phalange.

Red grimaced and let his anger fuel his spin.

Tick-tick-tick-tick-tick-tick-tick-tick-tick-tick.

The wheel finally slowed.

Tick… tick… tick… tick… tick.

Red's teary eyes scrunched closed with disappointment as he read the task to himself.

Fishhook in your pee-hole and reel! Jesus Christ!

It sounded just as outrageous as it did agonizing. Red didn't want to think about it, but he didn't have a choice. Gianni Lito had already appeared on the monitor again, ready to offer his tutorial.

"Ah, the great outdoors. While I myself may not be an outdoorsman, I can appreciate man's love of nature. For this task, you will retrieve the fishing pole under the table. The saltwater fishhook at the end of the line is a jagged, cruel thing. For our male competitors, the hook should be inserted directly into your pee-hole and pushed up until it pops out through the head of your cock."

"Nooooo!" Red cried. He was still not over chewing off his fingernail. As the tears continued to roll down his cheeks, Red reluctantly unbuckled his pants, hoping he might conserve some time.

"For our female competitors," Gianni continued, "it should slide right into your urethral opening and come out as close to your clit as possible. After the hook is set, simply reel the line in as quickly as you can. Once the top of the pole starts to bend you've completed the task. But there's a few steps to this one, so act fast."

Gianni disappeared from the screen and the clock instantly started to tick.

Red had already pulled the pole out from under the table and had the fishhook pinched between his fingers. The circular, saltwater hook was about the size of a quarter and looked like it'd been used a thousand times. The rusted metal was surely a doorway to tetanus. As Red looked from his pee-hole to the corroded tip, he knew there was no time to allow his dread to sway him.

As the point of the cold, uncomfortable metal slid into his urinary duct, it almost immediately curled into the roof of his tender tunnel. He felt the roughness of the tarnished metal bits breaking off. It felt like pieces of fiberglass were sliding into his flesh. A flaring, unscratchable itch was unleashed inside his cock—like an instant STD.

It was only when the unforgiving end of the hook poked into the tissue underneath the head of Red's mushroom tip that he hesitated. The piercing pain caught him off guard and forced his hand to involuntarily jerk backward. The sudden movement resulted in the barb below the tip of the hook ripping open his wiener duct. A disturbing V-shaped tear exposed the pink flesh on his penis. He stared down unable to believe what he'd done to himself.

Blood dribbled out of his dickhole.

Screams of agony filled the room.

Red peeked up at the clock.

Just 18 seconds left!

When faced with death, Red evolved into a piercing pro. He took a deep breath and pushed his continuous screams up to a higher pitch. Using all his willpower, Red curved the point of the hook forward until the bloody metal bore out of his cockhead like a worm pushing through damp soil in the morning.

The shocking sight and harsh pain caused Red's knees to weaken. As his joints buckled, he fell over sideways onto the floor. He landed in the slick of wet blood from the prior contestants, and the fishing pole fell by his side.

Despite the crippling pain and psychosocial horror of having hooked his own hog, Red wrapped one hand around the base of the pole and set his other on the reel.

4 seconds!

When he started to reel, his cock levitated like a snake charmer was blowing a flute in front of it. The hurt in his little head increased as the penis stretched to capacity. It was a battle of rods that concluded with Red's causing the end of the fishing pole to bend just as the time expired.

Red dropped the stick and fell over sideways but knew he couldn't rest long. Willing himself back to his feet, his mind raced. He wanted the rusty fishhook removed from his cock immediately. The filthy foreign object felt so unnatural clogging up his urethra. But when a new clip of Gianni appeared on the screen again, he knew he probably didn't have much time. He used the small knife on the table to sever the fishing line at the end of the eroded hook and turned to the old loon.

"A brief message around endurance. I didn't lay down any specific rules around how long of a break you may have in between spins. That was intentional. I hope you enjoyed your recovery time after your first two turns, because from here on out, it's a marathon. Now, after you complete a task, the lights around the wheel will flash ten times. If the wheel doesn't start spinning before the tenth flicker, well, let's just say you won't have to worry about what it lands on next. Good luck."

The screen went black and again prompted Red to spin.

Red wiped the tears from his eyes and zipped up his trousers. He hoped it would be the last time he had to do something that involved his cock or balls but there were no guarantees.

As the flashing lights around the wheel pulsated again, Red held his breath and spun. He tried to scale the spin, recalling how on his initial turn, a moderate amount of momentum went much farther than he'd anticipated.

Red watched carefully as the ticks started to slow before coming to a stop on a task that made his stomach turn.

Consume a plate of geriatric foot fungus! Noooooooooo!

Gianni returned to the screen.

"Ooo, my friend," Gianni said. The disgust was oozing off the old man's face. "There are few scents worse than the scent of neglect. Ironically, in this case, this elder's familial negligence has spawned your meal."

Red cringed as the sound of gears grinding came from the dumbwaiter. He approached the curtain and awaited Gianni's instructions.

"An unhealthy chunk of this man's foot lies in the dumbwaiter. The dead skin and fungus must be consumed in its entirety for you to survive. I wouldn't waste any time."

He set the tray down on the table and immediately removed the cover. When his task was revealed, Red's stomach bucked.

The skin hadn't been grated off the elder's fetid foot. When Gianni described it, Red imagined a parmesan cheese powder would be arriving. But instead, sat a fat slab of rancid skin and several thinner pieces. The big one was cracked with traces of dried blood as if when it had been harvested, the foot had been cut too deep and sliced into the layers of skin that were still alive. The parts that weren't affected by blood or black patches of fungus were the color of phlegm coughed up during the final stages of hospice.

Red shuddered.

He didn't have time to think about it, he just dove in head-first. When his fingers touched dead cells, the roughness caught him off guard. One piece was clearly the size of a heel, but it was difficult to tell the origin area of the other chunks. With only seconds to force it down, he grabbed as much as his mouth would fit and shoved it inside.

The grainy texture scraped against his gums. His saliva intermingled with some of the fresher skin, creating milk-like lube inside his mouth. The taste of death, mites, and unchanged bandages overpowered Red's palate.

He gagged, not expecting the skin to be so chewy, but continued to gnaw like a crazed animal. Drool leaked out of Red's mouth as his body tried to reject the dead flesh. He closed his watery eyes, trying his best to keep his repulsion in check. The wad of skin felt like it was starting to break down, becoming more malleable. It felt like he had a giant ball of fetid cookie dough in his mouth.

11 seconds!

He scraped up the remaining fragments of fungal foot chips off the tray and tossed them into the slimy ball in his mouth. Red was trying to condense the lump enough to swallow it whole, but he wasn't sure if it was passable. It was entirely plausible that he might choke on it.

3 seconds! Fuck it!

As he forced the ball of fungal flesh down his esophagus, Red was grateful for the milky fluid he'd generated. The creamy mixture of skin, blood, and liquidized black fungus greased the sides of his throat, allowing the clump to coast safely toward his digestive system.

The contaminated saliva oozed around his mouth as Red heaved. He kept his lips closed, ensuring his hard work wouldn't be revoked by a last-minute regurgitation.

His watery eyes found the wheel as the lights around it began to flash. Rushing up, he gave it a spin. Still distracted by the disgusting deed, Red was too flummoxed to focus on how hard he was spinning. He simply cranked it and hoped for the best.

When the ticker finally slowed, a new kind of fear found him. Up until that point, most of the things he'd done were fixable or small enough to not physically impact him long-term. But this next one would indefinitely change him.

Chop off one finger! Fuckin' shit!

Gianni was back in a flash. He bobbed his eyebrows as if excited to talk about the task.

"This one is a cutthroat classic. While we like to be creative with the wheel, we need a few things that don't require much explanation. Just cut a finger off." The image of Gianni on the screen had a cold look in his eyes. "Right now. It's as simple as that."

Red reached inside his jacket and removed more of the white powder. If he was going to find the gall to chop off a digit, he needed a little outside help. Some of the cocaine on Red's fingers got clumpy from the blood on his hands, but there was still enough dust on top to get a little more motivation up his nose.

Red sniffed hard and fast. The powdered areas as well as the clumps of blood blasted up into his nostrils. He moved in closer to the table and eyed the meat cleaver. There was surely no better choice if he wanted to quickly take off a finger. Red had seen it in the movies, but he never imagined how it might happen in real life.

As the sweat glistened off his brow, he knuckled up his right hand all but for his nail-less pinky.

May as well be this one. Looks like shit now anyway.

It only made sense to cut off the already wounded finger. But as he raised the cleaver, it was more than just the heft of the blade weighing him down. A permanent deformity wasn't something he ever aspired to acquire.

"Maybe I can reattach it later!" he screamed, driving the blade down just under the second pinky joint.

The sharp, heavy edge made short work of Red's bone, tendons, and blood vessels. Crimson spurted out of the finger nub as he dropped the cleaver. Red's horrified screams erupted as his face went ghostly white. The flashing of the wheel began immediately this time. Red rushed, pushing through his dizzy spell and stuffing the quivering digit into his jacket pocket. He staggered but kept his feet as he made his way back to the wheel of doom.

As Red gave it another spin, the blood rushing out of his hand painted the wheel. He was so traumatized by his gushing wound that he didn't even think about how hard he should spin it. As he watched the colorful sphere twirl and twirl, a nauseous sensation struck him hard. By the time he'd fought off the urge to vomit, the next torturous task was already being displayed.

Shoot yourself in the foot!

A light on the wall behind the TV screen turned green.

"Another simple one," Gianni's recorded image said. "Retrieve the handgun from the dumbwaiter on the wall. The hammer is already cocked, so all you have to do is just point and fire. There is only one bullet in the chamber so be sure not to miss. And remember, the task is to shoot yourself in the *foot,* not the toes."

Red rushed to the dumbwaiter and whipped open the curtain. A Beretta lay sideways there for the taking. He snatched up the gun with his five-fingered hand and returned to the center of the room.

He moaned looking down at his foot. The sneaker wasn't going to offer much protection from a bullet. Red felt uncomfortable in his own skin. The surging blood from his finger nub, the burning ooze leaking from his dickhole, the taste of fungus on his tongue, and now his foot already ached just thinking about what he had to do next.

Maybe I should just put the fuckin' thing in my mouth and be done with it. At least it'd be quick!

The faces of his ma and Dessi appeared in his mind, then suddenly, the idea was off the table. *Gotta save Ma and find Dessi, no matter how bad it gets.* The clock was displaying single digits; there wasn't much time left. Red pointed the gun directly at the top of his foot and pulled the trigger.

Blam!

Red immediately raised his leg off the ground and dropped the gun. He started to jump up and down on one foot as blood poured out of the other. He nearly slipped in the growing blood-slick below but balanced himself against the table. He screamed as he watched the bulbs on the edge of the wheel start blinking.

"Fuckin' Christ! Ju-just give me a second to think!"

No one was coming to his rescue. He limped his way to the wheel, feeling the hole in the bottom of his foot screwing with his balance. When the wheel was set in motion this time, he was just praying not to have to hurt himself again. In a way, he'd gotten his wish.

Chug a jug of garbage water.

Red was disgusted but wasn't upset. He didn't know if he could handle mutilating himself anymore. As the cocaine started to kick, he felt a surge of confidence. But then something dawned on him; if it was a gallon jug of garbage water—or any liquid for that matter—it was going to take a miraculous effort to ingest it in just a half minute.

The dumbwaiter returned.

"We get a lot of trash here at Shadows," Gianni said. "And I'm not just referring to our patrons. The compactors behind the scenes are always filled to capacity with filth. Whether it's rotten food or rotten people, it's *always* rotten. One can only imagine what kind of foul organisms are swimming in the fluid you're about to ingest. But there's only one way to find out! Oh, and a little puke is expected, but just don't abuse the leeway we're giving you. If you do, there will be repercussions."

The yellow words *Chug! Chug! Chug!* appeared on the monitor as the dumbwaiter displayed a transparent jug of discolored water. The vile hues swirling inside were all dingy, the normally translucent fluid clouded with globs of red and black. Particles floated in the areas where it was still clear enough to see them.

Red staggered over to the jug: a gallon container that was half-filled. He was relieved when he realized it wasn't a full gallon. Such a feat might not have been possible even with a drink he enjoyed. While he believed that he was up to the task, the thoughts of the rancid bacteria floating around inside the container made him squirm. Sure, he might survive the challenge, but would his gut survive the parasites?

As he unscrewed the cap, a wave of funk like he'd never witnessed found his nostrils. It smelled like rotten eggs, wormy pork, dehydrated urine, and burned hair had been fermenting inside a time capsule for a hundred years, only to be put into a blender and then have the pulp juiced into a pungent liquid.

Red's pelvis quaked. He did his best to keep the vomit down. Unfortunately, even holding his nose didn't make much of a difference. Some of the blood from his finger nub accidentally drizzled into the jug. As the water's color darkened, Red knew he needed to get moving.

He put the plastic to his lips and felt the tart, moldy taste of the wastewater hit his tongue. His belly buckled back and forth as the diseased fluid rained down his reluctant throat, but astonishingly, Red was able to keep it down. Maybe the shit-eating at the craps table had gotten him ready for the foul task, or maybe he was just born to eat shit.

He finished the entire jug with 4 seconds to spare.

With exhaustion knocking on his head, he didn't have much left in the tank. As the wheel started to flash, Red threw up violently. His watery puke and gelatinous wads of the foot fungus splattered all over the wheel and the front of his shirt and jacket.

God, what now?

He couldn't stop himself from gagging and choking on the sickening sauce. But while the vomit continued to spew, the wheel started to spin.

Red felt his brain becoming weaker. The fatigue that came with his injuries and the mental capacity it took to trudge forward had taken its toll. Falling onto all fours like a dog about to be taken out back, the garbage water continued to eject from his mouth. The wheel started to slow but he couldn't even focus on it.

As Red rested on the ground bleeding in a crimson puddle of blood and puke, the wheel finally come to a stop. He wiped the tears out of his eyes, barely able to lift his head and look. An unlocking sound came from the door to the right of the wheel, and a cackle of disbelief sprung from his mouth.

Advance to the next room.

MYSTERY PARLAY: BET 2

As the door closed behind Red, he took in the simple surroundings of the second room. Much like the first, a monitor was affixed to the wall, and the door to advance displayed 'Locked.' At the center of the room, similar to the blackjack area, stood a human-sized figure brought to life from a deck of cards. A statue of a joker held a power drill that rotated in his hands. The girthy drill bit spun, creating a deafening noise. It sounded much louder than any tool Red had ever held.

Beside the joker stood the suicide king. Just like the classic playing card, the king's white, curling hair and beard hung down each side of his face. He was positioned just as awkwardly, holding a knife that was stuck into the back of his crown, seemingly penetrating his skull.

A long, black table stood in front of them with ten solo cups flipped over. Red looked at the setup with a furrowed brow, unsure exactly what he was about to get himself into.

"Congratulations and welcome to the second bet of your mystery parlay," Gianni said, reappearing on the screen with his dashing smile. The volume was much higher than the monitor in the other room. It needed to be cranked for Red to hear his voice over the hum of the power drill.

"A gambling addict such as yourself," Gianni continued, "will most likely be familiar with the two figures at the front of the room. The one to your right, commonly referred to as the suicide king, is a misconstrued character. While many believe he's killing himself, the blade that looks to be buried in his brain is actually the result of bad copying techniques by English card makers. The king once held an ax, but as time went on, it disappeared into his head. No one wants to commit suicide, and you shouldn't either."

Red peeked around the side of the suicide king statue and noticed that there wasn't a knife in his head as it first appeared. After adjusting his vantage point, he saw the axe hidden behind it.

"The figure to your left is the joker. While many perceive the joker as no more than a fool, jokers are the most powerful cards in the entire deck. They're chameleon cards. They can be anything. They can't be beaten. You'll have the impossible task of defeating not just one, but *both* jokers in the final parts of your parlay."

The wicked grin of the joker almost looked ghoulish. The creative liberties used to produce that specific portrayal of the joker were nefarious in nature. Red examined it a few more moments before returning his gaze to the monitor.

"But let's not get ahead of ourselves. This is a simple bet. There are ten crushable cups lined up in front of you. Underneath nine of them are precision-point drill bits. Under one of the cups is nothing. You have three chances. If you find the cup with nothing, you advance forward. But to reveal the contents, you must smash the cup as hard as you can. You will use your hands on the first two attempts, and your head on the last. While the drills are no different from the one you see the trickster holding, they differ from a typical bit. The tips are extra refined to ensure they can easily bore through flesh. Should you locate the empty cup, the locked door will open, and you will be one final task from achieving your dreams. You'll begin at the conclusion of this video, and remember, don't keep us waiting."

Red blinked at the spinning bit under the joker's warped smile. While he didn't like the odds, there wasn't much he could do about it.

He was tired of crying.

He was tired of living.

Headbutting a drill might not be the worst thing—at least it would be over.

The drugs were hitting Red even harder, instilling a false sense of confidence and dulling his pain. He didn't even think about which cup he wanted to go for, he just drove his palm through the first one he looked at.

As the sound of plastic crunching blared out, blood sprayed up and drenched Red's face. The drill bit ate its way through his hand and kept spinning inside him eagerly, like a virgin fucking something warm for the first time.

Red screamed as he lifted the cavernous wound in his right hand off the spiraling steel. He looked at the hole with anger before the dread set in. Bloody shreds dangled out of the void of violence like a messy turd breaking away from an asshole.

With his adrenaline still pumping, Red shuffled two steps down the table and took aim at the third cup with his other hand. While he wasn't shocked, Red was disappointed when he felt another drill digging through his left palm. The point of the bit bullied its way through his extremity, leaving another shockwave of anguish flaring in both of his fists. Even with the assistance of the powder, his suffering had been too much.

Red fell to the ground as sweat poured out from the crown of his head. His throbbing hands oozed blood. His thoughts were heavy with the weight of his future. The gaping wounds continued to stack up. He wasn't sure if he could go on.

Suddenly, Red felt a soft material on the back of his neck and a tugging on his jacket. As his eyes peeped open, the suicide king's creepy mask looked into them.

Guess it wasn't a fuckin' statue.

"Pick a number between one and ten, you piece of shit," a raspy voice commanded.

Flashes of the day's events flooded Red's mind, bringing him all the way back to when he'd arrived at the parking garage. Space 7 was the only thing he could think of.

Lucky number seven, the shadowy man's voice echoed in his head. Red still couldn't quite focus enough to provide a response.

"Pick it or I'll pick it for you, stain-face!" the suicide king shouted.

"Seven… Lucky number seven," Red whispered.

The suicide king dragged him in front of the seventh cup and lifted him.

When Red felt his face smash into the table, the knot on his forehead instantly swelled. But as he slid off the surface, he realized that his head was drill-free. And just as his trembling body thudded against the ground, he heard the door to the final room unlocking.

MYSTERY PARLAY: BET 3

Red's body went tumbling through the door. The suicide king stood near the wall and watched Red squirm on the ground. His suffering was hellish as he stuck each of his hole-punched hands under his armpits, attempting to put pressure on them.

This just keeps getting' better, Red thought.

A familiar voice once again found him, and despite his general disorientation, Red's ears perked up.

"Degno di nota," Gianni said, slowly clapping his hands together.

Red shuffled onto his knees keeping his hands under his arms as he looked up at the screen with watery eyes.

"Impressive. Not many people have the will or sheer luck to make it this far. You're almost there." Gianni lit a cigar and took a few puffs. "It was during the first two parts of the parlay where the odds really aren't in your favor, but once you make it here… all that changes. This final bet is fifty-fifty, well, at least it starts out that way. You may have a chance to sway the odds in your favor."

The suicide king pulled a rope hanging near the corner of the room that triggered the black curtains in front of Red to part. Red's eyes popped with wonder and shock; he wasn't expecting such a grandiose visual.

"While dog tracks may be a dwindling form of gambling across the country, here at Shadows, the tradition remains alive and well. There are no protesters to fret over our rules. There are no lawsuits in the underground. I would even go as far as to say we've *enhanced* the races."

Red looked out at the track. The stadium seating ahead gave him an incredible vantage point to watch the would-be action. Just a short distance from the chairs were four separate lanes running parallel to each other. Red couldn't see exactly where the lanes began, but he noticed they curled out from his right before transitioning into an oval pattern and merging into a traditional, single-lane track.

"As you can see, the track is ready for use, so let's get to the last part of your bet."

The suicide king pulled a second rope that parted the curtains on the right side of the room. As the cloth drew farther apart, the suicide king returned to the second parlay room and locked the door behind him.

Red was alone again.

As the curtain revealed what would be involved in the final gamble, Red was consumed by dread and disgust. Four kennel cages were propped up against the wall, each of the cages containing a child that looked to be in the seven to twelve-year-old range. Their ages were made obvious to Red when he saw their underdeveloped bodies.

It looked like two girls and two boys. All the children were in their underwear or pajamas. Cartoon images of Scooby Doo were depicted on one boy's boxer briefs, while the Rugrats covered a young girl's shirt. The other two children had plain but juvenile clothing.

Each of the children trembled violently and had brown burlap sacks covering their entire heads.

What—what the fuck is this? Red was growing more concerned with each reveal.

The curtain continued moving past the cages to the end of the wall. When it finally stopped, one more puzzling figure was revealed.

As Gianni had promised in the prior room, the second joker statue stood. He held a large, silver platter in his arms. On the platter sat a single shotgun with four shells standing upright in front of it.

What the fuck?

Beside the joker, at Red's waist level, a stand had been erected. It had two big, round buttons on the top of it—one red and one black.

"It's a simple choice really: red or black," Gianni continued. "While you may just see four children on the cusp of teenage delinquency locked in the cages before you, I see something different. I see two jacks and two queens. I see the key to your dreams. These pups will all be competing against each other. The first to make it to the end of the track wins. You just have to pick the winner. So, what's the catch, you ask? I'll reveal that momentarily. Place your bet first by selecting the button of your choice. Once you've made your wager, my final instructional video will play, and then it won't be long before we find out if you're walking out of Shadows a millionaire."

The hyperventilation and cries of the children made Red's skin crawl. Their wails of horror sounded muffled like they might've been pleading through mouth gags. He couldn't help but think about one of the reasons he was there—Dessi. She couldn't have been much older than the caged children.

He looked down at the two buttons.

"How the fuck am I supposed to bet when I don't even know what I'm betting on?" Red yelled.

There was no response. The pre-recorded tutorial video remained paused.

He looked at the red button.

It called to him.

Red had seen every horror and pushed himself to the limit to get where he stood. He'd made it that far, so it only made sense to bet on himself.

I just gotta believe.

The gory hole in Red's hand smacked the red button, and as promised, Gianni appeared on the screen again.

"Wonderful. Now that the bet is in, I'm sure you're wondering what's next. This parlay is designed not only to test your physical durability, but your mental toughness as well."

Red squirmed in place, watching the cold-hearted bastard take several more puffs of his cigar.

"The joker holds a shotgun and four shells," Gianni continued. "While they may all look the same, rest assured, each shotgun shell has the capacity to do a varying degree of damage. One is birdshot, one is buckshot, one is a slug, and one is a blank. You'll fire the four shells from the exact same distance and—aside from the blank—each shot *must* hit. In essence, you're creating a random handicap. Once all the shells have been fired, the children will remove the bags from their heads, revealing their true colors. If you've bet red, then you'll be hoping that the tiny bodies of the red jack and queen are still operational. If you've bet black, then you're hoping the red jack and queen are as bloody as their designated color. Either way, you'll still have a chance in the race, but some chances are better than others. Should you choose not to fire the shots, then I assure you, what lies ahead for you isn't pleasant. You'd better put that fucking gun in your mouth and hope it kills you, because we'll keep you alive for *weeks*. Maybe months. We'll tear you apart then have the doctors put you back together, just so we can do it all over again."

Gianni took another long draw of his cigar. "Before I go, one final piece of advice. To make the right choice, you need to make the smart choice." Gianni winked. "Best of luck to you, my friend."

Red's blood-drenched hand slipped back into his pocket. He scrambled to sniff the clumpy powder he retrieved off his finger. *OD'ing wouldn't be the worst thing in the world.*

Red approached the deranged joker and carefully lifted the shotgun with his tender hands. He pushed each of the four shells into the magazine tube and pumped. Wincing in pain, he tried to ignore the drill holes in each of his hands.

When he returned to the front of the cages, the moaning children pulled at his heartstrings. Just the idea of pointing the gun at them caused tears to roll off his cheeks.

"I-I can't do it," Red muttered, closing his eyes.

Flash: the black, metal baseball bat smashed into Mrs. Blanchfield's toothless face, spraying blood all over the wall. Her head was covered in lumps, knots, and deep gashes. While laid out on her back, Buggs spread her wrinkly legs wide, revealing an old, hairy clam. He rubs the bat against her mangled face, lubing it up. As the slippery metal pressed against his mother's meat curtain, the vision ceased.

"No!!" Red screamed, shaking his head. "It's not real."

As Red's entire body trembled, he was unable to settle down. Even though he told himself that the violent images in his head weren't real, if he fucked up the last bet, they soon would be. The horrible things that Buggs said he was going to do, and so much more, were all looming on the final gamble.

I can't hurt a kid, they're... they're just fuckin' kids!

Red closed his eyes again and tried to reset his brain, but the drugs and blood loss were getting to him. He felt like he had a permanent hangover.

Flash: Brittany stood eating moldy fast food out of a garbage can. Dessi stood beside her, watching her pick the maggots off a piece of cheeseburger and begging her for the scraps. "Please, Mom," she cried.

Brittany slowly reached around the back of the can and whipped around. When she faced Dessi, Brittany was holding a shotgun—the same shotgun in Red's hands. She pointed the barrel at their daughter's face and pulled the trigger. Dessi's face turned into ground beef, blowing her cheeks and nose all over the brick wall behind them. His daughter's limp body dropped, the garble of ruined flesh smacking against the concrete and leaking all over the filthy alley. Brittany smiled, pumping the handle and reloading. Just when she put the gun in her mouth, the murder-suicide scene cut out.

Fuck, fuck, fuck, fuck! What am I gonna do?

Red felt a tightness in his chest.

A speaker in the corner of the room crackled. "I asked you before how far you were willing to go." Despite the digitization, the voice projecting was unmistakable. It was the voice of the woman who struck terror into every man inside Shadows—The Black Widow.

Red looked around with confusion, half expecting her to appear. The pressure continued to mount on him. Red felt as though he was reaching some kind of breaking point. "What the hell is wrong with you? They're…" Tears ran from his eyelids. "They're just kids…"

"Why should *they* be protected?" she asked.

The vitriol in her tone shook Red to the core.

"What makes them so fucking special? You know, there's a sad truth to life that only some of us figure out: it's all luck. Like me, I guess these little ones just happened to be unlucky."

"No!" Red cried.

"Yes! You should just be thankful that, because of their sacrifice, you can win. Dessi can win! You said you would do what needed to be done. So, go on then. You're so close. You're close to being who I hoped you'd be. You're almost my hero."

The drugs and torture had nudged his brain to the verge of psychosis. The Black Widow's words weren't what he wanted to hear; they were what he *needed* to hear.

Blam! Blam! Blam! Blam!

When Red unloaded the rounds from the shotgun, it took every ounce of evil in his body—evil he wasn't even aware he harbored—to pull the trigger. With each shot, he winced—not just for the children, but for the pain he had to endure while using his torn-up hands.

He wanted to get it over with as quickly as possible. There was no pleasure taken in firing the shots—his soul ached with each jarring release. But before he'd pulled the trigger, Red had made a calculated decision. One that was probably more selfish than most contestants in his position. Because, like Gianni said, for Red to make the right choice, he had to make the smart one.

At no point during the tutorial video did Gianni say that each child had to be shot. Blank aside, he stated that each shot had to land and be fired. In Red's eyes, putting all four shots into the same child gave him the best odds.

Wounding or killing three out of the four children could potentially leave him with two injured pups. But if he put every shot into the same kid, that would ensure he at least had one fully operational pup. He chose one of the girls because he wanted to keep his boy in the running. Judging by the size of the children, at that age, the boys were almost always going to be more athletic.

The first shot was the birdshot. It mostly landed on her legs, peppering her tender flesh with metal dots. The steel cage protected her some, but a sizable cluster of tiny holes oozed blood instantly. Imagery from Red's prior hallucination flashed in his head. The sickening sight of Dessi's noseless face made him scream but didn't stop the gunfire.

The second shot was buckshot. The spray hit the girl a bit higher, tearing open the meat on her shoulder. The pink, parted tissue broke away, exposing part of her collarbone. The strawberry spot of skeleton looked like a broken twig sticking out of crimson muck.

The third shot was the blank. It did no damage but did create a small amount of time between the shots. And just as Red was getting ready to fire the final round, the young girl slid forward in shock, aligning the brown sack covering her head directly with his hot barrel.

The fourth shot was the slug. The girthy hunk of metal blew through the sack. The slug exploded through the cloth sending the right side of her skull and brains vomiting out the back of her head all over the wall.

As the smoke rose from the barrel of the shotgun, Red stared at the massive hole and gore-caked mask. The waterfall of blood running down the child's entire body sickened him. It was horrific, but ironically it was also a better exit than most of the souls inside Shadows got.

Red felt a weight lift off him.

He knew he should've felt sick, but he didn't. He felt like he was finally taking what was his. He wasn't about to let his daughter rot away and die on the street, even if it meant he had to kill someone else's.

A loud bell rang. The piercing sound caused the remaining children to rip the sacks off their heads. Just like dogs, they'd been trained.

Red watched as each child revealed their colors, starting with the boys.

The first boy wore a black jack mask.

The second boy wore a red jack mask.

The first girl wore a black queen mask.

The second girl fittingly continued to ooze blood—a red, dead queen.

Red was horrified by the sight. He couldn't believe that he'd unleashed such violence on someone, never mind a child. A tear beaded over his eyelid. *Christ… what the fuck have I done…*

Once their masks came off, the steel doors on the wall that their cages were attached to slid open. "And they're off!" The Black Widow yelled over the intercom.

Rushing toward the stadium seating, he eagerly watched as the human dogs kept on all fours, churning through the track as fast as they could. It seemed less like it was about winning and more like it was about survival. Losing pups didn't seem like they would have a vivacious lifecycle in a place like Shadows.

Before long the children blended into the single lane. As each child reached that intersection, they switched to standing on two feet. They were all relatively in the same area of the track. Red watched the two boys in the creepy jack masks joust for position. His bet, the red jack, was in a hand fight with the black jack as they rounded the first corner. Red was just relieved to see he was still in contention to win.

C'mon, red, c'mon!

As they rounded the next corner, the black queen trailed. But she wasn't too far behind the battling boys.

Red put his blood-drenched hands together.

"Please, God, please, God," he whispered under his breath.

It was as if Red had forgotten he'd just left one of The Heavenly Father's creations filled with more holes than a graveyard. He watched the children intently, grinding his teeth as the two boys hit the last corner, still fighting. When the red jack pushed into the lead by just a stride, Red jumped up and down, pumping his crimson fist.

"Yes! Go! You're almost there!"

But as they closed in on the finish line, suddenly, the black jack lost his footing. As he went tumbling head-first, his arms got tangled in the red jack's legs. With just a few yards remaining in the race, both of the jacks hit the dirt, and the black queen blew past them to the finish line.

"Noooo! You fucked it up!" Red screamed, shaking his fist at the children from the balcony seating.

As the saliva flung from Red's lips, he suddenly realized he'd lost it all. But the darker epiphany came as he extended his middle finger in the direction of the three child slaves. Not only had he lost his chance at rescuing his mother and locating Dessi, but he'd also lost his humanity too. The frown of rage melted into sadness as he slowly brought his finger down.

He was the monster now.

The sound of a locking mechanism triggering behind him echoed in his eardrums.

"Hey, fella," said a gruff male voice. "You had a helluva run, but it's time to go."

When Red turned around, he saw the same toned and athletic black male from the roulette table. The fella that had smashed the one-eyed man's face in and helped drag him away. The memory of the beating and the fully erect collapsible baton currently in the security guard's hand kept Red from running. Escape wasn't an option. It was time to take his cough syrup.

Red's body was beat to shit. He could feel himself slipping. There was a part of him that knew he deserved whatever he got. His heart was in the right place, but he'd made his share of mistakes.

Red nodded in defeat. "Alright."

THE RED ROOM

The crimson door ahead looked like it had been painted with blood—an appropriate omen for a man in Red's shoes. Its dark, rich texture was highly unsettling, but Red figured the real horror lay beyond it.

Another security guard stood outside the door with a disgruntled look on his face. It was the other grizzled man from back at the roulette table. He opened the door for them, and Red reluctantly stepped through. The dim glow in the room outlined the silhouette of The Black Widow. He thought he might have seen the older man from the instructional videos too, but suddenly realized that wasn't possible.

There was a reason Gianni Lito's face looked familiar. Lilly's story about what The Black Widow had done to the former owner of Shadows came to mind. Red's eyes found a jar placed on the desk next to where she leaned. His gaze drifted to her elegant black dress then back to the container. The former owner's pruned and pickled privates hovered in semi-cloudy water.

She kept his cock and balls like a trinket on her desk, Lilly's voice echoed in his head. The taut skin stretched inside the case when he'd first entered the casino flashed in his mind. *His skin's pinned up in a glass box at the entrance.*

The terrible things Lilly had told him about The Black Widow's capabilities didn't leave him with much hope. After their ominous exchange at the roulette wheel, a seed of dread was planted inside him. Red figured it was only a matter of time until they met again.

To the left of the black desk were countless monitors mounted to the wall. It appeared that every inch of the casino was being recorded.

Red's eyes widened.

Fuck, he thought.

He saw a camera angle that covered the very seats inside The Doll House that he and Lilly had occupied earlier. Currently, the toothless woman with the blackened eyes and swollen face was in Lilly's seat, talking to a john who now sat in his old chair. The legless Asian girl in the wheelchair rolled by. The audio was low, but state-of-the-art. Not only could Red hear the conversation, but he heard the faint squeak of the wheels off in the distance.

That's how she knew.

Red looked away from the monitors to the other side of the desk. A unique table stood by itself. It reminded him of a crucifix—it was like the ones he'd seen on TV that they strapped people down to before giving them a lethal injection. He felt like he was on death row. He might've been right.

The variety of hateful devices that hung on the walls surrounding the table were even more concerning. Knives, swords, chainsaws, guns, spears, clubs, bats—anything that one might imagine assaulting a person with was there.

"So, there you are," The Black Widow said. "I had a feeling our paths would cross again." As she stepped out into the light, she toyed around with the oversized necklace dangling above her breasts. Its size and shape made the piece look more like a pocket watch.

"Lay down on the table," the security guard ordered.

Red looked into The Black Widow's cold eyes. There was something inside them that made him think she didn't want him to follow those instructions.

He looked back at the security guard. "I think I'd rather stand."

"Get your ass down, or I'll break your fuckin' legs—"

"Manx, it's okay," The Black Widow said. "Please, wait outside with Marty."

"Are you sure?" he asked.

"Yes. No need to worry. I can take care of this myself."

The security guard got close to the side of Red's face, almost touching his port wine stain.

"I'll be just outside, ma'am, in case you need anything," he snarled.

Silence filled the room after the door closed. As The Black Widow stared into Red's eyes, he wasn't sure what she wanted him to do. He was nervous to be in her presence but also strangely calm.

"So, I guess that's how you figured me out?" Red asked, pointing at the monitors. "But I don't get it. Why me?"

The Black Widow smiled. "In Shadows, there are always eyes watching and ears listening, even if you don't always see them. You have an interesting face. I suppose that's why you caught my eye initially."

Red reached up with his gory hand and itched at the port wine stain on his neck. He certainly was the type to stand out in a crowd. The powder still had him tweaking hard. But on the plus side, it kept the pain at bay just far enough to keep him conscious.

"Part of me took notice of your nobility," she continued. "Risking life and limb to locate your daughter and save your mother, that kind of thing… it speaks to me. But when I saw you nodding off in that theater, I couldn't help but wonder if you were the one that brought the trouble to them."

"I made my mistakes but—"

"Here me out. You'll get your chance to speak."

Red nodded.

"Despite all the violence and depravity inside these walls, do you know what I enjoy most about this place?"

"What's that?"

"The stories. There are hundreds of them scurrying around—more stories than a centipede has legs. Most of them are the same though, predictable reruns. I'd say close to ninety percent are just cases of simple selfishness, nothing more. So that gets quite boring, and after a while, I tend to lose interest. But every once in a while, I run into something that grabs me. A story that I maybe relate to a little more closely than I'd like to admit. I've had a pair like that today—both sides of the chip so to speak."

The Black Widow opened her necklace. A weathered chip with an 'S' on each side fell into her hand. One side was black, the other side was red.

"I've dealt with the first side already, and I've been waiting for you ever since. All I have is time in this place, but now and then it drags. But your story got me thinking…" The Black Widow was struck by emotion.

Red noticed the glossy coat welling over her wicked eyes. She was like a demon with feelings.

"I'd have given anything to have a father like you. I know you're not perfect, but just having a chance at life would've…" She turned to a circular mirror hanging on the wall beside her. "That would've meant the fucking world." Her lips quivered. "Who knows what I could've become. I certainly wouldn't have stayed here."

Red saw a deeply buried sadness unearthed. While The Black Widow may have had all the stroke in her demonic playland, Red could see none of that mattered to her. There was something she was missing—something that it seemed she would never find.

"What happened to you?" Red asked.

The care and concern in Red's voice were genuine, but at the same time, he was carefully strategizing. Since The Black Widow somehow related to his story, Red aimed to enrich their bond as much as possible. It was the only move that made sense—the only move he had. The closer she felt to him, the better the chance of him not taking a dirt nap on the murder table.

The Black Widow suddenly restrained her emotions. As her lips grew firm, she straightened up, and the gloss in her eyes dried.

Be cool. Just play it fuckin' cool. He desperately hoped he hadn't shown too much of his hand to her. This certainly wasn't her first rodeo.

"This isn't about me. It's about you. And there's only one question left for you to answer."

Red gulped, his plan had quickly blown up, and he wondered if the barbaric décor on the walls might soon be finding his flesh.

"Are you that piece of shit I saw passed out in the theater and the annex?" The Black Widow asked. "Or, are you the man looking to track down the daughter he lost and make her life worth living?"

"I'm the—"

"That was a rhetorical question. You answer when you bet. The chip never lies." She rubbed the haggard hunk of clay between her finger and thumb. "It's inevitable. Your truth shall be revealed, and your fate will be decided. Just like mine was."

The Black Widow slid the chip down to her thumb and let it rest.

"I don't do this for people, so consider yourself a lucky man. It's fifty-fifty. If you call the color, I'll get you enough financial support to ensure you can pay off your debts, the PI looking for Dessi, and still have enough left over to start a decent life. A life that you had damn well better not fuck up again."

Clenching his fists in angst made the holes in Red's hands ache. He swallowed hard and nodded at her.

"But if you don't call it," she continued, "well, let's just say you won't be leaving Shadows—ever. And whatever becomes of your mother and Dessi will remain an agonizing mystery. Got it?"

Red nodded again, but before he could even finish the first bob, the chip was already flipping through the air.

The Black Widow's eyes widened as she tried to track the chip in the air.

Red knew he was stuck in The Black Widow's web, but wondered if he was a fly or a caterpillar. Deep down, he wanted to believe the latter. He prayed that he'd blossom and that the butterfly inside him would break free, flying off to a better existence.

If The Black Widow didn't believe it was possible, she wouldn't have even given him the opportunity. But at that moment what she believed was irrelevant. Just like everyone else in that fucking casino, she was a slave to the stakes.

"Call it!" she commanded.

Red's eyes swelled and he opened his mouth. As he watched the black and red sides alternate and plummet closer to The Black Widow's hand, he knew it was time to make a choice.

THE GAMBLE

Hello dear reader, at this moment we ask that you locate a coin before continuing. If you are reading from the limited-edition hardcover of *Through the Eyes of Desperation,* then you should use the special Shadows casino chip included with your bundle. But if you are reading this in eBook, paper-back, or listening to audio, any coin will do.

There are two different potential conclusions to this story, and both are now in *your* hands. Designate each of the heads and tails sides of your coin as either red or black (those using a chip, your sides are already designated). Once you flip the coin/chip and determine what color it has landed on, use the below guide to read the ending that destiny has chosen for you.

THE BLACK ENDING: if your coin landed on black, flip to page 243 and read the black ending.

THE RED ENDING: if your coin landed on red, flip to page 269 and read the red ending.

B

THE BLACK ENDING

BLACK

As the coin flipped through the air, to Red, it seemed like everything was in slow motion. The flashes of each color flickered in his eyes. There was no right answer to give, just a guess that he was having trouble deciding on.

"I said, call it!" The Black Widow yelled.

"Red!" he finally blurted out. That was his color, surely it wouldn't fail him again.

The Black Widow snatched the coin out of the air and slapped it down on the top of her hand.

"Black always wins," The Black Widow said. A somber look came over her. "You should've known better."

"God damn it! Please… You-you've gotta give me another chance!" Red screamed.

"I wish I could. But it wouldn't be a bet if I just let you win. I'm afraid that was your last chance, dear," she said looking to the door. "Manx! Marty!"

Instantly the men burst into the room, Manx still with the baton ready in hand.

"I'm afraid you've lost, Red. Not only have you lost, but it seems you've made the same mistake twice on a fifty-fifty bet. It's probably for the best. If you screwed up twice here, odds are, you'd have done the same with Dessi."

"Don't you fuckin' talk about her!" Red yelled.

As he took a step toward The Black Widow, Manx came down with the steel baton against the side of his thigh.

"Ahh!" Red collapsed to the ground. "My fuckin' leg!" The drugs were wearing off. The burning pain from the gunshot wound in his foot, his missing pinky, and the holes in his hands and cock all started to rise.

Marty grabbed Red's arms and bent them behind his back. Red cried out from a kneeling position.

Lifting the baton, Manx glared at the top of Red's skull, like he was ready to crack it.

"Wait!" The Black Widow yelled.

Manx paused his rage, while Red remained on the ground clutching at his knee.

"It would be easy to give you the same fate as everyone else who lost the last stage of the Mystery Parlay, but when I ask myself what purpose that would serve, I can't seem to justify it."

A twinkle of hope was drowning in Red's watery eyes.

"I have another idea," The Black Widow said with her grin stretching ear to ear.

TIME'S UP

"Go fish," Dane said, glaring at Mrs. Blanchfield.

The old lady's frail hand trembled as it moved toward the pile of cards in the center of the table. It took her a painful amount of time to draw and play.

"For Christ's sake, grandma, would ya hurry up already!" Dane snapped.

He was tired of playing cards, sleeping on the old lady's scratchy couch, and eating frozen meatballs. But more than anything, he was tired of pretending that her fuck-up son was somehow going to arrive with enough money to make things square.

"I-I'm sorry, dear. I'm going as fast as I can," Mrs. Blanchfield replied.

"I think this has gone on long enough," Dane said, throwing his cards on the table and standing.

Buggs looked up from his hand. He was far calmer than his counterpart. The pair of flies hovering around his head finally decided to settle. One chose his shoulder and the other landed on the cards he held.

"A deal's a deal," Buggs said. "We said exactly four days which means the lump 'a shit's got another two hours and thirty-seven minutes until the time's up."

Dane rolled his eyes and exhaled, glaring angrily at Mrs. Blanchfield's confused mug. That was the only look she'd worn since her son had left her in the care of the two disgruntled and smelly men.

"C'mon, he ain't comin' back," Dane whined.

"We been here almost four days now, another couple hours ain't gonna kill ya," Buggs said as he turned his attention to the old lady. "But it'll kill *her* though!"

The pair of goons both let out thunderous cackles. They needed a good laugh after such a run of shit days.

While the thugs enjoyed their joke, Mrs. Blanchfield's hands shook. It was as if what she'd feared worst since her son left had finally been confirmed.

EXACTLY 2 HOURS AND 37 MINUTES LATER...

"Okay, you ready?" Dane asked.

"There wasn't a pitch thrown that I wasn't ready for," Buggs replied.

Dane tossed the softball up in the air and it sailed toward Buggs. Right as it entered his radius, Buggs blasted it with the bat. The big ball rocketed forward, flying past the chair Mrs. Blanchfield was tied to. It went into a cabinet behind the kitchen table and shattered a glass picture frame. When the keepsake toppled over, it revealed a picture of Red. In the snapshot, one of Red's eyes was black as the night, but he was still smiling. The picture was just like Red—always in some kind of trouble.

"Ain't that ironic," Buggs muttered.

Mrs. Blanchfield moaned with the gag in her mouth, begging them to spare her.

"Send me another," Buggs said. There wasn't an ounce of pity or forgiveness his heart.

He crushed the second one even harder. He was pissed about the first one not landing, so when it smacked into the old bat's kneecap, fragmenting it into multiple pieces and knocking half of it onto the side of her leg, Buggs couldn't suppress his glee.

"That a boy," Dane said, proud to see the hit connect. He'd been waiting for what felt like an eternity.

"You know, I ain't gonna lie, I'm kinda glad he didn't show," Buggs said. "We can always find more money, but a memory like this that the two of us get to share, I mean, that's priceless, ain't it?"

Dane grinned and nodded.

"Say, you got any regulation balls?" Buggs asked.

"A course, I knew we'd most likely get a shot at this, so I brought a little of everything."

"Do me a favor then, take the gag outta this old whore's mouth and put a ball in it for me."

Dane nodded. He enjoyed trying to figure out where Buggs was going with the request. When he removed the spit-soaked gag, Mrs. Blanchfield screamed bloody murder. Dane quickly shoved the baseball between her jaws and whispered, "If this ball falls outta your fuckin' mouth, you're gonna have bigger problems than that little knee-job, sweetheart."

As Dane stepped back, Buggs stepped up. When he took aim with the baseball bat, he hit his target dead on. The metal smacked Mrs. Blanchfield right in the mouth, knocking her dentures loose and pushing the baseball deep into her air passage.

Blood splashed Buggs' face and speckled Dane's coat. The extreme force behind the hit caused the old lady's chair to tip backward. She crashed against the floor, smacking the backside of her head.

"Oh, no, she's choking," Dane said sarcastically.

As Mrs. Blanchfield's eyes widened, she used her gawk of terror as a plea to her attackers. She had a look like she'd do anything to survive.

"No problem, I got this," Buggs replied windmilling the bat to exercise his wrist.

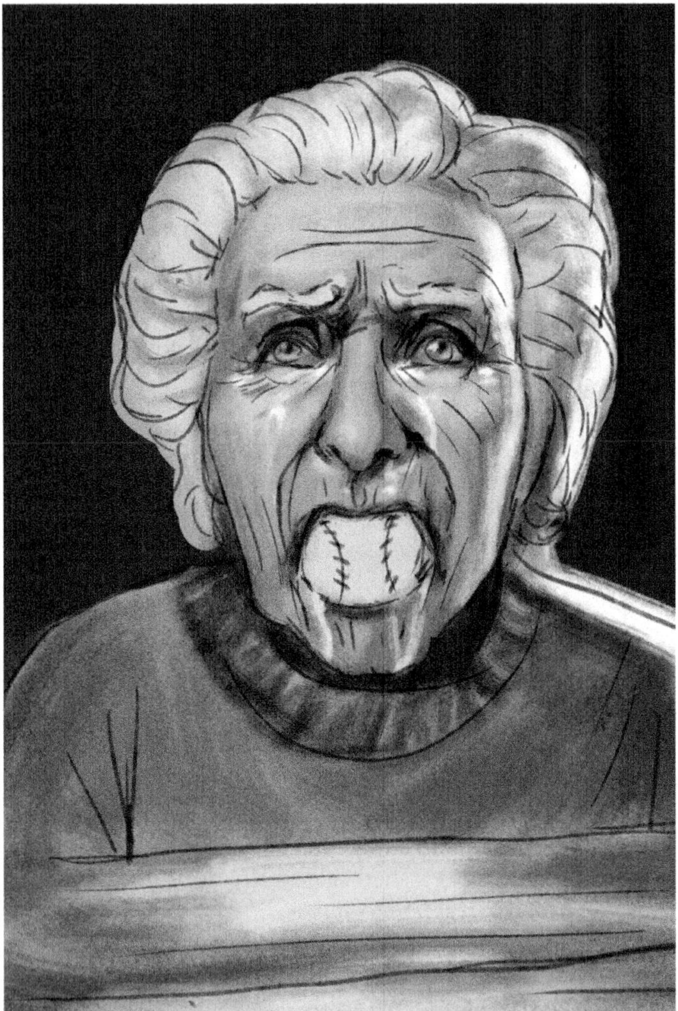

The big, stinky man stepped forward, still holding the slugger. From her side, he did a little bunny hop and dropped both of his heels on her chest. A sickening crack of several ribs breaking erupted, while the air in her lungs forced the baseball to shoot up.

The disturbing, bubbly moan that whistled out of Mrs. Blanchfield was accompanied by a gurgle of blood, courtesy of the fragmented rib shards puncturing her organs.

Dane squatted down and retrieved the switchblade from inside his jacket. As he cut the restraints off her, he whispered, "Now just remember this, old girl. Remember that everything we do to you is because of that lump 'a shit that fell outta your pussy all them years ago." Dane snapped his head back at Buggs. "And speakin' of pussy, wasn't that part of the deal you made with Red?"

"Afraid so," Buggs replied. "Why don't you cut that ratty dress off her? It's got blood all over it now anyhow."

Dane slid the knife from the bottom of her dress all the way up the side and tore big patches of the clothing away.

Buggs squatted beside Mrs. Blanchfield. "You know, when I was a kid, I never wanted to be a fuckin' degenerate. Guess what I wanted to do?"

Gurgles of blood and violent coughs were all Mrs. Blanchfield could offer.

"Don't got a guess? It shouldn't be hard. I wanted to play ball. Be out there on the field with all those people watching me on the TV. There was just something about holdin' a bat in my hands that felt so fuckin' right."

Buggs squeezed the fuck out of the handle and his knuckles popped.

"But," he continued, "sadly, I couldn't hit the broad side of a barn with a pitch. And my hand-eye coordination just wasn't what it quite needed to be. Kinda sad really when you stop and think about it. But I didn't let not being good beat me up too much. That loser fuckin' kid of yours though, he just couldn't figure out what he was good at. Might not've been good at nothin' really."

Buggs stuck the handle of the bat into the mix of blood and drool that leaked out of the massive gashes in and around her mouth. He coated the small end of the bat until it glistened with the cherry-red juices.

"Me, on the other hand," Buggs said. "I found what I was good at. Might not've been the prettiest gig in the world, but it gave me a purpose. And even though I never saw the field, I still get to play ball once in a while."

"You play like the best of 'em," Dane said.

As Dane ripped away the last piece of Mrs. Blanchfield's dress, both of the goons looked at the droopy, wrinkled skin that covered her frail body. The massive patch of gray, overgrown pubic hair between her legs stared back at them.

"Jesus, look at that bush," Buggs said. "I need my fuckin' lawn guy to see what's goin' on in there."

Dane chuckled as he watched Buggs bury the bloody bat handle between her legs. His eyes popped with enjoyment as Mrs. Blanchfield let out a guttural gasp.

"Oh, if this ain't some sour seafood. This clam ain't been opened in ages," Buggs said, as he gently nestled the bat in her cunt. The gooey juices of yesteryear dribbled out of her slit along with the blood and saliva used as lubricant. "But we can fix that, don't you worry."

The guttural moans that Mrs. Blanchfield expelled would've rattled any decent person. But Buggs and Dane kept on, excited to continue.

Buggs jerked the bat upward forcefully, trying to stretch her rubbery snatch to its limits. The smell of rotten cod and body odor only intensified as Buggs proceeded to ram the handle in and out of her.

Dane watched on with a smile, enjoying her funky scent and watching the mixture of colors creeping out of her glistening gash.

"Nasty, cunt." Buggs mumbled. "Fuckin' thing's tighter than I thought though. If we're gonna fit the big side in, like we promised ol' Red, we might have to open her up a little bit, if you know what I mean."

"Not a problem at all," Dane replied, crouching down while raising his switchblade.

He laid the blade deep into her labia without batting an eye. The knife sliced into the rancid pink and the blood oozed. As the slimy flesh continued to separate, the bat was soon given more range inside her hole.

"Things are gettin' a little fuckin' loose inside there now," Buggs said. "Might be time to turn this thing around. What do you say?"

As the drool dollop fell from Dane's lip, he continued yanking the blade up into her pussy meat. As he retracted the length of blood-smeared metal from the runny wound, Dane nodded. "Sounds like a plan to me."

Buggs removed the handle from Mrs. Blanchfield's cunt but before he was going to push the big end inside her, he took aim at her extremities. He raised the bat above his head and gritted his teeth.

Crack!

The first swing cracked her right forearm at the mid-point. Her old, brittle bone was sharp, the compound fracture looked as if it could rip through her leathery skin at any moment. The pool of blood inside her toothless mouth splattered up over her face, running into her eyes and hair.

Pop!

The next shot landed on the opposite side of her body—just above her bicep. The spin and torque Buggs laid into her with knocked Mrs. Blanchfield's shoulder clean out of the socket. The horrific bump raised her shoulder as high as a linebacker's pads and it ironically looked softball-sized.

Crack!

Thump!

Crack!

Thump!

Thump!

The next several shots came in a flurry. Most of the hits were bat on bone, leaving her legs looking like she'd just jumped out of a three-story building.

Through all the strikes, Mrs. Blanchfield stayed quiet. The occasional blow triggered a wheezing exhale to escape her mangled frame. She looked lifeless.

The bloody knots and swelling all over her body rose instantly. The breaks put the trajectory of her legs at angles that made a future walk in the park impossible.

"You think that cunt's ready for me now?" Buggs asked.

"You betcha," Dane said, kicking up her destroyed legs and watching them flop backward like noodles. "Look at that fuckin' thing." Dane growled suddenly excited by the mutilated muff. "Lemme make sure it's good to go."

Buggs had always figured himself the sicker of the two, but as he watched Dane's eager snout slip inside the hag's gushing cunt, he knew there was a new champion.

"That's a new one," Buggs mumbled.

Dane couldn't resist nibbling on the bleeding meat. It looked like a fresh roast beef sandwich—extra rare. The strange feminine cream creeping out of the haggard slit could've been the horseradish dressing on top. Dane attacked it like a rabid dog, biting down hard as the old woman continued to choke on her blood. Smears of gore, and slimy solutions cascaded over his face as he rammed his thumb into her puckered asshole. The taste of unhygienic hag-hole was like eating a fish sandwich out of a used diaper. But that didn't stop him from shaking his head madly, like a man who only grew further infatuated the filthier it got. He could taste her bowels beginning to falter. The prunes that she'd devoured just hours ago had left her ready to blow. Just as her odorous ring relaxed and prepared to open, a juicy sliver of diarrhea slipped.

"Hey, ya mind?" Buggs asked. "Can I put the big end of the fuckin' bat in the old bag before she croaks?"

Dane pulled away from the pair of rancid holes, a mixture of mustardy brown liquefied shit and blood painted his face. "Of course," he replied, licking his lips.

While the whole ass-eating spectacle was unexpected, Buggs was too excited about keeping his promise to Red to play psychologist with Dane. They both had their issues. Who was he to judge?

"Would you hold her fuckin' shit open already?!" Buggs demanded. "C'mon, I don't make a threat to a guy if I'm not gonna deliver. That's how you get a bad reputation. You understand?"

Dane smiled with his shit-eating grin and stuck his lumpy, diarrhea-drenched fingers into Mrs. Blanchfield's baby hatch. "I hear ya."

Buggs looked down at the old hag. The gurgling had stopped. Mrs. Blanchfield wasn't breathing anymore.

"She—she's dead. She's dead! We missed it! We fuckin' missed it!" Buggs yelled.

"We didn't miss shit. Relax," Dane said.

"Don't tell me to fuckin' relax!"

"Just put the fuckin' bat in her cunt. Dead or not, it'll make you feel better."

"I... I don't wanna," Buggs said, turning away from him.

They'd spent far too many years killing people together. Things seemed to be getting a little too elaborate lately. And when something didn't go right, they went at it like an old married couple.

Dane opened the mutilated hole a little wider. "I'm sure if you just stick it in for a few minutes, you'll forget about all of this, and everything'll be fine."

Buggs looked back at him and shifted the bat in his hands like a spoiled brat. He didn't want to believe Dane was right, and he was still a bit sore at him. But he knew he was. He crouched down slowly and extended the wide tip into the huge, runny hole.

"There you go. See? You can still fuck her with it. She's still shittin' and everything," Dane said.

As the bloody steel slipped over the mangled meat socket, Buggs felt better. Hearing the slick snatch strips queef as he ramped up the revolutions put him at ease. Buggs still wasn't quite ready to stop pouting, but he was feeling decent again.

"Great job, man. You're—"

"I don't need you to keep pattin' me on the ass, okay?" Buggs said. "I can see that it's good. I know what good looks like."

Dane smiled. "Oh, c'mon, don't stay sore at me."

Buggs started vigorously ramming the bat in and out of Mrs. Blanchfield, ignoring Dane's extension of the olive branch.

"I've got something that'll make you not sore at me anymore," Dane said.

"Like what," Buggs grumbled.

"An idea. Once you're done reaming her out, I've got one more thing that'll put you in a good place. I promise."

EXACTLY 13 MINUTES LATER

Buggs' eyes lit up with delight as he swung the bat as hard as he could. When the tip connected with Mrs. Blanchfield's head, the power behind the lick cracked her eye socket open. The bloody orb inside the cavern popped out nearly halfway.

"Look at that!" Dane yelled. "You almost knocked the fuckin' eyeball out of her goddamn head!"

Dane looked on in adoration as the head sailed forward through the air. Several long shoestrings were looped around one of the wings of the ceiling fans and tied to a curved metal hook that was screwed into the top of her head.

Buggs kept his eye on the prize as it headed back toward him. He crushed it a second time in nearly the exact same spot, forcing the eye to pounce out of the socket and dangle over her cheek by the nerve string.

"There it goes!" Dane yelled, celebrating the strike.

He lay on the ground next to Mrs. Blanchfield's nude, decapitated corpse. The limbs looked like Gumby's worst day. Her pussy was still bleeding, but the baseballs that Dane had stuffed inside her mutilated meat pocket had slowed some of the oozing.

"You know, I'm getting kinda hungry now," Dane said. "What do you say we clean up and go grab a bite?"

"That sounds good," Buggs said. "I'm actually starving myself."

Dane took one look at his bloated partner's disgusting physique and laughed to himself.

"What's so funny?" Buggs asked.

Bang! Bang! Bang!

A series of noises came from the floor underneath them.

"Hey! Keep it the fuck down up there!" a voice from the apartment below screamed. "I'm tired of listening to your bullshit!"

Buggs looked at Dane with wide eyes that said, 'this mother fucker's got some balls.'

Dane plucked the switchblade out of Mrs. Blanchfield's chest plate and looked back to his partner. "Say, Buggs, what do ya think about makin' one more stop before we get that bite?"

Buggs took a parting swing at Mrs. Blanchfield's head, adding another dent in her noggin and grinned. "I think that's the best fuckin' idea you've had all day."

THE BLOOD BANK

"Hey! I need to put down a bet, I-I don't have much time," the man said, looking over the counter.

No response.

The haggard, down on his luck degenerate slammed his hand down on the bell affixed to the station.

Ring! Ring! Ring! Ring! Ring!

"Where the fuck are you?!" he asked.

He went after the bell again like it owed him money.

Ring! Ring! Ring! Ring! Ring!

"Please! Wake up! Wake the fuck up!" the stressed-out man begged.

Red opened his eyes. The smell of piss, shit, body odor, and iron invaded his sinuses. The brash ring of the bell echoed inside his skull. His eyes were bloodshot. He hardly slept anymore. The filth, sweat stains, and dead skin embedded on his cot mattress used to make him want to puke every time he woke up, but not anymore. The nasty novelty of the myriad of foul scents had worn off.

Nothing disgusted him anymore.

Nothing shocked him anymore.

Nothing fostered hope anymore.

Nothing seemed real anymore.

"I know you're down there!" the man persisted. "I know you can hear me! How much can you take at once?"

As Red crawled out from underneath the table, his pale skin now only amplified the port wine stain on his neck that he was nicknamed after.

The gaping holes in his palms had healed. There was still a tiny hole at the head of his cock from when he'd torn the fish hook out of his pecker, but otherwise, it had mended nicely. The Black Widow's personal physician—Dr. Pollard—had stuffed him full of needles and stitches after the entire ordeal to ensure nothing rotted and fell off without her say so. He begged them to reattach his pinky, but The Black Widow said all severed flesh belonged to the house.

When Red stood up and positioned himself, he did so with a limp. The bullet that had gone through his foot left him with a permanent stagger. It didn't really matter, though; it wasn't as if he was going on nature hikes or anything. He'd survived The Mystery Parlay, but the plethora of scars and deformities were there to stay.

But what hurt much more than the physical scars were the mental ones. Red was continuously haunted by his failures. When he awoke each day, he remembered the damage done to his loved ones. The constant wonder of what Buggs and Dane had done with his mother. The infinite mystery of what had become of his little girl. Was she even *his* little girl? The question still antagonized him.

He would never learn the truth.

Red did a small bump of powder through a tiny straw off the end of the counter. The Black Widow only extended him enough drugs to keep him operational, never a quantity that would allow him to OD. Since he worked twenty-four hours a day, and could only sleep in between customers, the drugs were a necessity.

When Red stretched his back, a sickening crack escaped his brittle bones. There still weren't any clocks allowed inside Shadows, and he'd never gotten to use his ticket to get his father's watch back.

It would've been pointless anyway. The whole purpose of the watch was to keep him on a path of decency. Red wasn't anywhere near that path now. He'd fallen off the hill completely.

Still, with the absence of time, it was impossible to know how long he'd been there for. But the bruised, decaying tissue on his ankle that the shackle remained clamped around suggested a sizable stretch.

Each time Red moved, he grimaced. The slightest motion caused the rusted metal to rub against the raw, infected meat on his ankle. He groaned as he positioned his elbows down on the stand.

"Mister, please!" The man banged his hands on the counter. "I'm running out of fuckin' time! I'm begging you! Just tell me how much you can take at once!"

The desperation in the man's voice was as normal as noodles in a Japanese restaurant. The only thing Red saw anymore was desperation. He was bound to a station where he constantly came face-to-face with society's most frantic and destitute.

Red had never seen the grungy bastard standing before him in his life, yet, he knew the man all too well. It was just a short time ago that he was that man. Red had looked through the eyes of desperation, and he'd seen exactly what the man was seeing.

"Well, that's up to you," Red replied. "How much ya need?"

Red pointed up to the glowing crimson sign above his head. It read: *THE BLOOD BANK: TRADE BLOOD FOR IMMEDIATE CASH!*

"That sign says The Blood Bank, not doctor," Red said. "I don't know how much you need, but the payout pricing is listed here. You've gotta figure that safety shit out for yourself."

"C'mon, help me out man!" he begged. The savagery in his eyes was primal. The man was clearly on the edge. "How much do I need to live?! At least tell me that much."

Red felt little pity for the man. The scumbag probably had a sad story—everybody did. But so did Red, and that didn't change how things shook out for him. He wasn't a psychic, but he knew how the man's story was going to end. He didn't want to think about it anymore. He wanted the man to leave him be.

"Listen, buddy," Red said, tone growing more annoyed by the second. "I'll tell you the same thing I tell everyone, the only thing they told me when I started draining. The human body contains five liters of blood—"

"Okay, but what do I need to live?!" he interjected.

Red raised his eyebrows. "If you'd just fuckin' relax for a second, I'll tell ya."

The bummy man rubbed his hands and nodded.

Once Red was satisfied with his behavior, he continued. "You can die from losing anywhere between two and a half and four liters."

The man didn't seem to be in such a rush anymore. "Shit, that's a lot of wiggle room."

As he watched the creep scratch the side of his head, Red knew exactly why he'd suddenly slowed his role; the man was pondering his life.

Red fell back into his own thoughts of solitude. Often, he wondered why The Black Widow had even kept him around. Any asshole with two hands and half a brain could drain blood, so it begged the question, why him? The best he could figure was that she didn't relate to many people, but she related to him. Even though she ultimately left helping him up to chance, Red had something inside him that had been lost in her own life. Maybe she secretly wanted to keep him around.

The way she had them kids in cages, it was like she was jealous of them, Red thought. *Like she didn't want them to have the chance at life that she never did. She did the same to my Dessi. Fucking cunt.*

From time to time, when she checked in on him, he sprinkled a question here and there. One day he hoped to finally learn—or confirm—why she held him in that regard.

Quite frankly, if she'd have torn him apart inside The Red Room, he probably would've been better off.

Why'd she do it?

It was another mystery that remained. While it was the mystery that he was least interested in, it was the only one that was solvable any longer. In some ways, that question was all he had left.

"And it's a hundred a liter?" the man asked.

"Yup," Red replied.

"Hmm. Anyone ever go four and a half and live to bet?"

"Not since I been here."

The fidgety man looked like he was doing math in his head—probably calculating how much he'd get and how much he needed to win to get out of whatever hot water he was in. Suddenly, he rolled up his sleeve and jumped into the squeaky chair beside the stand.

"Let's do four liters right on the button!" he exclaimed.

"You got it," Red replied.

Red bent over and grabbed hold of the brown leather straps. He secured the restraints around the man's arms, legs, torso, and neck.

With the donor fully secured, Red retrieved the rusted needle from behind the counter. The tip was still wet with the blood of the last drain patient when he plunged it into the man's arm. The scumbag didn't seem too concerned about it. He clearly had more pressing matters than potentially contracting a blood disease; it didn't even generate a blip on his radar.

Red turned to the machinery mounted beside the chair. Punching the number four button then start, he triggered the machine to activate.

Four is sure pushin' it.

As the device sucked the crimson out from the man's arm, Red watched him lay back, close his eyes, and try to forget about his worries. He knew in the man's mind that the money his blood would give him was the answer.

Money was the answer to everything.

Money was the reason the vampiric machine had a built-in blood analysis system to funnel out the different blood types. Stealing blood from people wasn't just another sick thing to do to people desperate enough to find themselves at Shadows; it was an industry. There was a ridiculous demand on the black market for blood.

Money was the reason that body parts and organs were harvested with haste from the people who couldn't pay on their bets. Sure, Red believed The Black Widow still took pleasure in people's suffering, but surely the money didn't hurt either.

From time to time, Red chuckled at the thought. As much as The Black Widow hated Gianni Lito, in more than one way, she'd become just like him.

But who was Red to talk? Money—or the lack thereof—was the reason that he was where he was.

Red didn't even realize how lost in his thoughts he was. By the time he glanced over at the measurement meter, three and a half liters had already left the man's shitty little body.

"Shit, I feel high or somethin'," the man mumbled, opening his eyes and shutting them again.

"Yeah, it feels like that sometimes," Red replied.

"Where am I?"

Red grinned. "You're home."

Every time Red looked at the medical machinery beside the chair, it reminded him of the hospital. And whenever he thought about the hospital, he thought about his mother. It was a cruel, cyclical, domino effect that he relived many times each day, like a person with short-term memory loss who kept having to be told their life was a steaming pile of garbage.

"I'm… I think I'm gonna pass out… maybe," the man whispered, eyelids starting to twitch.

Red stared into the little man's pale face. He didn't look well. Regardless, he ignored the man's statement and continued with his own thoughts.

Was his poor mother rotting away in some mite-infested room with every bone in her body broken? Had her cunt been ripped open with the tip of the baseball bat like Buggs had promised? Red was the only person his mother had left. One of his last promises to her was that he'd always be there to take care of her.

As the machine stopped at exactly four liters, a deep hiss escaped the man's body. It was a noise he was intimately familiar with—the rattle of death.

Red watched the man's pasty face as a smile appeared. There was an elusive relief, one that Red had always thought about but never believed he had the will to attain. Still, he enjoyed living vicariously through others.

"You got off easy, fella," he said looking at the man's closed eyes. How he longed to rest like him. "You got off easier than you know."

Red punched the number one into the keypad on the machine. "I guess you won't be needing the rest of this." There was no sense in letting the last liter of blood go to waste. After all, he didn't know who it might eventually go on to save.

His finger hovered over the start button but couldn't seem to push it.

The fuck am I doing? How long can I keep on going with this shit?

Sure, Red might've been spared, but in so many ways, he was just like Lilly. Just like Mr. Don. Just like the bald man. Just like the soccer mom. Just like Lane. For all intents and purposes, his life was over.

Something about watching the pathetic man die flipped a switch in Red's head. When he passed, it wasn't like the others—he looked peaceful. It felt like a subliminal message that had been constantly reiterated to him, except suddenly, it finally clicked.

For the first time, Red wondered if maybe the answers that tortured him all day and night were within arm's reach. It just depended on one question he could never seem to settle on; was there life after death?

Red undid the straps and pulled the man out of the chair. He sat down and grabbed the bloody needle. Solving the mystery of The Black Widow's motive wasn't enough to keep him around any longer.

It's time to find Ma and Dessi, Red thought as he inserted the bloody prick into his vein.

Red updated the number of liters from one to five on the device and found his finger hovering over the start button. A strange sensation stirred from his gut up to his heart. He couldn't be sure why he felt the way he did, but he was grateful.

Even if they aren't there yet, waiting there—or anywhere—is better than here. Even if they never arrive, maybe this will somehow bring us closer.

Red relaxed his body and set all the tension and anxiety inside him free.

"Fuck it."

He pressed the start button.

THE END

R
R

THE RED ENDING

RED

As the coin flipped through the air, to Red, it seemed like everything was in slow motion. The flashes of each color flickered in his eyes. There was no right answer to give, just a guess that he was having trouble deciding on.

"I said, call it!" The Black Widow yelled.

"Red!" he finally blurted out. The color he was named after couldn't fail him twice in a row, could it?

The Black Widow snatched the coin out of the air and slapped it down on the top of her hand.

"You should never bet red. Black always wins… but not this time," The Black Widow said.

A wave of relief cooled over Red but then halted. Could she be trusted to be true to her word? Would she do as she'd promised? Based on everything that Lilly had told him—and her own grisly demise—The Black Widow wasn't to be believed. She was a tortured soul that existed only to reciprocate her torment.

"Marty! Manx!" she yelled.

The door burst open. The intimidating security guards were ready for her command.

"Prepare a car for our friend," she said. "And get a hold of Dr. Pollard. We'll need to get him patched up before—"

Red grimaced. "I ain't got time for a doctor. I've already wasted too much! I've gotta get back right now."

"Friend, you've had enough stops at the buffet table to put you on cloud nine," The Black Widow said. "You'll probably go to sleep before the dope wears off. If you *actually* want to save that mother of yours, you'll need to be alive, right?"

Red looked down at his bloody foot and gory hands. Those factors, along with the stinging sensation in his peehole reminding him he'd just hooked his worm not too long ago, kept him quiet.

She looked back at the men. "I'll have a few other requests once you complete those, but get started."

"Yes, ma'am." Marty and Manx left the room.

As the door closed, Red was a cyclone of sentiments. He didn't know how to feel about the woman before him. Sure, she was helping him achieve what he'd come to Shadows to achieve. But how could someone offer such generosity and kindness in one instance only to be the catalyst for utter carnage in so many others?

She'd sacrificed Lilly to a bloodthirsty crowd.

She'd forced Red to painstakingly destroy his body.

She'd made him murder a child to try and save another.

"Why-why are you doing this?" Red asked.

"Because I wanted to be rescued too," she replied. "But instead, I got left in the hands of a psychopath. Sounds like your daughter may be in a similar predicament. Maybe it doesn't have to be that way."

"I sure hope not." Red wasn't sure if he should say what he had in mind. He decided to anyway. "But so was Lilly. Why didn't you feel that way about her?"

"Lilly was a worthless whore who you know very little about. Unlike her, despite the horrible circumstances of my situation, I persevered. Lilly fell victim to hers, in some ways because of her demons.

"But people change. There's gotta be some kinda road to redemption, right?"

"Well of course, but we all must carve that path out ourselves." The Black Widow gestured toward Gianni's severed cock and testicles. The graying junk remained floating amid a flurry of dead skin particles inside a jar of fluid on the desk. "And still, even though I was able to do that, I would've preferred that *this* not be my legacy."

"And what about that kid you…" Red's lips trembled, and his eyes glossed over. "The kid you made me kill."

The Black Widow grinned. "In fairness, I didn't *make* you do anything." She tapped the jar of sexual organs gently. "That's one thing I must give Gianni credit for. As is the case with you, outside of a few extenuating circumstances, most everything people do to themselves inside Shadows is voluntary. Make no mistake about it, Red; *you* killed that child—not me."

"But you made it possible!" Red yelled. "What the fuck are kids even doing inside this place to begin with?"

She pointed to the monitor affixed to the wall beside her desk, more specifically the one focused on the bar inside The Doll House. "I know you've heard about me. I listened to that whore tell you my story. If I ended up here…" Her eyes grew blacker. "Then why should age act as a shield for any other child?"

Red couldn't believe what she was saying. She sounded so convinced of her argument.

"Now if the parent of a child—such as yourself—is willing to make the ultimate wager to regain their bond, then so be it. The doors of Shadows are open to guardians with grit. Otherwise, their babies will just have to be like me." She lifted the jar. "And carve out a path of their own."

Red's lip curled with disgust. He could hardly stand to listen to her. "You're fuckin' sick, lady—"

"I think the dopamine receptors in your little brain are hitting too hard. I've been beyond generous with you, but your remarks and questions are testing my patience. I suggest you forget about your feelings and focus on why you came here in the first place."

While the trauma was fresh in his mind, there was no doubt, she was right. Anything that had transpired during his time inside Shadows couldn't be changed. As much as he didn't want to admit it, she was right.

He needed to get patched up and get back to his mother as quickly as possible. Once she was safe, he could move on to finding Dessi. He'd already pressed his luck far enough. There would be time to cope with the losses later. For now, it would be best to count his winnings.

"You're right," Red said.

The Black Widow set Gianni's cock and balls back on the desk and glared at Red. "I know."

The door flew open again.

Manx stood with the baton still in hand as if hoping she would give him the okay to beat the shit out of Red. "The car's waiting outside, and doc is ready for him."

"Alright," The Black Widow said. She looked at Red. "This is where we say goodbye. While I'm sure you won't miss me, you'll certainly remember me. Best of luck, Red."

Red thought she might expect him to thank her for sparing him. But after everything she'd put him through, there was no way. He reached into his jacket and dug around. A bloody ticket stub and severed pinky dusted with cocaine emerged. He looked at the series of numbers inked at the bottom.

"I left a watch with the bank on my way in," Red explained. "I'd really appreciate if you'd let me—"

"Manx will make sure your property is returned," The Black Widow replied.

Red nodded, looking down at the severed pinky. "And what about my fuckin' finger?"

"If you move along quickly enough, I'm sure Dr. Pollard can have it reattached. He's one of the best." The Black Widow narrowed her eyes. "I've certainly seen him work *miracles* before."

Manx approached Red. "C'mon, let's go."

Turning, Red followed his order.

"Oh, just one more thing," The Black Widow said to Manx. "Have Marty bring down his money to the car, but after he gets patched up, take him by the weapons vault. Let him pick out whatever he needs." The Black Widow looked at Red and smirked. "Unfortunately, his fight has only just begun."

EXIT PLAN

Two large black gun cases sat on the curb beside Red. He looked back at the wall of mountain.

You'd never even know it was here, Red thought.

A black shuttle bus with the windows blocked out hissed to a stop a few yards away. As players exited, Red looked at the jigsaw of stitches that covered his hands, trying his best not to move his reattached pinky too much.

Hopefully they're as lucky as me.

Exhaling, Red winced in pain. Looking down at his father's watch, he tapped the face. He was just grateful to be in the realm of time again.

Even as Marty approached him in a gray Lincoln, Red couldn't believe he'd made it out. He looked back at the gun cases. What became of his life was up to him now.

Marty exited the vehicle. He carried over a Samsonite briefcase and held it up. "Here's your money." He popped the trunk and walked around to the back of the car. Setting the money in the boot, he and Red each grabbed one of the gun cases and loaded them.

"Have a look," Marty said, showing him the money.

There were more Benjamins inside than he'd ever seen before.

Red nodded.

"Alright. Let's go." Marty said.

He closed the trunk and they both got inside the car.

As they traveled through the rugged terrain, Red saw the outlines of the mountains in the darkness. It took some time before they finally reached the decrepit parking garage, Red wouldn't have bet on reentering it.

"Where you parked?" Marty asked.

"Space number seven," Red mumbled.

Marty slowed near Red's vehicle. As they finished transferring the money and guns, something distracted them.

Back when Red was waiting in his parking space to be taken into Shadows, he'd heard a mysterious noise coming from the car beside him.

"You hear that?" Red asked.

The sounds of a female struggling and crying grew louder.

Marty looked at the number eight spray-painted on the concrete in front of the blue Cadillac. His eyes widened. "Shit, he wasn't lying."

"What?" Red asked.

Marty moved to the driver's side window and removed a handgun from his jacket. He pistol-whipped the window, opened the door, and popped the trunk.

Red's face crinkled with horror and disgust. A young girl, probably no older than Dessi would be, lay inside the trunk. She was hog-tied and terrified. It was easy to tell since her clothing was saturated in her own urine and feces.

His first reaction was to untie her, but as he moved in, he heard a gun cocking. When Red looked to the side, Marty's barrel was aimed between his eyes.

"That girl's property of the casino," Marty said.

Red looked back at the trunk. The child begged him with his eyes.

"I'm not fucking asking you. I'm telling you," Marty continued. "You've got your own war to fight. Rest assured, she'll be looked after."

"In that fuckin' place?" Red asked, pointing back in the direction they came from. "Are you kidding me?"

"This ain't none of your business," Marty said.

The girl continued to cry and moan, biting down on the gag in her mouth as tears streaked down her face.

Red thought about the gun cases in his car. "I could make it my business."

Marty backed up, putting some space between himself and Red. "You've got exactly three seconds to get in that car and drive away. One… two…"

He didn't have much of a choice. The weapons Red had been gifted weren't within reach. And though he didn't believe the child was at fault, he didn't know all the particulars of the situation.

As he stepped away from the trunk of the Caddy with his hands raised, he felt like he was betraying the girl. But Marty was right, he had his own war to fight. Buggs and Dane Fuller could be tearing his mother apart any moment. Dessi was still waiting on him.

Red closed the trunk of his car and slipped into the driver's seat. When he made his way out of the parking lot, Red was certain of only one thing: he'd never look back.

GUNS BLAZIN'

"Go fish," Dane said, glaring at Mrs. Blanchfield.

The old lady's frail hand trembled as it moved toward the pile of cards in the center of the table. It took her an incredibly long time to draw and play.

"For Christ's sake, lady, would ya hurry up already!" Dane snapped.

He was tired of playing cards, sleeping on the old lady's scratchy couch, and eating frozen meatballs. But more than anything, he was tired of pretending that her fuck-up son was somehow going to arrive with enough money to make things square.

"I-I'm sorry, dear, I'm going as fast as I can," Mrs. Blanchfield replied.

"I think this has gone on long enough," Dane said, throwing his cards on the table and standing.

Buggs looked up from his cards. He was far calmer than his counterpart. The pair of flies hovering around his head finally decided to settle. One chose his shoulder and the other landed on the cards he held.

"A deal's a deal," Buggs said. "We said exactly four days which means the lump 'a shit's got another two hours and thirty-seven minutes."

Dane rolled his eyes and exhaled glaring angrily at Mrs. Blanchfield's confused mug. That was the only look she'd known since her son had left her in the care of the two disgruntled and smelly men.

"C'mon, he ain't comin' back," Dane whined.

"We been here almost four days now, another couple hours ain't gonna kill ya," Buggs said turning his attention to the old lady. "But it'll kill *her* though!"

The pair of goons both let out thunderous cackles. But their laughter was interrupted by a heavy knock at the door.

Dane's eyes narrowed. "Could it be him?" he asked reaching for his holster and retrieving his piece.

Buggs was already cocking his gun. He put the barrel to Mrs. Blanchfield's temple. "Anyone you forgot to tell us about?"

Mrs. Blanchfield started to tremble and cry. "I… please, no one's supposed to be here, I swear, I-I don't know what's going on."

"Listen ya old bag," Buggs whispered, "I'll tell ya exactly what's going on. You're gonna go over to that door, and if it's that fuck-up son of yours, you're gonna let him in. If it's anyone else, you'd better get 'em outta here fast." Buggs pointed to the barrel. "Or I'm gonna stick this up that old, pruned asshole of yours and let the shots rip."

"We'll be listening," Dane added, slapping her face gingerly. "Now lose the tears and make it natural, ya hear?"

The old woman used her sleeves and wiped the tears away from her face as the pounding on the door continued. "I'll do my best."

"Do it right, or else…" Buggs said.

Dane grabbed her by the arm, forcing Mrs. Blanchfield to stand up. He hung back with his partner, their weapons ready as he listened intently.

As she made her way around the corner of the living room and into the kitchen, Mrs. Blanchfield did her best to keep herself composed. "Ah, just a minute, please. I'm—I'm coming."

Gritting her dentures, she reached for the lock with one hand and doorknob with the other.

With his eyebrows raised, Buggs looked at Dane as they listened to the front door squeak open. But when no words were exchanged, he gestured to Dane to check on it.

Dane raised his gun and nestled up against the paneling that led into the kitchen. He wanted to get a peek around the corner at the hallway before he started letting off shots indiscriminately, but right as his head popped around the doorway, a barrage of automatic gunfire ripped through the apartment.

The fedora flew off Dane's head along with part of his skull. When he fell onto the floor, Buggs saw what the hail of bullets had done. His partner's brow had been turned to mush. Crimson oozed from the countless cracks in his skull while wads of knotty brains pulsated.

Buggs flipped the table on its side and took cover, peering out at his mangled friend. He watched Dane lift his gun above his squirting head into the air—the dying degenerate was all instincts. But as the piece elevated, another storm of lead penetrated his forearm and wrist.

The joint below his hand shattered, and Dane's limb went limp. As the gaping wound on the backside of his arm smacked against the floor, blood gushed from the holes followed by an eruption of spasms.

"Fucker!" Buggs yelled. While he watched his fallen partner's violent tremors, rage and vengeance took hold of him. But before Buggs could get his gun aimed around the table, the clanging of metal hitting against the floor behind him drew his attention.

He only had a second to register it. Buggs had seen flash-bang grenades during raids in the past. What came next happened too quickly for him to prepare. An explosion of white blinded him. He dropped his gun impulsively shielding his ears with his hands. But as the deafening noise resonated throughout the room, his eardrums popped like kernels in a microwave.

***

Red took his fingers out of his ears and picked up the Uzi from the stove. When he jammed another magazine inside the submachine gun, he felt grateful. The Black Widow didn't have to allow him his parting gifts, but it was the least she could do for him after the hell he'd been through. Without the guns, the stun grenade, and a fuckload of painkillers, Red knew he wouldn't have been able to go to war with Buggs and Dane.

As he limped around the corner, Red clenched his bandaged hands around the Uzi. He was no longer afraid like before. The man stepping inside the living room on that morning wasn't the same man that had nearly pissed himself there days earlier.

He was hurt.

He was angry.

He was hardened.

And he was tired of being everyone's punching bag.

While Buggs scrambled and felt around for his gun, Red peppered his knees and thighs with shots. The blood splattered all over the floor as Red kicked the gun away from his stunned adversary.

"Ahhhh, fuck!" Buggs cried. "You—you fuckin' shot me! My legs!"

"I got your money," Red said. "Ain't that what you should be concerned about? Isn't that the only thing the entire planet cares about?"

"Please don't kill me, please!"

"Tell Mad Dog I got his cash, and he ain't gettin' a fuckin' cent."

"I got a mother too," Buggs said. "Okay, maybe not, but I got a dog! You can't fuckin' kill me!"

Red suddenly realized that the goon wasn't hearing a word he said.

Flash bang must've popped his ears good, Red thought.

As Buggs continued to beg for his life, Red raised the Uzi. "Fuck it. I guess I'll tell 'em myself."

As the hail of gunfire shredded through Buggs' torso, blood painted the floor. Small holes were scattered all over his front side while his back tissue separated, leaving deep voids that were a gateway to his organs. Suddenly, the man who'd sent so many people to the insects was finally headed for them himself.

Red retreated into the kitchen. At the doorway of the apartment he picked the gas canister off the floor.

"Patrick, can we leave yet?" Mrs. Blanchfield asked peeking around the door.

"Jesus, Ma, I told you to go out the back of the building!" Red said. "It's still dangerous."

"But I—"

"No buts, go out back and wait for me in the car!"

"Al-alright, dear."

While his mother headed to the rear exit, Red turned his attention to Dane. He was still gurgling blood as Red stood over his body with the canister.

Red poured gas all over the hollowed-out area where his forehead used to be. As Dane's blood mixed with the accelerant, Red pulled a lighter out of his jacket.

When the flames engulfed Dane, he was already too broken to scream. Red liked to imagine the evil gangster could still feel the heat liquefying his skin as he watched him twitch uncontrollably. Collecting the phlegm in his throat, he readied the mucus on his tongue. He spat on Dane and watched the loogie land on his cheek and start to sizzle.

"Fuckin' scumbag," Red mumbled.

While flames devoured Dane's body, Red dumped more gas around the apartment. Much of Red's life and history up until that moment were largely forgettable. They were just an agonizing series of blunders, selfish anecdotes, and nightmarish consequences. There wasn't a whole lot that was worth saving.

Today's a new day.

Burning all his heartache and horrible memories down was the easiest thing he'd done in days, especially since he had enough money to become someone better—someone who didn't have to gamble any longer. A man who he could stand to look at in the mirror. A man who no longer wondered 'what if?' and wasn't afraid to shed light on the mysteries that haunted him.

As Red exited the apartment, he looked at the fire alarm on the wall, then to the exit at the rear of the building. He could hear the uproar and screams of other people who lived there.

Hopefully they all make it out.

Red pulled the alarm handle and ran for the exit.

BETTER DAYS

"You look like you seen better days," Jack Tunney said stuffing a breakfast sausage into his mouth.

"Well, looks can be deceiving," Red replied.

Red watched as Jack took him in. From Red's purple eye to his bandaged hands and reattached pinky. But even setting the bruises and cuts aside, there was something beyond the physical traits that was different about him.

After swallowing his bite, Jack had to ask. "The fuck happened to you? And why the hell we meetin' all the way out here all of a sudden? Drivin' this far out of the city is a bit of an inconvenience."

Red slid an envelope across the table to Jack.

"How about you stop with all the goddamn questions and just tell me what I'm payin' you to find out. I put a little extra in there for you going out of your way and your *inconvenience.* But I need you to shoot straight with me. I've had a bit of a reawakening, and since this reawakening, I got to thinkin' about our little arrangement. It seems to me that this has gone on a lot longer than it should've. And I'm in no mood to further prolong your efforts."

Jack raised his greasy fork. "I explained this up front already, these things take time."

"And I've given you that and then some. I gave you so much that terrible things have occurred as a result. Yet here we sit, and you just keep stringing me along." Red cracked his knuckles. "We've reached a point where you've become a liability. And I can't afford to watch you keep dragging your dick any longer."

"I-I ain't stringin' you along, Red, I—"

"Quiet for a second. I'm making a point."

Red watched him closely. Jack was starting to sweat. The only reason for him to be scared was if there was some truth to Red's accusations.

"So, what I'm saying is, you can only string someone along so long until that rope ends up around your own neck. You follow me?"

Jack's brow glistened as he nodded solemnly. He looked like he didn't know how to respond.

Red interlocked his fingers, being gentle with his pinky. "Good, then for your sake, I hope you're about tell me what I've been waiting to hear."

"Well, I supposed we can get right to it." Jack slid the envelope off the table and into the pocket of his trench coat resting on his chair. From the pocket, he removed a folded piece of paper and set it on the table.

"What's that?" Red asked.

"An address."

Red picked up the piece of paper and opened it.

"A very reliable source said Brittany's been selling her ass around there, living on one of the upper floors of the building," Jack said.

Red looked up from the paper and squinted. "One of the upper floors? Which fuckin' one is it?"

"They couldn't say. It ain't like she's gettin' mail there; the building's abandoned."

He nodded and slid the paper into his jacket. "Anything else I should know about?"

Jack took a sip of his coffee and anxiously exhaled. He looked scared.

"Just that it ain't a particularly nice part of town, if you know what I mean," Jack said.

Red grinned for the first time during their meeting. "Well, that shouldn't be a problem. Cuz I ain't a particularly nice fella anymore."

GOODBYE AND HELLO

At most funerals, people cried but not Mad Dog; he drooled. As the two caskets got lowered into the ground, he looked to his left. There were four other goons dressed in their best suits standing around the graves.

Mad Dog used his handkerchief to absorb the slobber on the side of his mouth while he listened to a priest recite a Catholic prayer.

"Son-of-a-bitch took my left and right hands," he mumbled. "Took 'em both."

"What's that boss?" the man beside him said.

"I said you're the big dick now, Claudio!" Mad Dog yelled. "And you better be ready to fuckin' kill. Cuz guys like Buggs and Dane don't grow on fuckin' trees. So if they're both layin' here, you better be on your toes with this bastard. The fact you ain't found this piece of shit yet's a sin. Look at 'em, they're already turnin' over in their graves!"

The priest raised his eyebrows, quickly made the sign of the cross, and jogged away.

"I'm-I'm on it, boss," Claudio said. "It'll be taken care of, rest assured."

Mad Dog stuck his finger into Claudio's chest. "It damn well better be. Cuz if it ain't, then it's your ass."

Claudio nodded. "It's gonna happen, and just like you wanted—slow."

Mad Dog looked at the graves. "Guys like them… this life was all they had. That's why you don't see no one else here but us. We were family."

"You takin' care of their arrangements was really swell, boss," Claudio said.

Mad Dog raised the rag to the corner of his mouth again. "It was the least I could do for their loyalty. They deserved better than they got. They—"

The squeal of tires halting on concrete overshadowed the statement, followed by a thunderous explosion. Mad Dog and Claudio hit the deck as a collection of screams escaped the henchmen.

Mad Dog looked up to face a scene out of a war movie. Gore littered the graveyard. A leg blown off from the thigh down lay on the ground beside him. His eyes bulged. "What the fuck is going on?!"

PUTTING THE DOG DOWN

Red steadied the grenade launcher out the window of the car and continued the assault. He was grateful Marty imparted some of his military experience and explained how to use the guns. Several more rounds blew up the cluster of screaming men. The sheer force of the shots exploded the windshield and rear window of the vehicle. When the blast erupted, it turned the bodies into one big, repulsive puddle.

One of the men was coughing up blood and missing both of his legs. Another had a piece of shrapnel stuck inside his skull. The others looked like they'd been pulled apart by giants. Much of their skeletons were exposed and various extremities were strewn everywhere.

Red grinned. Drunk off power, he could taste vengeance. He only had one grenade left and could see Mad Dog and one of his other men hiding behind a larger monument. He wasn't sure if the shot would connect, so he waited and listened.

"Go, now, damnit!" Mad Dog yelled.

Red squinted and watched as the goon made a run for the car. He was sure that the boss had told his final henchman to pull the vehicle up and rescue him, so Red allowed him to get into it. Just as the goon got in the driver's seat, Red looked down at his father's watch.

"Watch this," Red whispered.

The shot connected with the car's gas tank, turning it into an orange fireball. The goon's body was launched out of the car, onto the grass. He remained motionless and enveloped by the fire.

"Mother fucker!" Mad Dog yelled coming out from around the headstone with his gun raised. He used his cane to keep himself steady as he fired indiscriminately.

Red dropped the grenade launcher and ducked down. The vehicle got peppered with shots from the boss' handgun, but the action didn't rattle Red. He was battle tested. Lifting the Desert Eagle off the passenger seat, Red slipped out of the car. He listened closely as he took cover behind the tire and waited for his cue.

When Mad Dog's gun clicked, he dropped his cane and reached inside his pocket. He scrambled to reload, but usually he wasn't the one firing the gun, he was telling other people to.

Red whipped around the car and let off a pair of shots. Even though they missed, it caused Mad Dog to drop the magazine he was trying to insert. As he realized Red was getting ready to shoot again, the old man turned around and ran for his life.

He didn't get two steps before the bullet struck him in the lower back. As Red approached him, blood leaked through and darkened the backside of the gangster's suit. Looking at Mad Dog's cane, Red bent over and picked it up. Then he used the point of it to roll him over.

Red reveled in the shock on the old son-of-a-bitch's face. He'd dreamed about getting him out of his life. What was about to happen should've felt unbelievable, but after what he'd been through, it just felt right.

"Kind of ironic, isn't it?" Red asked. "You shot my father in the back. Guess it all kind of works out one way or another."

Mad Dog gurgled as blood spilled over the side of his face. "You're… you're makin' a mistake."

Red laughed as he shook his head. "Nah, I been makin' those my entire life. I know what those feel like. And this definitely ain't one."

"Please, I-I need medical attention!" Mad Dog yelled.

Red could see panic setting in as Mad Dog's drooling mouth dropped open. Realization dawned on the old man's face that he had no one left to manipulate. No one left to hide behind. Red was loving every minute of it.

"Remember how you talked about diggin' up my dad's bones?" Red asked. "I guess you didn't know, but, he never got a grave—we didn't have money like that. After you shot him, we had to cremate him. So, since he didn't get a grave, neither do you."

"What the fuck are you talkin' about?" Mad Dog asked.

"I'm talkin' about this fancy little private cemetery of yours. Nice and secluded—I bet it was fuckin' expensive. But that's too bad, cuz your dirty bones ain't never gonna rest here. They ain't never gonna rest period."

"Red, Jesus, I'm a resourceful man. There's got to be some kinda agreement we can reach!"

"I'm just doin' what you do."

"What do you mean?"

"Makin' 'em feel it. Remember? That fear and pain you made me live with, now *you're* gonna feel it."

"I've-I've got plenty I can offer you. You could be set for life! Money beyond what you—"

Red rammed the pointed end of the cane into Mad Dog's mouth. The old man choked as the sound of his teeth breaking rang out. The blood bubbled and flooded up like a water fountain.

"What you got, I don't want."

Red exhaled, pushing the tip of the cane deeper into the back of Mad Dog's throat.

"My ma's gonna be sad. She was a big fan of your tomato sauce. And since you ain't gonna be around anymore to make it, that part kinda sucks."

As Red watched Mad Dog choke and beg with his eyes, another thought came to him.

"Although, when I walked in on her that day and she was eating from that special batch we put Buddy in, I can't say I ever wanted to look at the stuff again."

Tears streamed from Mad Dog's eyes, and bloody drool overflowed down his cheeks. He truly looked the part.

Red looked back at the trunk of his car and grinned. "Even though poor ol' Ma won't be able to eat it, there's gonna be one last batch. And rest assured, I'll make sure it reaches your family."

LONG TIME NO SEE

As Red parked his car in the dilapidated alley, he thought about the events that had brought him to that point. He was grateful that no one else had burned up in the fire he'd started besides Buggs and Dane. He was happy that his ma was safe again.

To the cops, the scene back at the apartment complex probably looked like some kind of organized crime caper gone horribly wrong. Red was a small-time bookie, not a kingpin. His disappearance and the murder of Mad Dog's scumbag henchmen were low on the list of police priorities in a city of rampant violence and corruption. But following that up by going to war with and assassinating Mad Dog—private cemetery or not—was going to force law enforcement on his trail.

Thankfully, Red had connections. He'd already gotten in contact with a few shady characters from his past. The kind that could provide a new life for him and his ma. Names, birth certificates, social securities, identification—whatever he needed. It was best to move on from the persona that had held him back his entire life. Not only for his well-being but for his mental health as well.

Forget about all that, he thought.

Red wasn't sure how he felt after sending the final case of MD Sauce to the old man's wife. She was probably in the dark about what kind of person Mad Dog was. Half of those mob ladies were stay at home wives, clueless to the violence and horror their husbands pulled the strings on.

As Red loaded the handgun and slipped it into his jacket, he stepped out of the car into the frigid air. He'd seen the front doors of the place chained up and imagined the ratty folk were making their way in via the alley. Looking up at the rotten building was upsetting. The last thing he wanted to think about was Dessi staying in a shithole with a bunch of creepy transients and drug addicts roaming around.

Jesus, what the fuck have you gotten her into, Britt?

The environment would put any kid on the fast track to being a junkhead. Rusty needles, funky garbage, and broken bottles littered the alley. He hadn't even been there for five minutes and hated the place.

"Hey, mister, you got fifty cents?" a toothless vagrant asked, gums chattering.

"Get lost." Red glared at the man. The look in Red's eyes was a warning in itself.

The creep was smart enough not to press him.

He passed more cardboard homes and dirty clothing en route to the staircase. The smell of neglect was profound, a mixture of human rot and moldy feces. The open manhole cover beside him might have had something to do with it. He continued to inspect the area, investigating the abyss of waste, that would've disgusted most to the core.

Red shook his head. *This fuckin' place.*

His blood pressure rose the longer he studied it. Red didn't want to stay any longer than he had to, and he wanted the same for Dessi.

It's so cold. Dessi must be freezing.

As he entered what seemed like an old factory building, a broken door lay on the floor beside a woman shivering in a puddle of her own urine. Her pale body was covered in rags, and her vomit crusted lips were turning blue.

Red ascended the steps, his imagination running wild. As his brain simulated potential scenarios, each pace he took elevated his anger.

Jack Tunney's source had claimed that Brittany had been spotted on the upper floors, but Red wasn't leaving anything to chance. He wanted to be thorough. Process of elimination, from top to bottom, he'd find her. After what he'd been through to reach that juncture, he'd be damned if he didn't.

The first and second floors were more of the same—drug addicts, whores, and degenerates. The selfishness that he recalled in his own life fit right in with the rotten building. Red passed one guy that clearly had stopped breathing. But he wasn't there on a crusade to rescue the randoms. He pushed the woes of all the other street dwellers aside and climbed the staircase again.

When he reached the third floor, Red heard a faint groaning. Making his way through the doorway, he drew closer to the moans. He passed several vacant rooms before reaching the source of the sound.

Aw fuck.

He'd had a sneaking suspicion that the noise was a little too hushed to be a cry for help. But he didn't expect the sight that confronted him. On a mattress that had been chewed to pieces by the rats, within a pile of moldy blankets, was Brittany. But she wasn't alone. There was a skinny man bent over in front of her. His ass was raised in the air and positioned in front of Brittany's hips.

The smell in the room was stomach-churning. A mixture of rotten food, unwashed flesh, musky lube, and aged excrement. Red put his hand over his mouth, attempting to thwart the vile aroma.

Brittany wore a long sleeve shirt that nearly reached her bare bottom. Her ass rocked back and forth as she drove the long, black strap-on deeper inside the skinny man. He was completely nude and shivering. Each time he exhaled a whimper, a cloud of smoke escaped his lips.

Brittany lifted one leg up and reached around his thigh to jerk him off. "You like that? You like it when I fuck your ass, little bitch?"

In some ways, it was the same old Britt. Red would've never let her do anything like what he was seeing to him, but he knew that kind of intensity and animosity had always lived inside her. She was domineering by nature. She was a cheater and a whore. Her suffocating personality was probably the biggest contributing factor in the collapse of their liaison. After all, it fostered a double murder.

"God, you smell like fucking shit!" Brittany said.

She cupped her hand below his rectum and collected some of the freshly moistened anal crust and juice that she was milking out of the scummy man's asshole.

"Smell it!" she yelled.

Red watched in horror as she pulled the skinny man's head back by his hair and rubbed the anal ooze all over his nose and eye sockets.

"Where the fuck is Dessi?" Red asked, letting his voice boom through the room.

Startled, Brittany turned around. She looked far worse than he remembered. Her teeth were black as coal and her face was covered in scabs. Some were freshly picked and bleeding, while others were covered by a brownish yellow crust. Many of the blood vessels in one of her eyes had burst. She didn't just look like hell, she looked like the people who went there.

The demon that she'd hidden from him for so long had finally forced its way to the surface. The look of coldness in her eyes from the night of the double murder remained. It was like it had never left.

The shiny, shit-caked dildo made a sickening slurp noise as Brittany pulled out of her friend. The skinny man's asshole remained gaping while the unpleasant, red innards of the chasm winked at Red.

"Well, well," Brittany said. "There's a fuckin' freakshow face I never thought I'd see again."

She turned to the backpack at the side of the bed and pulled a small baggie and overused pipe from a pouch. Dumping the meth into the glass bulb, she grabbed the lighter and flicked it.

She upgraded.

"Who the fuck is this?" the skinny man asked, nonchalantly slipping his pants on.

"Quiet, Todd," Brittany commanded. "I'll take care of it." She took another massive pull from the pipe before handing it to her friend. "I can't imagine what brings you here." She grinned, but it quickly melted off her face. An unsettling seriousness resurfaced. "And I've gotta a pretty good fuckin' imagination when I smoke this shit."

"I think you might've smoked too much of that shit," Red replied. "I figure after decades, your brain's probably about ready to turn to dust."

"Well, you figured wrong, cuz I'm gonna live forever!" She laughed, brandishing the broken, black enamel.

Todd took another big hit and raised his arm slightly. "Forever," he whispered.

"Where's Dessi?" Red asked.

Brittany giggled.

Red tightened his jaw and pulled out the gun and cocked it. "I ain't gonna ask you again, bitch! Now, where the fuck is she?!"

"Whoa, hey, man, chill out," Todd said.

Red pointed the gun at Todd. "Shut your mouth and don't move. You got that, ass-fuck?"

"Y-yeah," he said, closing his eyes.

"Don't be afraid of this fuckin' pussy," Brittany said. "He wouldn't hurt a fly."

"Don't test me, Britt. I promise you, I ain't the fella you remember."

She stood up, the large dildo flapping up and down with Todd's drizzle still running off the side of it. "So what, after all this time you came back to play daddy? Do I got that right? You're about as good a father as your old man."

Red narrowed his eyes.

"But he was dead," Brittany continued. "At least he had an excuse. What's your fuckin' excuse?"

Red looked at the old-style silver watch wrapped around his arm and reminded himself why he was there. No matter what mind games Brittany tried on him, he would not become his father. She could say whatever she wanted, but his actions spoke louder than her words. And after how he'd left Mad Dog, he suddenly felt impervious to such ignorant comments.

"That shit ain't gonna work this time around." Red shook his head. "Now get to talkin', or I can skip right to the ugly stuff. Your choice."

Brittany's manic, thousand-yard stare vanished and her mouth flat-lined. "I honestly don't even understand why you'd care."

"I know it's hard to understand in your little psycho fuckin' head, but most people feel guilt. Most people got a conscience—"

She grinned as she cut him off. "But she wasn't even yours."

The weight of those five words hit him hard. It felt like a nuclear bomb had just gone off inside him. All the inner turmoil and deep suspicions were finally validated. But what did it all mean? Did the man he was and the man he'd become look at those five words differently?

Jesus Chr—

"Todd, now!" Brittany yelled.

The long-haired creep drew a pistol from a towel on the side of the bed. He moved quicker than Red would've imagined him capable of.

But he wasn't quick enough.

Despite the bombshell Brittany had dropped, Red was far more focused than the pair of smoke-heads. Before Todd could get the shot lined up, a pair of bullets had entered his body. One blew a gaping hole in his elbow joint and the other lodged in his ribcage.

"Ahhh!" Todd screamed. "He-he fuckin' shot me! He fuckin' shot me!"

"We can see that!" Brittany yelled.

Red kept the gun on Todd as he took the pistol from his dangling forearm. The blood gushed inside the hole, offering a window into the junkie's ligaments and muscle. Red looked at Brittany and the pissy look on her face, then back to the gory forearm. "Maybe if you won't talk, your little butt-boy will."

He stepped on the destroyed joint, pulling the dangling limb down with his heel. Each time Red stomped, it yanked at the dwindling connective tissues, creating an excruciating pain that he was glad he wasn't familiar with.

"Where's the fuckin' girl?!" Red asked.

Brittany gritted her teeth. "Don't tell him shit!"

As the tears streaked down Todd's face his screams eventually turned into words. "I-I don't know what you're talkin' about—"

Red applied more pressure. "I'll rip this fuckin' thing off. I promise you."

Todd wailed even louder. The agony wasn't something he could get past. "She-she fuckin' sold her, man! Please, stop, it hurts!"

"You don't know what hurt is, you piece of shit!" Red yelled. "Sold her to who!"

"Shut the fuck up, Todd!" Brittany yelled.

Red looked back at her. "So help me god, you say another word, and I'll unload this entire fuckin' thing on your smelly ass." He stomped on Todd again. "Who?!"

"I don't… I don't fuckin' know!" he cried. "Some fuckin' bum. H-he-he used to be a cobbler or somethin'! It was a while ago, I swear! That's all I fuckin' know, man! I swear!"

Red furrowed his brow and glared at Brittany. "Sold her, huh? You fuckin' scunt."

Brittany stuck her tongue out at him. It seemed as if she still couldn't take him seriously. Red was ready to see how long that lasted. He looked back at Todd. "Whereabouts?"

"Right around here, just—just like two alleys over. It was a while back but I'm-I'm sure you can find 'em if you ask around!"

"Well, that's swell news. I shouldn't need to keep you around then." Red lifted the gun to Todd's head and pulled the trigger twice.

One shot went through his eye and lodged inside his skull and the second blew the nose off his face and collapsed his sinus cavity. The explosion of gore speckled his cheek. He looked down at the mass exodus of blood raining out of the void in his face. After what he'd witnessed during his time inside Shadows, the violence didn't faze him.

Brittany watched how nonchalantly he murdered the man. And for the first time, through the fog in her drugged-out eyes, Brittany seemed to finally see him clearly.

Red was no longer the one to fuck with.

She tried to run past him, but Red stuck his leg out. Landing flat on her face, Brittany scraped at the floorboards trying to lift herself back up. By the time got to her feet, Red had already cycled his gun. The handle connected with her scabby cheek full force.

"Here's another cut for the scab patch," he said.

She hit the floor harder this time. Red rolled her to the side and took in her bloody, disoriented expression. Again, he raised the handle of his gun and brought it into her rotten teeth. The vile chicklets exploded everywhere.

"You know," Red said. "There's a lotta things I imagined I might say to you if I ever saw you again. But today, this stops being about you."

Red pistol whipped her repeatedly.

One time for every life she ruined.

One time for every bad memory he relived.

One time for every ounce of pain he felt inside Shadows.

Until Brittany was a pile of scabs and gore. She looked like murder yet somehow remained alive.

Red wiped the bloody handle of the gun on her shirt and stood.

As he looked through the broken glass and tried to catch his breath, he saw something poetic. The steam exiting the open manhole in the alley below called to him, but more specifically, to Brittany.

Grabbing her by the throat, Red balanced the garble of flesh that was Brittany's face and aimed it toward the open sewer. "I guess it didn't take you long to blow through the dope and whatever cash you got from it. But that wasn't enough. You sold your fuckin' daughter to a stranger."

Tears welled in Red's eyes.

"Our daughter," he corrected himself. "You can say she wasn't mine, and maybe that's so, but I was still hers. I was there for her when no one else was. And she was there for me." Red sobbed hysterically before composing himself. "We had a bond that a heartless cunt like you could never comprehend."

Brittany spit up blood and several rotten teeth. Her face continued to leak but no words came.

"I didn't need her to be my blood to give a fuck about her," Red continued. "You understand me!"

When he squeezed her neck tighter more blood bubbled around her lips, but she remained unresponsive.

He looked out the window again then over to his father's watch. "I think it's about that time." Reaching under her legs, Red elevated Brittany into the broken glass. "Time to finally put you where you belong."

As he forced her legs over her head, the cracked glass shattered, cutting into the runny mess of gore that was her face. Brittany tumbled out of the window and plummeted toward the alley, splatting several feet beside the open manhole. The back of her head sprayed the tar and surrounding garbage with a thick coat of blood.

"Holy fuckin' shit!" a vagrant yelled.

Watching below, Red saw all the homeless folks scatter. The savvy transients knew better—when something like that went down, it was always better not to be a witness.

He squinted at her corpse. "Nah, that ain't right."

Red left his place at the window and went back downstairs to the spot where the dead man rested. He ripped the scarf off his icy face and reversed it. Wincing in disgust, Red wrapped it around his own. There was enough cloth to obscure his facial features and his glaring port wine stain.

He made his way out to where Brittany's destroyed body lay. One of her legs was snapped in half and the other was bent in a direction contrary to standard anatomy. The evil brains once inside her skull had been strewn everywhere.

Red grabbed her legs—careful not to pull the one with the compound fracture off—and dragged her closer to the steaming chasm.

"I guess this is goodbye."

Red rolled her into the hole and watched her body vanish in the gray sewer water. Bending over, he used all his strength to muscle the manhole cap over the opening.

Upon returning to his car, he felt a weight lifted off his shoulders. Red started the engine and promptly headed for the highway. He wanted nothing more than to look for Dessi right away, but it wasn't the best idea to stick around after a double murder—a lesson that he'd had too much experience with now. He needed to disappear and regroup. Maybe he could enlist the services of Jack Tunney again to help him get a lead on the cobbler character he needed help locating.

He looked at his watch.

Gotta check on Ma.

For the first time, Red wasn't looking at the watch as a reminder. It was now merely a timepiece. Even though he didn't need it for its original purpose any longer, Red considered keeping it.

Exhaling, he finally felt whole. He'd become the man he never imagined he could. As he drove down the trash littered road, Red recognized that there was no magic way to change the things that had happened in the past. They were with him for the long haul. He couldn't ignore them. He needed to face them.

The lies he'd told.

The drugs he'd done.

The money he'd stolen.

The crimes he'd covered up.

The girlfriend he'd let control him.

The child he'd abandoned.

The people he'd scammed.

The kid he'd shot.

The finger he'd chopped.

The people he'd murdered.

The mishmash of horrors still swirled in his head, but as horrible as they were, Red was confident that he wouldn't let them be his undoing.

He didn't want any of those horrible things to go down the way they did, and he would do everything he could to right his wrongs. After all the time that Red had spent wallowing in his failures, there was one thing he figured out about the world: if people knew you fucked up, they were quick to burn you at the stake. People didn't tend to leave a whole lot of room for paths to redemption.

When Red flicked his turn signal to get on the highway, he thought back to something The Black Widow told him.

Maybe there was some truth to what she said.

The faces of the lives he'd taken over the last several days flashed in his mind.

Sometimes you gotta carve out your own path.

As Red entered the on-ramp, he got a glimpse at the city of violence and thought about Dessi. Back when he wasn't sure if she was his daughter, Red's entire journey had been predicated on finding her. But now that he knew Dessi wasn't his blood, for the first time, he realized finding her wasn't the most important thing.

It was wanting to.

THE END

THROUGH THE EYES
OF DESPERATION
THE BLACK VERSION
DANIEL J. VOLPE

To learn The Black Widow's full story
and reveal many other Easter eggs read:

THROUGH THE EYES OF DESPERATION:
THE BLACK VERSION

By Daniel J. Volpe

Both novels are completely different stories, each with two completely different endings transpiring over a simultaneous timeline.

To learn more about the cobbler read:

SEW SORRY

By Aron Beauregard & Daniel J. Volpe

Author Note:

Use of the word 'scunt' in the final chapter of this book is entirely intentional.

Scunt: /skuhnt/ *noun*

1. A slang term used to describe a contemptuous person.
2. A combination of scumbag and cunt.

ABOUT THE AUTHOR

Aron Beauregard is the 2x Splatterpunk Award-winning author of *Playground* and many others. Nearly three years ago, Beauregard quit his day job of 12 years, and with no college education, set off to pursue his passion and become a full-time horror writer. Against all odds, he's since reached #1 Bestseller status in horror. His work has generated controversy and intrigue. Love him or hate him—there is no in-between.

JASON PARENT
THEY FEED

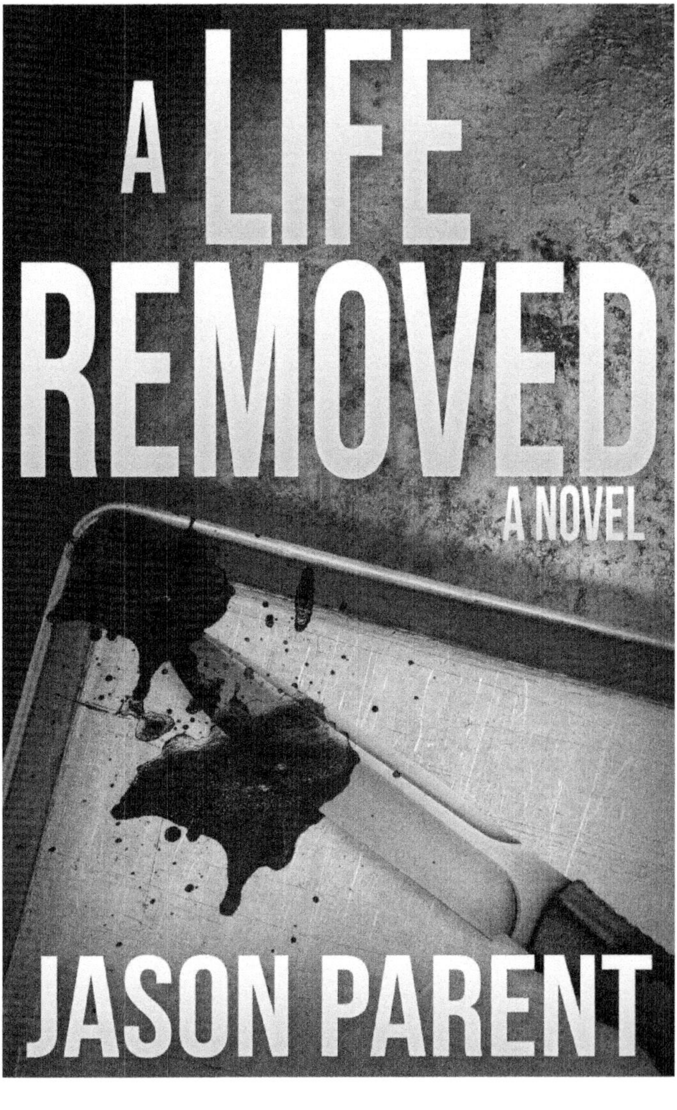
A LIFE
REMOVED
A NOVEL
JASON PARENT

Printed in Great Britain
by Amazon

38999181R00182